Festival in Croftwood Park

Victoria Walker

Copyright © 2024 Victoria Walker

All rights reserved.

ISBN: 978-1-7399441-6-2

No part of this publication may be reproduced, distributed, or transmitted in any form or by any means, including photocopying, recording, or other electronic or mechanical methods, without permission.

The story, all names, characters, and incidents portrayed in this production are fictitious. No identification with actual persons (living or deceased), places, buildings, and products is intended or should be inferred.

For my Festival buddies
You know who you are!

1

Oliver's coffee house had never been busier. Jess Taylor was squeezed onto a bench seat at a table for four with five other people and it was only bearable because she'd enjoyed this month's book so much. The group situation she found herself in went against the principles of the book club which was supposed to be just two people who'd read the same book having a chat about it over a coffee or a glass of wine, hence its name; the date-with-a-book club. Such was the popularity of the club, it was harder and harder to keep it to its original format when they were so tight for space.

Jess had been a regular at the book club since Lois Morgan, manager of Croftwood Library, had started it over a year ago. What she loved was that it wasn't an especially literary book club. Every month, Lois and her colleagues chose one book from three different genres: biography, thriller or crime, and romance. It was a rare month where Jess didn't choose the romance book and it was brilliant to come to the book club and talk to other romance readers without feeling like they should be ashamed to admit that they preferred a good love story over the latest Booker prize winner.

Tonight Jess was sharing her table with five other women who had enjoyed the latest Christina Lauren book as much as she had. They'd also snagged a bottle of red wine for their table thanks to Jess being a regular at Oliver's and having an in with the eponymous owner.

'Who do you imagine would play the male lead if they made a film out of it?' Patsy asked. The discussion often circled around to this topic.

'I imagined him as Ryan Reynolds,' said Linda.

'You always say Ryan Reynolds,' said Zoe, laughing. 'I was thinking of Will Smith.'

'Good choice,' said Patsy. 'And just to keep things even, how about the female lead?'

'Reece Witherspoon. Hands down the only woman for that job,' said Jess, perhaps influenced by the film she'd watched on Netflix the night before, which starred Reece alongside Ashton Kutcher.

'Or Jenna, the one who was Queen Victoria and the sidekick in Doctor Who.'

'Coleman.'

'Olivia Coleman's too old,' said Linda.

'No, I totally agree,' said Zoe. 'That woman's name is Jenna Coleman. Presumably no relation to Olivia. Anyone for a top-up?'

At nine o'clock, people started to drift away, but Jess stayed behind to help Oliver and Patsy tidy up. As fellow town traders, it was one of the few chances they had to chat. Between running The Croftwood Haberdashery and sewing workshops, Jess sometimes felt as if she didn't have a minute to herself, although she loved being busy, especially if sewing was involved. But sometimes she craved the company of people who were in the same boat as her. They discussed everything from what they were doing for the Christmas window competition to whether a week of lower takings was anything to worry about or if it was just the weather keeping people away from the town.

Jess went around the table collecting empty mugs and glasses while Patsy made inroads into the washing up and Oliver started re-stocking ready for the morning.

The door opened and a shattered looking Lois walked in.

'How was it over at the Courtyard tonight?' Jess asked her. The book club had outgrown Oliver's almost as soon as it had started, so they'd added a second venue. The Courtyard Café was just a short walk away, further down on the other side of the high street.

'Heaving,' smiled Lois. 'I've left Rosemary to boot the stragglers out.'

'I'm sure they'll already be tucked up in their beds then,' said Jess. Rosemary, who'd had Lois's job before she'd retired, had a no-nonsense approach to everything.

Lois laughed. 'Probably.' She sat down at the nearest table. 'I need to come up with a plan, Jess. This is mad. The book club's too big. It's taken on a life of its own, but it's morphed into any old book club. It's not the date-with-a-book club anymore.'

'I thought you were limiting it here to people who'd officially signed up at the library?'

'That was the plan. Since we've rolled it out at some of the other local libraries, I think people have decided they'd rather come here than wherever their local meeting is.'

'You can't argue with people who have good taste.' Oliver bent down to kiss Lois. They'd come up with the idea of the book club together, which was how it came to be hosted at the coffee house and how their relationship had begun. 'But it was busier than ever tonight. It's a shame, but I think we might have to turn people away if it happens again, or organise shifts.'

'Well, no-one can say it hasn't been a roaring success. It did save the library, don't forget,' Patsy said, slumping into a chair next to Lois.

'Finished the washing-up, Pats?' Oliver asked.

'Sod off. Of course I have. You're lucky Alice was front-of-house at the cinema tonight, otherwise you'd have been on your own.'

'As if you didn't arrange that so you could come and talk romance books with Jess.'

'Alright you two,' Lois admonished them affectionately. 'I've got bigger problems than our book club.'

Oliver pulled up a chair with a look of concern on his face. 'What's up?'

'Now that we've rolled out the date-with-a-book club across the library network, they want to have a big launch event.'

'Who's they?' Jess asked, feeling like it might be a stupid question.

'The British Library,' Lois said, as if that wasn't a big deal.

'Oh, right,' said Jess, slightly awed that Lois was moving in those circles since Croftwood Library had won the Library of the Year award the previous year.

'For some reason, they think I have the answer to everything and I have no idea what they're expecting or how on earth they think one small library can showcase to the entire country how the book club works.' Her voice was rising as she spoke, the frustration and anxiety obvious to her friends, who immediately chipped in with suggestions.

'Couldn't they do some kind of online video? Like a social media campaign?' Patsy suggested.

'Mmm, maybe,' said Lois.

'Why can't the librarians spread the word like you did when we started?' Oliver asked.

'Because they don't all have an Oliver to help them out,' Lois said affectionately. 'And that could take ages, and they want it to be one big launch.'

'How about one huge date-with-a-book meeting?

Something where literally thousands of people can come,' Jess said, an idea beginning to form. 'Almost like a festival weekend.'

'A book festival, like Hay or Cheltenham?' Lois asked, more interested now.

'Not exactly. Maybe along the lines of a music festival? You could have one enormous book club during the daytime and then have music at night.'

'I like that idea,' Oliver said. 'Even if you don't go with the festival idea, the fact that the British Library is looking at you to come up with an idea is a great opportunity to put Croftwood on the map.'

Jess smiled. That was typical Oliver: serial entrepreneur but always wanting to give back and do great things for the town.

'He's right,' she said. 'I bet the traders would love to be involved. If you did do something along the lines of a festival, we could have a local market, so even if people didn't venture into the town, it would still benefit all of us.'

'That's a great idea,' Patsy said. 'Books and crafts are the perfect mix for a lot of people.'

'Thanks for the input, guys,' said Lois, looking less defeated than when she'd arrived. 'I'll mull it over and come up with something.'

'Don't worry,' Oliver said in a loud whisper to Jess. 'I'll talk her into the festival idea.'

'I already like that idea,' Lois said, smiling and biffing him on the arm. 'I just need to think about the wider strategy and make sure that a festival is going to meet the brief.'

'Fair enough,' Jess said. 'But whatever you decide, if you need a hand with anything, let me know.'

'Thanks, Jess.'

'And thanks for helping tonight,' said Oliver. 'At this rate, we might need to spill over into your place next month.'

'Red wine and coffee is not conducive to a relaxing evening in the haberdashery. At least not for me.'

Jess pulled her coat, hat and gloves on, said goodnight, and made her way across the road to the car park behind the church. It was always creepy taking a shortcut through the churchyard, especially in the dark, but that's what she always did, as it was quicker than walking all the way around. Over the years she'd toyed with the idea of moving to Croftwood, but actually, she liked the separation between work and home that the drive gave her.

Her little Mini, Madge, was an oldie but a goodie. It had been her grandmother's car and then her auntie's and now it was hers. There were a few rust spots which were threatening to overwhelm the blue paint in some places, but somehow it always got through the MOT with next to nothing needing doing, and the insurance was a pittance. She'd made seat covers out of hot pink jumbo corduroy fabric, which was cosy in the winter and practical in the summer by saving her thighs from third-degree burns from the original vinyl seats.

Jess chucked her bag onto the passenger seat and turned over the engine, before she flicked the lights on, turned the heater up, not that it would make much difference, and made sure the radio was on. She loved listening to Jo Whiley on her way home from the book club. Because Madge was so old, the radio struggled to find a signal through the aged arial but thankfully there was a cassette player for times when the static got too much, and it just added to her charm.

It was only a ten-minute drive to the village of Old Hollow, nestled on the side of the Malvern Hills, where Jess lived in a small cottage that had originally been built for workers from the local granite quarries. It wasn't the warmest house in the world, so Jess lit the wood-burner most nights from September to May until the sun was strong enough to warm the stone house from the outside in.

The house was full of fabric and other craft paraphernalia. Jess's first love was sewing, but she enjoyed having a go at anything creative, so there was a spinning wheel in the corner of the lounge and a small weaving loom on the coffee table. Her spare room was where she kept her sewing machine and dressmaker's dummy. Contrary to popular belief, owning a haberdashery shop didn't mean she could spend every day sewing, but she needed to produce garments to give her customers ideas of what they could make with the fabric and patterns that she sold and that had to happen in the evenings. Most of the time she made clothes she would want to wear herself and happily her eye for what looked good caught the attention of her customers. Only on a rare occasion would she sew something she wouldn't end up keeping for herself, but she still enjoyed making things, even if they weren't for her.

Even though it was late, Jess settled down to sew. She was making a long dress with three-quarter length sleeves and a tiered skirt out of some drapey floral viscose fabric. It would be a perfect dress for spring days where the sun might be warm, but it could be worn with a cardigan or denim jacket if it was chilly. She could already envisage how it was going to look on her, and she knew she'd want more of the same dress in a variety of fabrics.

Jess limited herself to an hour of sewing and then checked her emails before she went to bed. She'd listed her latest batch of workshops over the weekend and there were several emails booking places which she responded to. The classes were held at the shop or at Croftwood Cinema, which was owned by Oliver and Patsy and meant she could cater for larger numbers. The flexible space was perfect for her and it was easier to leave the shop in the capable hands of her colleague Penny rather than try to hold all the workshops in the shop by herself during opening hours.

If Lois went with the festival idea, Jess wondered whether

they could offer workshops as well. After all, people might not want two or three days of solid books. It might be good to add other things into the mix. Books, crafts and music. It sounded like the perfect weekend. Hopefully Oliver could talk Lois into the idea. But even if he couldn't, Jess wondered why they couldn't do some version of it anyway. Oliver was right. Something like this would put the town on the map. It would encourage visitors and, selfishly, would help her weather the summer slump where crafters tended to abandon their indoor activities for gardening. The Croftwood Festival could be the perfect answer to her own problems, as well as Lois's.

2

It wasn't until the following week that Jess heard about the outcome of the discussion they'd had after the date-with-a-book club. She'd forced herself not to quiz Oliver about it every time she went into the coffee house, but today she was at Croftwood Cinema running a workshop and she was sure Patsy would know what the latest was.

'What are you up to today?' Patsy asked, as they arranged the tables in two rows that faced the cinema screen.

'It's the monthly group where people can sew whatever they like, but I'm on hand to help and give advice. You ought to join in, Patsy, you've been saying you want to learn to sew. I'll let you know next time I have a space.'

'The way things are going, that day won't come! You seem to be busier than ever with the workshops.'

'Only since I've started holding them here. I think people much prefer the extra space to working in the shop.'

'And they can still pop in to the shop at lunchtime or afterwards. Win-win. Anyway, I fully intend to get started with the sewing. I've been looking at summer dresses on Instagram.'

They went over to a storage cupboard at the side of the auditorium and started pulling out the sewing machines.

'How many do you need today?' Patsy asked.

'Only three. Everyone else is bringing their own.'

They always used more machines at the Learn to Sew workshops than they did at this one. Luckily Jess had managed to buy some cheap ex-display models from one of her suppliers which was another reason her workshops were so popular. Not everyone had their own machine when they were starting out.

'Have you heard anything about Lois's book club launch plans?' she asked Patsy.

Patsy hauled a machine up onto a table in the front row. 'Well, apparently the British Library loved the festival idea, but they think it could be too expensive and they don't want to wait until next year to launch.'

'Next year? I thought it'd be this summer.'

'They reckon there's no way you can organise a festival in less than a year. But Lois mentioned the idea of a social media campaign and Linda has already made a TikTok.'

'Wow, good for Linda.' She had no idea how Linda had navigated her way around TikTok when it was only about a year ago that she'd started tweeting and posting to Instagram.

'Oliver's gutted. He loved the festival idea, but he doesn't want to put any pressure on Lois by pushing it. She's already stressed out trying to juggle the library and being the date-with-a-book club champion.' Patsy began pulling chairs from the side of the room to sit behind the tables.

'Yes, it's a lot. The library's busier than ever and there's still only Linda and Rosemary working there with her.'

'I suppose saving the library is one thing. It doesn't necessarily translate into extra money, though.'

'Exactly. They're lucky Rosemary was willing to start back part-time after she retired, otherwise they'd be really stuck.'

They finished setting up, Patsy making sure that all the

sewing machine cables were routed safely underneath the rubber matting while Jess connected her laptop to the audio system so she could play some background music and play tutorial videos on the big screen if she needed to.

'Have you got time for coffee?' Patsy asked.

'I've got half an hour before anyone's likely to arrive,' said Jess, checking her phone as she followed Patsy into the room behind the screen that they called the Backstage Bar.

Patsy expertly made two lattes, and they sat at the bar together.

'How was your holiday?'

Patsy and her partner Matt had taken his two children on holiday to Disneyland Paris for February half term.

'It feels like a lifetime ago now, but we had a great time. The kids are good fun. They wanted to go on everything, even the rollercoasters, but they're too small for all of them apart from the runaway train ride. We spent a lot of time on that,' she said with a smile.

'I can't picture you at Disneyland, somehow,' Jess said, teasing.

'I know! It wouldn't have been my first choice of places to go, but actually it was brilliant. It lets you embrace your inner child with no judgement.' Patsy was beaming. She and Matt had had a rocky start, having met just when Patsy's controlling ex-husband had come back into her life. But they'd weathered the storm and had been happily living together for well over a year, sharing the care of his children with their mother.

'And how are things with you, aside from your burgeoning business?'

'Not bad, thanks. Work is busy, but I love that.'

'Anything outside of work?' Patsy raised a questioning eyebrow.

'Not at the moment.'

'You're on the lookout, though?'

Jess smiled and nodded. She'd been perusing dating apps for the past few years. Not in search of meaningless hookups, but in search of distraction. She wasn't in the market for a partner. She liked to meet someone for a drink, maybe dinner on the second date, and then that was usually it. A bit of company and good conversation, if she was lucky, and so far no-one she'd met had made her crave anything more. She fully expected it to stay that way.

'Well good. You need someone to drag you away from the sewing machine sometimes,' said Patsy. 'I'm glad that business with Dan didn't put you off.'

Jess had unwittingly matched with Patsy's ex-husband on a dating app when he was trying to track her down the summer before. She'd found out on their third date and she'd already suspected by then that he was too perfectly charming to be true. Even if Patsy hadn't told her, she'd resolved it was their last date, but it didn't stop Patsy from feeling guilty and bringing it up every time they discussed Jess's love life.

'It didn't, you know that.'

Patsy shrugged. 'I know, I just worry that he made you wary that other men might be hiding a dark side like him.'

'I think he's in the minority on that score,' Jess said, giving Patsy a reassuring smile. 'I'm too busy with the shop at the moment anyway, so I'm giving the apps a break. Maybe in the summer when there's the usual lull.'

'Matt might have a friend or colleague we could introduce you to?' Patsy said, hopefully.

'Oh no, that's okay. It might make things awkward.' It definitely would, because breaking away after a couple of dates if it was a friend of Matt's wouldn't be so easy.

'I can't think who I would suggest, anyway. He works on site so much I don't often meet the people he works with and I wouldn't trust him to pick someone nice for you.'

Jess laughed. 'I can just imagine.'

'What about Toby?' Patsy suggested. 'He's so lovely and I don't think he's seeing anyone.'

Again, awkward.

'He is lovely, but not my type. Perhaps too serious?' Toby would be someone she would absolutely be attracted to if things were different. He was a lawyer who used Oliver's coffee house as a makeshift office during the week where he quietly gave free legal advice to people on a website he'd founded. That was attractive enough aside from the fact he was well-groomed, wore dark jeans and a shirt, sometimes with a fine wool jumper. Jess couldn't deny he had the potential to be her perfect man. If only she hadn't already found, but lost, the perfect man.

'Right, I'd better get up to the foyer in case they start arriving,' Jess said, drawing a line under the conversation with some relief.

'I'll be here for a couple of hours doing some work, so shout if you need anything and send them all in for a coffee on the house when they get here.' Patsy said.

Jess gave the auditorium a cursory glance on her way through to make sure she hadn't forgotten anything, then carried on to the foyer. She unlocked the door and took a seat in the ticket booth, scrolling on her phone while she waited for her customers to arrive. She loved looking through Instagram at people with mainly sewing and knitting on their accounts. It was a great source of inspiration and a fantastic way to connect with people. The Instagram account she ran for the shop had a good following and she found that whatever she posted on there sold well, if not to people who visited the shop, to customers further afield via her website.

The website had been Patsy's idea. She'd built one for the cinema when she and Oliver launched it last year and then had been keen to start on one for Jess, to keep her hand in, she'd said. The cinema website was basic from a shopping point of view, simply needing to list what was on and sell tickets. Patsy wanted the challenge of a proper shopping cart project, as she'd put it. She'd refused to let Jess pay her for it, which was an amazing opportunity for The Croftwood Haberdashery to have an online presence that Jess couldn't have afforded otherwise. But it meant that Jess had to match Patsy's voracious pace and had to produce photos and item descriptions for everything in the shop in a very short space of time. Ultimately, she was grateful to Patsy for pushing her into it because it might mean that the lean summer months might not be quite so lean now that she had a bigger reach.

She checked to see whether any orders had come in overnight and saw that Penny had already marked them as picked and ready to dispatch, which was brilliant. She had no idea how she'd managed before Penny started working with her.

'Hello?' someone called tentatively as they pushed the door open.

'Morning!' Patsy said, coming out from the booth to hold the door open while her first customer manhandled herself, her sewing machine, and an enormous bag of fabric through the door.

'It's a long walk from the car park,' she said, breathlessly.

'I know. I'm sorry about that. I'll have to think about organising a porter or something,' Jess said with a smile, taking the woman's machine off her.

'Oh, no, it keeps me fit! I'm Cherry.'

'Nice to meet you. I'm Jess. We're just in here,' she said, leading the way into the auditorium. 'Choose any table you like.'

'It's a real treat to have so much space to sew,' said Cherry. 'I'm making a dress with an invisible zip and the thought of it has terrified me into stagnation.'

'We'll get you started on that as soon as everyone's here. If you head down to that door in the corner,' Jess pointed, 'Patsy will make you a coffee.'

Cherry dumped her bags at a table in the back row, and Jess set the machine down for her before she headed back to the foyer. She got a buzz out of this. Cherry wasn't the only person she'd meet today who was stymied by a sewing problem that Jess could solve in her sleep. And Jess knew that Cherry and the others would bond over a shared enjoyment of their hobby, and some of them would probably even stay in touch. It was wonderful to feel part of that process of bringing people together.

She took her place behind the desk in the ticket booth again, thinking that her workshops were much the same as Lois and the book club. When Lois had started it, it had been limited to the few people who frequented Croftwood Library, but it had grown and brought people together. There had even been a romance, aside from Lois and Oliver's. And it wasn't quite the same thing, but Jess could understand how daunted Lois must feel to be launching something that had started so small, far and wide. She wasn't sure she would fare any better if it were her trying to do that with a sewing or knitting club. But what she could picture, very strongly, was bringing like-minded people together at a festival. There was no reason why it had to be linked to the date-with-a-book club launch. Why didn't they do it anyway?

3

After the workshop ended, with all twelve of her participants happy, and half of them planning to head over to the haberdashery to choose their next project, Jess locked up the cinema behind them and walked briskly through the park back to the shop. It was dusk and without the March sunshine, the temperature had begun to drop. The trees and borders all looked bare, yet to spring into life, so there was nothing to linger and look at anyway but Jess did spot clumps of snowdrops here and there and a wonderful patch of purple crocuses that had sprouted underneath an ancient oak tree.

Once she got back to the shop, she spent a happy hour helping Penny serve everyone before they closed the doors for the day.

'Oh my goodness,' Penny said. 'That was a busy couple of hours. Before you came over, I had a group from Worcester College in buying patterns and fabric for their GCSE textiles project.'

'I'm sorry you had to manage that on your own,' Jess said. 'I know how hard it is when you've got a queue.'

'I love it,' Penny said, grinning. 'There's no better feeling than filling that till with money. Or credit card slips.'

'I'll cash up. You get home. You haven't even had a lunch break.'

'Neither have you, and I bet you're heading back to the cinema to clear up.'

'There's not much to do. They were a tidy bunch today.' But she'd have to hoover the auditorium, put the tables away and help Alice rearrange the chairs before the cinema opened for the evening. 'Go on, honestly, I can close up. Thanks so much for today.'

She pressed a twenty-pound note into Penny's hand. It wasn't her wages, just an extra thank you for holding the fort all day by herself. It was one thing for Jess to work all hours with no break, but she always felt guilty that Penny did the same.

'Jess, no,' Penny said, pushing her hand away.

'Yes. Don't argue.'

Penny took the money with some reluctance, knowing from experience that she wouldn't win. 'Thanks. I'll see you on Thursday?'

'Great. See you then.'

She locked the door behind Penny and turned most of the lights off so that it looked as if the shop was closed and deserted. She loved this time of day. It was so peaceful and as much as she loved talking to her customers, she also relished this time in the shop where no-one would ask her anything.

She set the till to run the end of day report and wandered around tidying rolls of fabric and returning rogue balls of wool to their rightful places.

Lost in a world of her own, she jumped when there was a knock on the door. She could see Oliver peering through the glass. He waved when he saw her.

'Hey,' she said, opening the door. 'Are you after an emergency ball of wool?' She held the door open for him to come inside and then dropped the latch behind him. It wasn't unusual for customers to try to come in after closing time if they were desperate for something.

'You know me so well,' he said with a smile. 'I've been talking to Pats, and she mentioned you were keen on the festival idea we talked about the other night.'

Jess could see by Oliver's face that the idea had him gripped as well. He had the same bright-eyed enthusiasm radiating from him as he'd had when he'd first bought the cinema.

'I am. I know Patsy said Lois can't do it for her launch of the book club, but it's a good idea and I'd love to see something like that in the town.'

'Me too!' Oliver looked ecstatic. 'So what do you think? Can we pull it off?'

'I don't know the first thing about organising a festival. I've been to a couple, but I'm not sure how much help that will be.'

'I haven't got anything more than a vague idea to offer myself, but we can't let that stop us.'

Jess knew from conversations she'd had with Patsy at the time they were renovating the cinema, that knowing nothing was no barrier as far as Oliver was concerned. He was a force of nature for getting anything done; a bit like Patsy and the Croftwood Haberdashery website.

'Where would we start?' she said. 'Both of us have our hands full with our businesses. We can't organise a festival.'

'No, you're right. The thing is, it would be great for the town, so I wonder if there's a way to get all the traders involved. Spread the load,' he suggested.

'It's a good idea. Some of them would definitely be interested. We could have a traders' meeting to suss out what the feeling is.' The traders met around once every couple of months to discuss all sorts of things that impacted the town. There had been lots of occasions when it had benefitted all of them to work together and present a united front to the Council.

'Okay. I'll put something out on the WhatsApp group and we'll get a date in the diary. I think before the meeting we ought to flesh out exactly what we're proposing. We need to be ready to sell it to them. I'll see if Matt's willing to help. I'm pretty sure he told me he did some work for Glastonbury once. I don't know what exactly, but he might fill some of our gaps.'

'That sounds great. Count me in,' Jess said, feeling excited at the prospect of trying to capture the ideas that she'd been mulling over and turning them into a solid plan.

'Brilliant. I'll catch up with you tomorrow.'

He let himself out of the shop, and Jess locked the door behind him. She finished her tidying up and went over to the counter to pick up her phone and her bag. There was a missed call from her mum. Her parents lived in Dorset, where she'd grown up. Almost the only thing she missed about living in Croftwood, aside from her parents, was living near the sea. Croftwood was about as far from the sea as you could get, situated almost in the middle of the country. But even so, she didn't go home very often. She told herself and her parents that it was because she didn't have time but the truth was that home held too many memories and it felt like a dangerous place to be because of that.

Once she'd moved to Worcestershire and opened the shop eight years ago, her parents had eventually realised that they were only going to see her more regularly than every Christmas if they came to her. And that's what had happened ever since. It suited Jess. Maybe one day she'd be able to go back. Maybe one day the memories wouldn't floor her like she knew they would, even now, so long after everything that had happened. It was easier to stay where she was, in a place where no-one knew. She was Jess from the Croftwood

Haberdashery and that was all. Her support came from the friends she had made through the shop; from the knitting club to the other traders. That was enough. Anything more than that was leaving herself open to the same thing happening again. She knew she'd distanced herself from her parents for the same reason, that perhaps losing them as well, as would inevitably happen at some point, might not hurt as much if she closed herself off from them.

Because Jess knew what loss was. She knew how much it could hurt, and she also knew that she wouldn't survive if it happened again. So she kept her life carefully balanced, with not too much of herself invested in anyone. Just in case.

'Hi, Mum.' She was sitting at the table at the back of the shop where the knitting club usually met, but at other times was a handy place for customers to browse through pattern books or for long-suffering partners to sit and wait.

'Jessie! How are you? Did you have a workshop today?'

'Yep, the one where they bring their own project, so it was good fun.'

'At the cinema?'

'Yes, we're holding hardly any in the shop now. It's working out really well.'

'I can't wait to see it.'

Cue having to extend an invitation.

'Next time you come, we'll go there, whatever film's on. Maybe in a few weeks when the shop isn't so busy. Then we'll have more time.'

'That sounds lovely. And you're alright? Not doing too much?'

'I'm fine, Mum.' Her mum knew her too well. She knew that most of Jess's life was a distraction technique to avoid allowing herself to feel anything too deeply. Since Jon had died, they'd had numerous tearful conversations where her mum had begged her to take the time to grieve properly. To lean into the feelings rather than avoid them. 'It's been busy since Christmas, but that's good, and I've had Penny working more hours so that I can concentrate on the workshops. I'm enjoying myself.'

'Good, that's what I want to hear.'

There was a pause. Jess could feel her mum working up to something.

'Do you think you'll make it home for a few days over the summer, when things are quieter at the shop?'

'Probably not. We're thinking about launching a festival on the back of the book club I told you about. If it happens, I might be helping to organise it.' Not exactly a lie, more of a hopeful prediction.

'Oh, because Sara is hoping to come home for a couple of weeks and it would be great if we could all get together, wouldn't it?' Sara was her sister who lived in Australia. She had married an Aussie and had two small children, which was why she hadn't visited for years.

'That would be fab, actually,' Jess agreed. 'Let me know the dates and I'll see if I can work something out.'

They ended the call with a tentative plan for her parents to visit at the end of April. At least it gave her some breathing space.

Jess felt guilty at how grateful her mum was to hear that she might go home. Perhaps she was being selfish by avoiding it, but everything there held memories of Jon.

They'd grown up together and had been going out since they were fifteen. Even now, he was in every corner of Corfe Bay, the small seaside town where they'd grown up. Beaches where they'd spent endless sunny days laughing, swimming and hanging out with their friends. Shops where they'd tried to buy cider, thwarted because everyone knew everyone. The ramshackle, abandoned beach huts where they all hung out when the weather turned and where they'd shared their first kiss. Everyone had said it wouldn't last, that they were idiots to try to keep their relationship going through the university years when they were almost living on opposite sides of the country, with Jon studying medicine in London while she was studying textiles in Bristol. They were wasting the best years of their lives for something that would fizzle out because of the distance between them, people said. His parents said. But they'd been wrong because their love had lasted the rest of Jon's life. And that was why it was difficult for Jess to imagine loving anyone else.

It wasn't that her parents hadn't understood how devastated she'd been when Jon had died, but they'd expected her to bounce back more quickly than she had because she'd been young. She had the rest of her life to live and Jon wouldn't want her to be sad forever. She knew that was true, and she wasn't as sad as she'd been back then, but she wasn't the same person either.

Corfe Bay was still full of people who she'd grown up with. Her mum provided regular updates as to what everyone was up to, including Jon's family, probably to keep Jess connected or perhaps to ignite some curiosity for her to visit and find out for herself.

The summer was ages away. She'd worry about what to do if Sara came home closer to the time. For now, she'd message her sister and say she was thrilled they were thinking about coming for a visit. That was enough to keep everyone happy for now.

4

The following day, the traders' WhatsApp account was buzzing with activity and eventually a meeting was arranged for Thursday evening at six, after most of the shops had closed. That was only two days away; great that they didn't have to wait long to introduce their idea because if they had any hope of pulling it off for the summer, they needed to start working on it straight away. But it also meant that Oliver, Jess, and Matt only had two evenings to work on a plan that was fleshed out enough for them to answer the inevitable questions that would be asked.

'Matt has his kids tonight, so he thought it'd be easier if we went round there,' Oliver said when Jess arrived at the coffee house on Wednesday night after she'd closed up. 'You okay to close up, Jack?'

'Course, Boss.' Jack was in his early twenties and was Oliver's star barista now that Patsy and Oliver had their hands full with the cinema, as well as the coffee house. He was furiously polishing the chrome on the coffee machine.

Oliver grabbed his rucksack from behind the counter. 'Right. Let's go.'

'I'll drive, if you like?' offered Jess. She didn't want to waste time later having to walk back into town to collect

Madge.

'Great, thanks. Lois is working late, so she's going to pick me up from Matt and Patsy's later. Ah, I forgot your car is the tiniest car in the world,' he laughed, as they walked across the car park. 'Am I going to fit?'

'Push the seat back. You'll fit,' she said, trying to sound stern, affronted on Madge's behalf.

It was only a five-minute drive to Matt's. He and Patsy had the most amazing house, designed by him, on the outskirts of Croftwood. It was like a ski-lodge that would look more at home in Aspen than in rural Worcestershire, but it nestled into the woods that it backed onto beautifully. And as much as Jess loved her cottage, she couldn't help but envy Matt and Patsy.

'Had any more thoughts?' Oliver asked. She couldn't see him since he had slid the seat back as far as it would go and may as well be sitting in the back of the car.

'Only that the priority for tonight probably ought to be coming up with a list of potential venues.'

'That's what I thought,' he said. 'Given that we want it to benefit the town, it seems crazy to commandeer a field that's too far away for anyone to think about popping into Croftwood. Somehow, I think we need to use the town as the festival venue.'

'Have you ever been to the Hay book festival or Cheltenham literary festival? That's what they do, although they're not festivals in the sense that we're planning. Cheltenham doesn't have camping or anything like that.' Jess pulled the car onto Matt and Patsy's substantial driveway.

'Lois mentioned that. She's been to Cheltenham a few times, not that she'd be interested in camping.'

'I'm not sure I would either. It's miserable if it rains,' Jess said, ringing the doorbell.

'True. But the festival will be so amazing, no-one will care about the weather.'

Jess pulled her best 'I doubt it' face.

'Hey, come in,' said Matt, opening the door looking a bit flustered. 'Sorry, I'm in the middle of bedtime stories. Patsy's at the cinema. Won't be a minute.'

'Carry on, we'll make ourselves at home,' Oliver said.

'Cheers!' shouted Matt as he took the stairs two at a time.

Oliver shut the door behind them and they took their shoes off. The underfloor heating felt divine.

'God, this is so nice, isn't it?' Jess said, taking her coat off and hanging it on one of the hooks next to the door.

'Yes, it beats our house. It's a bit draughty compared to this.' Lois and Oliver lived on the outskirts of Worcester in a Victorian semi.

'Mine too.'

The house almost glowed with its cosiness. Oliver led the way into the kitchen where the big table was covered with the detritus of the children's dinner, which Matt hadn't had chance to clear up.

'The lounge might be better,' he said, leading the way through, where a huge stone chimney-breast housed a fireplace. The fire was suffering from lack of attention, so Oliver took a couple of logs from the basket and revived it into a blaze.

Jess revelled in the warmth. There was a real danger that she might fall asleep before Matt came down to join them.

'I've only ever been here in the summer,' she said. 'This house really comes into its own in the winter.'

'It does,' agreed Oliver. 'Lois is pretty wedded to the Victorian vibe, though. I can't see her living here. If we move, I think it'd be to a bigger version of where we are now.'

'Okay,' Matt said, appearing in the doorway. 'Anyone want a cuppa?'

Once they'd settled back into the lounge with their drinks,

Oliver kicked things off, explaining to Matt what their vague plan was.

'Sounds good, I don't think I've seen any festivals around here and it's not clashing with other book-related festivals if we have it in the summer. Hay is in the spring and Cheltenham is in the autumn. The only thing is, if you're thinking of doing it this year, you might come up against supply problems.'

'Supplies of what?' Jess asked.

'The biggest things are tents, marquees and toilets. You'll definitely have to wait until after Glastonbury because they basically use the entire country's supply of all of that kind of thing.'

'We hadn't got as far as thinking about what we'd need to source.' Jess was worried. 'It's one thing to come up with an idea like this, but there's a lot we don't know. We could be walking into all sorts of problems.'

'It's definitely a risk,' said Oliver. 'But there will always be teething problems with something like this. Planning for it to be an annual event means you can learn from the first year and carry that expertise forward.'

'In the meantime, putting on a rubbish event.'

'What you really need is an expert from the start,' Matt said. 'You've got no hope of getting this off the ground for this summer without an events management company helping you.'

'That sounds expensive,' said Jess.

'It might be,' Matt agreed, 'but you'll be selling tickets, presumably?'

Jess looked at Oliver. Surely he could already see where this was going. They'd come up with a great idea that was impractical. A logistical nightmare, especially if they thought they had a chance of doing it this summer.

'Perhaps we should start smaller,' she suggested. 'Maybe

do a one-day event with the book club and a small craft workshop at the same time. We could do it in the park, have a couple of marquees and perhaps show a film in the cinema as part of it too?' She felt more comfortable with that idea. It was realistic. They wouldn't need to worry about camping, toilets, lots of tents, food vendors, parking or any of the other myriad things Matt had mentioned and which, until tonight, neither she nor Oliver had thought about.

'Come on, Jess,' Oliver said, his eyes shining in a way that Jess knew meant he already had the bit between his teeth and had already made his mind up. 'None of these things are insurmountable. We do what Matt suggests and find a company to do all of this difficult stuff for us. We get to manage them, which means we don't have the stress ourselves.'

He was blatantly trying to talk her into it. And the entrepreneur in her couldn't ignore the exciting little seed that he was cultivating right in front of her, tempting her to put practicality to the side. He was playing on the fact that she, like most of the traders in Croftwood, had that creative spark that had driven them to conjure up a business from nothing. This felt the same; another chance to start something from the very beginning, just like she had with the haberdashery. What did she have to lose?

She exhaled and began to smile.

'You're in, aren't you?' Oliver said.

'Of course she is. Your enthusiasm is nothing if not infectious,' said Matt.

'I'm in. For now,' she said. 'If it goes down like a lead balloon with the traders or if we can't find an events company that is going to fit, I'll have to reconsider, okay?' She wanted to be sure that Oliver was listening to her.

'Understood,' he said, momentarily managing to look serious.

'Let's do it then,' she said. 'Let's plan it exactly as we envisage it, and then we can be advised whether it's even possible. And you never know, when we present it at the traders' meeting there might be all kinds of expertise we can draw on that we don't even know about yet.'

'That's true. Pats could probably do the website for us,' said Oliver.

'Let's take a step back,' Matt said. 'The first thing we need to do is draft a proposal. Something you can present at your meeting and something we can use as a guide when we're asking events companies to quote.'

They spent a couple of hours talking through the ideas they had so far and cobbled it together into a coherent plan.

'I can send this to a few companies I know from the work I did at Glastonbury and see what they come back with,' Matt said.

'What did you do at Glastonbury?' asked Jess, intrigued as to why a festival would need an architect.

'I designed a nightclub based on warehouses in New York.'

'An actual building for just that week?'

'You haven't been?'

'No, I might have more of a clue about our festival if I had,' she smiled.

'Our nightclub looked like it was bricks and mortar, but a lot of it was clever painting, a bit like set design. But the inside structure needs to be sound and meet all the standards and that's my job. Glastonbury is like a small city. There are all sorts of things, like the nightclub, that take months to conceive and build just for that one week. It's an incredible thing to be involved in. The scale is just immense. Anyway, there are numerous events teams working there. Some of them exist just because of Glastonbury, but I'm sure we can come up with someone that's right for us.'

Jess was exhausted but excited as she headed for home not

long after they'd tidied up their plan enough for Matt to send it off to his contacts. There was so much to think about. Jess knew that whatever the scale of the event they ended up going with, and regardless of how much work the events company might do to help, it was going to be a huge commitment. As long as Penny was on board to help in the shop, it'd be fine. Things would be quieter once late spring arrived, and her workshop schedule would thin out a bit with the warmer weather, so if there was ever a good time to take on a big project, it was at least the right time of year.

Even though it was late and hardly seemed worth lighting the fire, she did anyway. She relished the cosiness it spread into the dark cottage, despite it being a far cry from the level of snugness at Matt's house. Then she made a cup of tea and a piece of toast as a late-night snack.

Jess curled up in the corner of her squashy old sofa and turned the TV on, choosing an episode of Friends at random. She never tired of watching them and had seen the entire collection more times than she had kept count of. It was soothing. A million miles away from serious or challenging television that might trigger unwelcome memories. Things she used to watch, like ER and Grey's Anatomy, were no longer on her list of favourites and she never watched soaps; why watch someone else living through the kind of misery that she'd had to go through? She had discovered a long time ago that the best way to cope with carrying on was to avoid anything like that. It also helped that no-one in Croftwood knew what had happened before she'd moved here. Because if they did, she wondered whether she'd be able to be as happy here as she was.

5

Sebastian Thorne had his head in his hands. The headache that had been niggling since he'd got up that morning was less to do with the couple of large whiskies he'd had last night, and more to do with the letter that was lying on his desk. It was from the landlord of the industrial unit that he operated out of and was threatening him with eviction if he didn't pay the rent he owed by the end of the month. Was he really five months behind?

His events company had been struggling for the past year. The events industry had been particularly hard hit during the pandemic when the whole country shut down for the best part of two years. Just as he was ready to get back to normal, a lot of his regular work had dried up and it had been an uphill struggle to find contracts to replace what he'd lost.

Aside from the letter about the rent arrears, he also had the bank to worry about. They were chasing him for last month's payment of his bounce back loan. Couldn't they see he was operating almost entirely using his overdraft facility? What did they think he could do?

He exhaled and wearily got to his feet, heading out of the office that was in one corner of the unit and into the tiny kitchen next door. He needed coffee to clear his head and help him warm up. It was too much of a luxury these days to turn on the fan heater. While he waited for the kettle to boil, he put a couple of slices of bread in the toaster and warmed his hands over the rising air until it was too hot to bear.

Seb took the coffee and toast back into the office and shut the door in the vain hope that it might create some extra warmth, then sat down to scroll through his emails. He went down the list, deleting most of them without opening them, not wanting to read the emails from suppliers asking whether he needed anything as they hadn't heard from him in a while, or the updates from other events companies telling him cheerily what they were busy doing. The only reason he checked his inbox these days was in the vain hope that one of the contracts he had quoted for would come good and he could go back to doing what he loved. The anxiety-ridden person who bore little resemblance to the Sebastian of three years ago was someone he was tired of being.

Scanning through the emails, his finger clicked the delete button before his brain had the chance to process that this email might be different to the others. He opened the trash bin and scrolled down until he found it. The name rang a bell — Matt Garvey — but it was the subject of the email that had caught his eye: New festival query.

He dragged the email back into his inbox and opened it.

Hi Sebastian,

We met a few years ago at Glasto — I was the architect on that bloody nightclub project! I'm involved with a group who are hoping to get a festival off the ground for this summer. I know, the timescale is more than tight. We're after an events company to be involved right from the start. We don't have much experience ourselves and will need input every step of the way. I've attached a document that outlines the ideas so far but we could do with guidance on practicalities and logistics of this. Let me know — a long shot as I'm sure you're booked up for this summer already. Or if you can suggest anyone else we could approach? You probably have more idea than me of companies who would be a good fit for this kind of thing. Look forward to hearing from you, Matt Garvey.

A festival for this summer? Were they mad? No-one could organise a festival, even a small one, in a few months. But he pushed that thought aside because, mad or not, this was an opportunity that he couldn't afford to miss. If he could get a contract to run the event, that could be exactly what he needed to solve all the problems piling up on his desk.

6

Croftwood Church hall was a cacophony of chatter. The traders' meetings were always a welcome chance for everyone to catch up with each other and compare notes, and no-one ever expected them to start on time. The chairs were arranged in a large circle since nobody was in charge, and that was fine because they were an affable bunch of people who were, for the most part, all on the same side.

'Can we all take a seat?' Oliver called, because if you had to say who the leader was, it was him, particularly tonight, which Jess was grateful for.

The chatting died down once everyone was seated, and they turned expectantly to look at Oliver since he was the one who had called this meeting out of the blue.

'Thanks for coming. Jess and I have got an idea to share,' he began. 'You all know about the date-with-a-book club.' There was a murmur of agreement. 'The library was looking for a way to launch the club nationwide and one of the proposals was to hold a huge date-with-a book club, almost like a festival weekend.'

'That's a great idea,' said Jen, who owned the Courtyard Café, where the bookclub nights were held along with Oliver's.

'Well, it wasn't an idea that worked for the British Library in the end because of timescales, but Jess and I thought it was too good to pass up. We wondered what you all think about us, the traders, organising a festival in Croftwood.'

There was an immediate resumption of the chatter levels there had been at the start of the meeting, cut through by Brian from the newsagents.

'How much is it going to cost us?' he asked. His arms were crossed, and Jess knew from experience that he was probably the hardest nut to crack.

'We don't know a lot of the detail yet,' Oliver admitted. 'But what we do have is an outline of what we're proposing that I've posted on the WhatsApp group.'

People started pulling their phones out of their pockets to look at the details.

'What we hope is that we can get a commitment from you to help. Not financially, but with some of the organisation. I know we're all busy with our own businesses, but any time you can offer will make all the difference.'

'And what's in it for us?' Another stalwart of the town, Rob, who owned the music shop.

'We need to work out the details,' said Oliver. 'Toby, we might need your advice on some of this, but I envisage some sort of profit share amongst the traders who want to take part.'

Toby, sat next to Jess, nodded. Although not strictly a Croftwood trader in that he didn't have business premises, he worked out of Oliver's every day and knew everyone and everything that went on in the town.

'Let's take a short break so that everyone can digest the information and then we can take questions after that.'

'I'm not sure it's blowing everyone away yet,' Toby said to Jess.

'No, but there's always the odd few who never want to get

involved with anything. I reckon we'll get enough interest to at least make it to the next step.'

'Which is what?'

'Getting an events company on board. Matt's sent out a few enquiries so we'll see if anything comes of that.'

'Wise idea. I can start looking into the different ways to set it up. Presumably it needs to be some sort of community interest company or a cooperative, something like that.'

'I have no clue at all,' Jess said. 'I did wonder whether we ought to start a bit smaller, grow it gradually.'

'Can you see Oliver going for that?' Toby grinned.

'No,' Jess sighed, 'and that's what brings us together tonight.'

'I'm looking forward to it, to be honest. It'll be the first thing that's happened in the town since I moved here that I can get involved in.'

'Maybe that's because we've never done anything on this scale before. Normally, it's someone else's thing, like when Patsy and Oliver opened the cinema, or when Jen organised the food market last summer in the park. And we're all willing to support those things, but I think the support this festival will need is on a whole other level.'

'How did you come to be Oliver's sidekick then, if you've got misgivings?' Toby had no hint of criticism in his voice. He was genuinely curious.

'I got carried away thinking about how cool it would be to have a huge date-with-a-book club meeting, then I started imagining a craft market, workshops, all that kind of thing.'

'Well, yes, I can see the vision is there,' he teased.

'I suppose I hadn't factored in all the nuts and bolts of it, like toilets. Apparently, it's hard to get toilets until Glastonbury's over. Who thinks of any of that when they're imagining themselves sitting in a field talking about books and doing a bit of knitting?'

'Quite.' Toby's brow was creased in a way that made him look as if he was taking Jess seriously, but she knew he was still teasing.

'Anyway, hopefully we'll find the events company of our dreams to do all the rubbish bits,' she said, 'and I can do all the fun bits.'

'Yes, I'm certain that's how it works,' he said.

Jess gave him a gentle shove in the arm and he laughed just as Oliver began calling the meeting to order again.

'Hopefully everyone's got a feel now for what we're proposing. The aim is to benefit the town and by running this ourselves, we can make sure that everything is being done with our interests in mind. Yes, Jen?'

'So, it's open for us to suggest ideas, even if they're blatantly only serving our own purpose? Sorry Jess, but craft workshops are only going to benefit you.'

Jess could feel her face flushing, but she also saw Jen's point. Everyone was looking at her as if she needed to say something to defend herself. She had nothing to be ashamed of, so stood up to respond.

'Obviously, when we were talking about initial ideas, that was one that came to me because of what I do. All of us probably have ideas to put forward that relate to our businesses and that's great, but even if you don't, we want to drive the festival goers into town. That's the point.'

'Where's it going to be?' Brian called out.

'We don't know. Everything's up for negotiation and we could do with suggestions on that front.' Oliver said.

People started chatting amongst themselves again, and Jess began to feel frustrated.

'Guys! Why don't we call it a night, take the information and what we've discussed tonight and think about how you feel about this in relation to your own businesses,' she said, ignoring the smirk on Oliver's face. 'You could, I don't know, do baking workshops or something like that, Jen. Have a pop-up newsagent, Brian. Organise some music, Rob. The point is that the book club was the starting point and I think we can all agree that it's going to be the biggest draw. Anything else is a bonus, and Oliver's right, it's up to all of us how it looks in the end.' She sat down with a thud, surprised at herself for speaking out when she hadn't planned to.

'Thanks, Jess,' said Oliver. 'I think it's a good idea for us to take some time to think about everything. In the meantime, Matt and I will collate whatever we get back from the events companies he's contacted and Toby is going to have a look at how we can structure the business end of things. Thanks for coming, everyone.'

Despite the misgivings that Jess knew some traders had, they all clapped before they got up and left.

'Jess, I didn't mean to sound like I was having a go at you,' Jen said, looking mortified. 'I know it came out like that, but I was really asking whether we could all put forward ideas of our own.'

'It's fine. I didn't think anything of it,' Jess lied. 'It was just the first thing that came to mind when we started talking about it.'

'And I know no-one sounded particularly enthusiastic, but we'll all be behind it, you know that.'

Jess wasn't sure she *did* know that, but she smiled at Jen as if she did. 'Thanks.'

'You might want to have a word with Mo from The Book Croft. She wasn't here tonight, but she might be interested in running a pop-up bookshop for you. Might feed in nicely with the book club.'

'That's a good idea, thanks.'

Jess wasn't at all sure how Mo would take the idea of supporting the book club, which was essentially promoting books with mass market appeal. The books that Lois and her team chose were popular fiction, romance, crime, thrillers and celebrity biographies whereas Mo's shop was full of prize-winning books that Jess had never heard of. When she did venture in there in search of something in particular, it usually had to be ordered. Not that she minded, because it was important to her to support the other independent traders in Croftwood, but sometimes she felt the romance novels that she loved were looked down upon by Mo.

'Fancy a drink at the coffee house on the way home?' Oliver asked Patsy, Jess and Toby as they started stacking the chairs against the wall at the back of the hall.

'I need to get home. Matt's been complaining he's barely seen me this week,' said Patsy.

'Really? He told me he was enjoying the peace,' Oliver said, earning himself an incredulous look from Patsy and a shove that almost toppled him.

Patsy and Oliver used to work in the coffee house together all the time before she started managing the Croftwood Cinema. Jess knew they both missed the good-natured but constant niggling at each other, and nowadays they took any opportunity to resurrect it wherever they were.

'As much as I'd love to, I have some work to do tonight. Another time,' Toby said.

Jess had a dress that was begging to be made, but she felt as keen as Oliver was to have a bit of a wash-up conversation.

'I'm in,' she said. 'I'll just get the car and park outside the shop to save me coming back over here later.'

The parking spaces outside the shops on the high street were restricted to just half an hour, but after six in the evening, you could park for as long as you liked. There was the perfect space waiting for her right outside Oliver's and she pulled Madge in just as Oliver was crossing the road. The doors of the coffee house were closed, but some of the lights were still on and Jack was behind the counter cleaning the coffee machine.

'We'll go round the back and have a drink upstairs,' said Oliver. 'Lois is coming to meet me here when the library closes.'

Jess locked the car and followed him down the alley in between his shop and the music shop next door.

'You're not living up here now, though. Aren't you at Lois's most of the time?'

'Yeah, it's just handy to have a base here and I wouldn't get much renting it out. It's more of an office than anything else, but we do stay the odd night, like in January when it snowed. We had no hope of getting back to Worcester that night.'

'I know. I ended up staying at Penny's. Madge doesn't like the cold.'

'Must be her age,' Oliver said, laughing.

It was cold in the flat, but once Oliver had switched on the fake flame gas fire, it was bearable and warmed up quickly. It helped that the decor in the flat oozed cosiness with the tweed fabric curtains and cushions, warm wooden furniture and worn leather sofas. The walls were dark; Jess couldn't remember if they were dark green or navy and it was hard to tell in the low-light.

'Tea or something stronger?' he asked.

'Tea's great, thanks.' She sat in one corner of the sofa that was closest to the fire.

'I thought it went well,' he said.

'Did you? I thought they seemed a bit anti, if anything.'

'I reckon once they all have a chance to think about what could be in it for them, they'll be right behind us.'

'That's what Jen said. I suppose we did have a head start on them, but I thought we'd have more ideas chucked into the mix tonight.'

'Maybe it's for the best not to have to yay or nay ideas just yet. It'll be hard for us to tell any of them if their idea's rubbish. Once we get an events company organised, that can be their job.'

'Good point.'

Lois arrived just as Jess finished her tea and was keen to hear all about the meeting.

'I wish I could have come, but Rosemary's a bit under the weather, so I sent her home early. What did they think?'

With his typical enthusiasm, Oliver painted the best possible scenario of how the meeting had gone without actually lying to her.

'It's okay,' Lois said to Jess. 'I know he's constantly wearing rose-coloured glasses.'

Jess laughed. 'I was just wondering whether we'd been at the same meeting.'

'Alright, so they weren't that keen.' Oliver held his hands up in surrender. 'But they will be and we'll keep planning, ready for when they are. The Croftwood Festival is going to be the best thing that ever happened to this town.'

And Jess couldn't help but believe him.

7

The following Wednesday was one of the rare occasions where Jess employed someone else to run one of her workshops. Although the shop stocked knitting wool, knitting wasn't something she was skilled in enough to teach. She'd known what brands she wanted to stock to complement the ethos she had on the fabric side, but the reps from the yarn companies, and more recently Patsy, had guided her as to what she ought to stock. She knew from her customers that she'd got most things right, and over the years, she'd tweaked the rest to make it a successful balance between profitability and customer satisfaction.

They had six ladies in today who were learning how to sew up their knitted garments to give them a professional finish. As far as Jess knew, it was mainly something called mattress stitch, which was yet to have a need for. She enjoyed knitting in the round, which was basically knitting tubes rather than flat pieces that needed sewing together. It was popular, but still considered a modern technique by lots of stalwart knitters, and lots of Jess's customers.

Being able to use the shop as the venue, since they could all get round the table in the back, was perfect. It meant Jess didn't need Penny to work, and it created more sales if the workshop attendees spent all day sitting amongst the wool.

The tutor, Fi, had been to Croftwood Haberdashery a couple of times before. One of the yarn companies had recommended her, and Jess loved the way she took charge of the customers as soon as they arrived. It was a welcome relief from having to run the workshop herself, but she also loved being a fly on the wall and the buzz in the shop on a workshop day was something she enjoyed. When they held the workshops in the shop, it was a fantastic advert to anyone who came into the shop, and Jess knew she'd get a few extra bookings from today.

'Morning!' Fi called, coming into the shop half an hour before she was due to start, as Jess had known she would.

'Hey, come in!' Jess came out from behind the counter to greet Fi, who felt more like a friend every time they met. 'I've just picked up coffee and pastries for us. Let's get stuck in before anyone comes.'

'Thanks, that's fab. I was planning to nip to that lovely coffee shop up the road once I'd set up and now I don't have to.'

Fi took a sip of coffee and then started unpacking her bag. 'I've brought some really cool sewing-up needles with me that I had as a sample. Is it okay if I give them to the ladies?'

'Yes,' Jess said, picking one up and studying it, struggling to see what made these needles any better than the ones she already stocked. 'Is it the bent tip?'

'It's perfect for mattress stitch,' said Fi. 'And it doesn't hurt that they're purple, does it?'

'No, that is cool. I'll take your word for the mattress stitch thing, though. Can I get these yet?'

'I think they'll be available in a couple of weeks.' She placed sets of instructions for each person around the table, and Jess placed a bowl of odd balls of yarn in the middle, along with a couple of plates of biscuits; the most essential thing.

Fi assessed the table. 'Yep, I think we're ready.' She sat down and pulled a pain au chocolat from the bag Jess had handed her. 'Ooh, this looks delish.'

'Can I book you for another date in April?' Jess asked before she tucked into a custard danish.

'I'm away in April. I'm going on a knitting cruise as the resident tutor.' She was grinning like the cat who got the cream. 'It's along the east coast of Canada, so it'll still be knitting weather and there's meant to be amazing scenery and wildlife.'

'Oh my god, how did you get a gig like that?' Jess couldn't believe there was even such a thing as knitting cruises.

'It's quite a new thing, at least for the cruise line I'm working with. They contacted one of the yarn companies I work for, and a couple of us applied. It sounds too good to be true, but I'm willing to give it a go to see. It's like a paid holiday because knitting never feels like work. They need sewing tutors too, you ought to apply. I know they're still looking.'

How exciting would that be? Jess quickly calculated that she could ask Penny to cover the shop, and perhaps ask a couple of the knitting club ladies to help. It would be amazing advertising for the shop and she'd be having the best working holiday she could imagine.

Then, almost at the same time, she brought herself down to earth. 'That does sound amazing, but I can't leave the shop for that long.'

'They do shorter Mediterranean cruises too. You should go for it.'

Jess shook her head, as much to emphasise to Fi, as to dislodge the painful images that the conversation had conjured up. 'No, I can't.'

Just then, the first two ladies arrived and Fi leapt up to

greet them while Jess tidied away the remnants of their coffee break, pleased that she didn't have to think anymore about cruises or holidays. She hadn't been on holiday since Jon died. For her, he was inextricably linked to sunshine, beaches and adventure and not just because they'd grown up at the seaside. Before he'd died, they'd toured around Europe in a camper van. They'd taken ferries between Greek islands, watched the sunset over the sea while they lay in each other's arms. They'd driven down Italy, clinging to the coast as much as they could, because they both felt at home when they were near the sea. After university, it was supposed to have been the first step on the way to bringing their lives back together and in the end, it was the only part they'd had. It was still difficult for Jess to look back on those months with any sense of bittersweet nostalgia because it still broke her heart to think about how perfect that summer had been and how that made everything that had come afterwards so much harder to accept.

The rest of the workshop ladies arrived and Jess busied herself taking orders for tea and coffee while Fi settled everyone around the table and they got started. When she delivered their drinks to the table, she also handed out small slips of paper for them to choose their lunch order, which she'd pop to Oliver's with straight away so that they would be ready for collection later.

She sat behind the counter and checked the website for orders. There were a few, so she spent a happy half an hour picking the orders from the shelves, cutting lengths of fabric and making a little pile for each order, including a Croftwood Haberdashery postcard on which she wrote a message to each customer. Something as simple as, 'I love the fabric you've picked!' added a personal touch that could make a connection, and hopefully they'd remember to buy from Croftwood Haberdashery the next time. It was one of her favourite jobs and more often than not she had to leave it to Penny because she was busy doing something else.

'I'm just going to pop to Oliver's with the lunch orders and go to the Post Office,' she said to Fi, once she'd packed everything up. It had been a fairly quiet morning, and she thought it unlikely that there would be a rush in the ten minutes she'd be away. 'If anyone needs a hand, ask them to wait, but if someone just needs to pay, you okay to do that?'

'Sure, I remember from last time. Don't worry, we can hold the fort.'

'Thanks, won't be long.'

It was a bright and relatively mild March day, so Jess didn't bother with a coat. She was wearing a long dress made of a fine wool fabric and had a thermal vest underneath. Her woolly tights and a petticoat edged with black broderie anglaise that peeked out from underneath the skirt kept her extra toasty.

The high street was fairly quiet, which was a good sign that there wouldn't be a huge queue in the Post Office and thankfully, that was the case. Once she'd dropped the parcels off, she headed to Oliver's.

Toby was sitting at his usual table near the window, busily typing on his laptop with his headphones on, but he smiled when Jess caught his eye. Oliver and Jack were behind the counter making up sandwiches and panini ready to be toasted during the lunch rush.

'Morning, guys,' she said, handing over the lunch orders to Jack.

He scanned through them and said, 'Yep, that's all fine. We can drop them round. It's not that busy today.'

'Famous last words,' said Oliver. 'Are you around later? Matt's had some quotes back from events companies and he thought we might like to have a look and arrange to meet a couple of the frontrunners.'

Jess agreed to pop into the coffee house after work and then headed back to the haberdashery, slightly worried that she seemed to have gone from a chat about having a festival to being full-on involved in the planning of it, with only an evening of brainstorming in between. It was starting to feel as if she might have bitten off more than she could chew. So far, it had been one meeting a week, but they'd barely started and she could see her precious evening sewing time becoming a distant memory. But maybe it would be different when they got the events company on board. Surely then they could take a more supervisory role that would take up a lot less time. They all had businesses they couldn't afford to neglect; after all, wasn't that the whole point of putting the festival on in the first place, to help their businesses and the town thrive?

Back at the shop, Fi was still sat at the table with her ladies, all of whom were now marvelling at their newly gained mattress stitching abilities, swearing never to use back-stitch again on their knitted garments. There were a couple of customers looking at wool, but they were contentedly browsing and didn't need any help when Jess checked.

It had been on her mind since earlier that morning, like an itch needing to be scratched. She sat down at the computer and googled 'knitting cruises'. The familiar feelings crept into her mind, the same way they did whenever she looked at holidays. It was unfortunate in so many ways that the first and only time she'd ever been abroad was with Jon. The whole idea of a holiday abroad was so inextricably linked to the memory of him it had been hard to contemplate doing the same again without him.

But this wasn't the same. This might be work, if she allowed herself to think about it like that. Not a holiday at all, and perhaps a way to reset herself. She was all too aware that her relationship with Jon still affected so much of her life, even all these years later. Something like this, something totally out of her comfort zone, might be a way to gain some closure.

'Would you mind passing my name on to that holiday company?' she asked Fi when they were tidying up together after the very satisfied group of ladies had left.

'Not at all! I'm so glad you're up for it, Jess. It'd be fantastic publicity for the shop, and who knows what it might lead to? I'm hoping to grow a bit of a following from it so I can look at getting my knitting patterns picked up by a publisher. As much as I love doing workshops, there's no future in it unless you have something to push off the back of them.'

'I suppose that's true. I didn't know you wrote your own patterns. Are they on Ravelry?' Ravelry was a website dedicated to knitting where almost every knitting pattern was listed. Knitters had a profile on there and could keep track of what they'd knitted, what yarn they used and it was an amazing resource for finding your next project, or seeing how a pattern you like had turned out for other people.

'Yes, I'll send you a link,' said Fi.

'Great. I'm just wondering whether we could do something together, put some kits together with your patterns and whatever yarn you think.'

'I love that idea, thanks Jess. I'll put some ideas together and let you know.'

Once Fi had gone, Jess locked the door behind her, leant against it and sighed, smiling to herself. This was just how things were if you had your own business. The very reason you did, was because it had once been an idea that you couldn't let go of. Those ideas didn't stop arriving just because you'd seen through one of the other ones. The festival was no different to what had just happened with Fi and the knitting patterns, and that was what Jess needed to remind herself. It might seem overwhelming at the moment, but it had been an idea that wouldn't leave her after the last date-with-a-book club meeting. It would still be needling at her if she and Oliver hadn't decided to get the festival off the ground.

Jess headed to Oliver's with a renewed excitement, resolving to take things one step at a time. She had come through worse, and now the town, her business, her friends were all things she loved. The festival was about all of that coming together, and it was going to be joyful to be part of bringing it to life.

8

Sebastian had spent the past few days obsessed by the email from Matt Garvey. The job felt like a hair's breadth from his grasp. He'd put a quote in and he was sure he'd nailed it. It was competitive; too competitive for him to make much of a profit, but it would give him the cash flow he needed to get through this bad patch. And if he got this job, it would be easier to get others off the back of it.

His finger hovered over the call button on his phone. Matt had said they'd let him know when they'd made a decision, but it felt too risky to wait until the decision had been made. If he could meet them, he could persuade them he was the right man for the job. He had nothing to lose.

'Hi Matt, it's Sebastian Thorne.'

'Sebastian, funnily enough, we've just been discussing the quotes.'

His stomach turned over at the thought they were in the midst of deciding his fate. 'Any decisions yet?' He tried to keep his tone light-hearted, as if the future of his business didn't depend on it.

'Not yet, but I must say, your quote is very competitive, so we'd definitely like to meet to discuss it in more depth.'

This was his chance. 'I can come now, if that's any good?'

Was he being too pushy? He must have sounded desperate. He held his breath while the muffled voices at the other end of the line discussed it, before Matt came back to him.

'If you're sure, that'd be helpful,' Matt said, going on to explain where they were.

Croftwood was half-an-hour away, but at this point, Seb didn't care if it was at the other end of the country. It could be the chance he'd been waiting for. He hung up the phone and grabbed his keys. He climbed into his truck, then caught sight of himself in the side mirror. He looked a mess. He hadn't brushed his hair or had a shave in... It said it all that he couldn't remember. His jeans were covered in a fine dusting of wood shavings from the storage he'd been building for the mezzanine level in the unit. If he turned up like this, he'd never get the job. He climbed out of the truck and went back inside the unit, ran upstairs to the mezzanine and found some clean trousers, a long-sleeved t-shirt and a fine wool jumper that he didn't remember. He took the clothes back downstairs, had the quickest strip-wash and shave he'd ever had at the sink in the tiny toilet, brushed his hair and rubbed some wax through the front to give the impression it was a hairstyle rather than just an unkempt mess. He dressed, locked-up and got back in the truck. Now, he looked more like the credible boss of a successful events company instead of the down-on-his-luck person who he was.

The sun had set, leaving the sky a fiery orangey-pink which Sebastian found beautiful enough that it took the edge off his nerves. It was a few years since he'd been to Croftwood, and as he turned down the high street, he was pleased to see that nothing much had changed, aside from a few of the shops. It had the look of a thriving little town dominated, from what he could see, by independent retailers, which meant that there were no gaping holes where chain stores had pulled out leaving large units empty.

He was looking for a coffee shop called Oliver's. Matt had said it was on the high street opposite the church and he found it easily. It was a slick-looking operation, and Sebastian already had respect for whoever owned this business, bringing their vision to life in a modern, attractive way that was sure to be paying dividends for them. Spotting a parking space just beyond the coffee shop, he pulled in, picked his laptop up from the passenger seat, took a deep breath, and got out of the truck. He could do this. He'd done it countless times before. Just not recently.

The sign on the door said closed, but he tried it and it opened.

'Hi there!' he called.

Three people emerged from a table, which was partially hidden from sight by an open shelving unit full of trailing plants. He recognised Matt straight away as he came over, holding his hand out with a big smile on his face.

'Great to see you, Sebastian. Thanks for coming.'

'No problem. It sounds like a really interesting project.'

They shook hands, then Matt introduced him to Oliver, owner of the coffee shop, and Jess, who owned a haberdashery shop. Did those even exist anymore? Bit of a throwback to the nineteen-fifties and probably full of grey-haired little old ladies. To be fair, she looked nothing like that herself. She was attractive, and he liked how she was dressed. Nothing she wore looked like anything he'd seen before. Her dress and cardigan weren't exactly fashionable, but she looked great. Her hair was in a messy bun with escaped tendrils falling in waves around her face. He found himself having to drag his eyes away from her.

'I assume this place is yours?' he asked, concentrating on Oliver instead as they shook hands.

'What gave it away?' Oliver said, laughing. He seemed like a good bloke, and Sebastian was pleased on some level that the owner of the coffee shop was as cool as the place he ran.

'He owns the cinema too, and you can blame him for getting all of us involved in this festival idea,' Matt said.

'Ah, I read about the cinema last year, I guess around the time you opened. What a great thing to bring back to the town.' Sebastian was aware he sounded like he was sucking up, but he had to win these people over.

He waited for Jess to come forward to say hello like Oliver had, but she didn't. She hung back on the other side of the table they'd been sitting at. Should he offer his hand? Somehow, it felt too formal. He'd rather have left it at an introduction and a friendly smile, but it didn't seem as if he was likely to get even that. Perhaps Oliver and Matt were the driving force behind the project, in which case he probably didn't need to worry about Jess's first impressions of him. In the end, he plumped for shooting her a quick smile, hoping to receive one in return. It didn't come.

'Can I get you a drink?' Oliver asked.

'Latte, if that's no trouble?' It had been some weeks, maybe months, since he'd had a decent cup of coffee. Instant with questionable milk was how he took it these days.

'No trouble.'

Oliver replenished the others' drinks while Matt looked through the quote Sebastian had sent in. Seeing his figures right there in front of them made his chest feel tight. He had to justify why he'd come in cheaper. That's what they'd want to know.

'I guess the main thing we're wondering is, how you can do such a good price. What's the catch?'

Matt still had the hint of a smile on his face, but Sebastian was under no illusion that the serious discussion had started. He needed to think on his toes and secure this contract before he left this coffee shop tonight.

Jess leaned forward, one elbow resting on the table,

waiting for his answer. Her blue eyes felt like they were boring into him, seeing everything he was trying to hide. His nerve faltered, and he had to look away from her before he answered Matt.

'I know it seems too good to be true, but for me, the biggest job is putting together an Events Management Plan. You'll need that before you can do anything. At the very least, it's your ticket to getting sign-off from the local Council. I had a contract for a festival in 2020, very similar to yours, that didn't happen in the end, but the EMP is as good as ready to go.'

Matt raised his eyebrows as if he bought into that story, giving Sebastian the confidence to continue.

'That means I don't need a hefty deposit. You're a new venture, so there's more work involved for an events company without an EMP template ready. They're likely to want big payments up front.' He was taking a punt on that being true and on the fact that, like him, his competitors probably hadn't put in their quote what the initial deposit would be.

'That's fair. We're still looking into how we go about raising the money for that. I mean, obviously we'll be selling tickets, but we're a long way from having a business plan that tells us how much we need to charge,' Oliver said, delivering the drinks to the table.

'We need to know the costs before we're able to get to that point,' Jess said. She addressed him directly, almost accusingly.

Sebastian's heart sank. This was a new venture for them and he should have realised they wouldn't be in a position to put down any money yet. He had to turn this around.

'I know it's your first year, and there's a lot to think about. But also, it's a lot to achieve if you want to do it this summer. By now, most festivals would have everything booked. You're going to be up against it.'

'We do know that,' Jess said defensively.

What was it about this woman? She was infuriating him by refusing to be won over by anything he said, unwilling to give him the benefit of the doubt about anything. But at the same time, he had a grudging respect for that. 'With an EMP that's ready to go, well, that's half the battle.'

'We did think about starting smaller and building up over the next couple of years, but we want to go for it,' said Oliver.

'I'm just playing devil's advocate,' Sebastian said, holding his hands up, and looking pointedly at Jess. 'When we speak to the council, they're going to say the same thing. Obviously I'd love to work with you on this and genuinely, I think I can help you win against this tight timeline, but if you decide to play the long game and aim for next year, I respect that.' It was a risky strategy. But what he hoped was they'd feel he was acting in their best interests and begin to trust him.

'Whichever company we go with,' she said, leaving him in no doubt that if it was anything to do with her, they wouldn't be choosing him, 'we'll be expecting them to deal with all the regulations with the council as well as manage all the suppliers and the landowner. That's the kind of experience we're looking for.'

'To be fair,' said Oliver, 'if Sebastian or anyone else can pull it off at the price he's quoting, we might need to give them a hand with some of it to make that work.'

Sebastian could have kissed Oliver. He was on side. 'If you did go with me, I'm happy to take all of that on and I stand by the quote I've given you.'

'It's just as well,' said Jess. 'We haven't got time to take any of that on, Oliver. If we didn't have our own businesses to run, we might not need an events company in the first place.'

Sebastian snorted. He couldn't help himself. Didn't she realise that there was no way a bunch of rookies could pull off an event of this kind with no experience in a matter of months? The EMP alone would be beyond them. Obviously, Matt and Oliver understood to some extent. And anyway, how busy could she be running her old ladies' sewing shop?

Deliberately avoiding the stare that he knew he was getting from Jess, Sebastian stood up. 'Look, I'll leave you to it. You've got a lot to discuss, but if you need any more information from me to make your decision, give me a call.'

'We appreciate you coming over. It's been a huge help,' said Oliver, clapping him on the shoulder as he showed him to the door.

'I'm not sure your friend thinks so,' Sebastian said once they were out of earshot of Jess and Matt.

'No, Jess is keen, she's just the voice of reality. She knows I'll do it whatever, so she's taking charge of the fact-finding. She'll be fine when you get to know her.'

'Okay, I won't take it personally then,' he said with a grin. 'It was great to meet you.'

'We'll be in touch.'

She'll be fine when you get to know her. Was that a sign from Oliver that he was going to get the job? He left the coffee house with a spring in his step. He wasn't going to tempt fate by celebrating too soon, but he knew he'd given himself the best possible chance of winning the contract, and it felt great.

9

'That was a stroke of luck finding Sebastian,' Oliver said, walking back to the table.

'Was it? Didn't he just tell us it's a terrible idea to try to do it this summer and that if we do, he's our only hope?' Jess was stunned that Oliver thought Sebastian had given them a credible quote, given how much lower it was than the others. And now that she'd met him, she had no confidence that he was the right person for the job.

'Um,' Oliver rubbed his chin thoughtfully. 'I don't know. Is that what you thought, Matt?'

'I thought he was—'

'Cocky?' Jess interrupted. She was damned if she was going to let this all-boys-together vibe get any traction.

Matt laughed. 'I was going to say confident he could help us pull it off. Look, I've done a bit of digging since the quotes came in and I think he's come in cheap because he's taking a hit on his own profit margin. Everyone in the business has had a hard time bouncing back from the pandemic. If he needs to cut his margin to get the contract, that's up to him, but I think he'll do a good job for us. As long as he comes up with the EMP like he said he would, that's the biggest hurdle for us.'

Jess trusted Matt. 'Okay, you know better than me,' she sighed. 'And anyway, Oliver likes him.'

'What's not to like?' Oliver said, holding his hands out and shrugging. 'We don't have to go with his suggestions on everything, but we need to remember, we don't know what we don't know.'

'And he knows?'

'He knows what we don't know,' Oliver laughed.

'We don't know what he knows,' Matt said.

'God, enough! Fine, let's go with Sebastian then,' Jess said.

'You don't want to meet any of the others? See the whites of their eyes?' Matt asked.

'Do you?' Jess asked Oliver, already predicting that he was keen on having a bromance with Sebastian.

'No,' he said. 'Let's go with Sebastian. He took the trouble to come over tonight. He cared enough about the job to call Matt to follow up, which is a great sign.'

'Okay. You can tell him.'

'Are you sure? I think he'd love to hear from you again, since you were so nice to him,' Oliver teased.

Oliver promised he'd ring Sebastian in the morning, and they made plans to arrange another traders' meeting before Jess and Matt left Oliver to lock up.

'Funny that you didn't hit it off with Sebastian,' Matt said, as he and Jess walked together to her car.

'Maybe I got the wrong impression of him, but he seemed like he was trying too hard. You know him and I trust you'd be able to tell if there was something weird going on.' She didn't phrase it as a question, but once they reached Madge, she turned to face him. 'Because Oliver is too excited to care. And he doesn't mind problems that come and bite him on the arse. He revels in the challenge.'

'That is true,' Matt said, smiling.

'I could do with someone else on my side, another voice of

reason, just until I get the measure of Sebastian. Until I know I can trust him.'

'To be honest, with work and the kids, I haven't got the time to get involved in it to that degree, but if you think something seems off, run it by me. Sorry, but Patsy will kill me if I take on another project.'

'Fair enough,' said Jess. 'Perhaps I'm overreacting. I think now that we're talking about money, it's made me realise that we're really doing this.'

'It seems like a huge risk, I know that, and it will be a lot of work, but you guys have hit on a great idea. I'm sure it'll be successful, otherwise I wouldn't have suggested you go for it. You only live once, Jess.'

Matt declined a lift home, so Jess turned Madge towards the hills and headed to her cottage. She mulled over what Matt had said. She knew better than anyone that you only live once. That was one thing that had brought her some comfort after Jon died. At least he'd really lived that last summer. They'd both had the time of their lives and she felt sure that if either of them had known what was coming, they would still have spent those last months doing exactly the same.

Jess pulled the car into the parking spot next to her cottage, took her bag from the back seat, and unlocked the door. She sighed and turned on a lamp in a vain attempt to bring some warmth to the lounge until she got the fire going.

She put the kettle on and made a pot of tea, leaving it to brew while she piled some paper and kindling onto the fire and lit it. Once it had taken, she added a couple of small logs and then poured herself a cup of tea, taking it to her favourite chair close to the fire.

When had she forgotten to live? She hadn't even noticed until today. Coming to Croftwood and starting her shop had been an enormous step at the time, and that had felt like living. She'd relished the challenge of growing her business, finding her feet in a new place and living a different life. It had been a life that had allowed her to leave some of the hurt behind and she'd loved it. She still loved it, but was she still living her best life? Had things become a little stagnant? Did she have any dreams anymore?

It wasn't even the festival that had started her feeling like this. It was Fi's suggestion about the sewing workshop holidays that had made her think. The idea of a cruise took her dangerously close to memories that still felt too tender to look back on with nostalgia, but after such a long time, perhaps that wouldn't be the case anymore. Should she be braver? Explore how she really felt now, instead of leaving everything that happened ten years ago locked in a little box in her mind and assuming that it was all exactly as she'd left it. Because maybe, she admitted to herself for the first time, maybe it wouldn't be.

She finished her tea and put another log on the fire. There was a built-in cupboard on each side of the chimney breast. One of them was full of half-finished craft projects and the other was full of all sorts of things that Jess never looked at but would never get rid of. Including a scrapbook she'd made for Jon of their summer holiday. She pulled out a few things that she'd stuffed in more recently, and then saw the spine of the scrapbook.

For most of the Greek island part of their holiday, Jess had worn a sarong over her bikini. She'd spotted it in a small gift shop on the first tiny island they'd visited. The shop was right on the beach and the floor had been covered in sand that had drifted in from outside. The outside of the shop was shaded by a simple awning of wood and canvas. The sarong itself was made from light, gauzy fabric and was decorated in a batik print of a turtle with waves of blue and green colour that perfectly captured the sunshine, water and beauty of where they'd found themselves.

Now, those colours were peeking out at her from the cupboard. The sarong, flimsy as it was, had torn. But Jess had kept it, feeling that it was perhaps the best souvenir of the holiday for her, despite not being useable any more. And then she'd decided on another use for it, and covered the plain scrapbook she bought, turning it from ordinary to something that linked them both to those precious months.

She gently eased it out of the cupboard, careful not to pull too hard in case she damaged the fabric. The turtle that she'd mostly managed to fit on the cover made her smile as she ran her fingers over it. Putting the book aside, she packed everything else back into the cupboard and then sat back in her chair, bringing the book to rest on her lap, poised to begin looking through the pages. But she couldn't. She knew exactly what was inside; every photograph, every note she'd written, every ticket she'd saved and stuck inside, all of them were ingrained in her memory. She didn't need to open the book to see what was inside.

Standing up, she put the book on the side. She'd leave it there for now. It was a step in the right direction, at least. She'd had a realisation today. That was the important thing. She didn't need to deal with everything tonight.

She poured herself another cup of tea from the pot and headed upstairs. It was only eight o'clock, there was still time to do some sewing. The spare bedroom was always cosy since it housed the chimney breast. She switched on the daylight lamp and started her favourite podcast, "Fortunately", on her phone. They'd had some ready-quilted fabrics delivered this week. Jess loved them, that's why she'd bought them, plus she had a vision of what she was going to make, and she needed to show her customers what that was. Then she was confident these fabrics would fly off the shelves. They were loose-weave Indian cottons that were quilted with a thin layer of wadding between them, making them slightly padded. One side was floral and the other a contrasting plain shade and she was making a simple, short, boxy jacket that would be reversible. That was the plan anyway, and it was putting Jess's binding skills to the test as she covered the raw edges of the front of the jacket with a plain strip of folded fabric to enclose them. By ten o'clock she'd almost finished, with just the pockets and the hems of the sleeves to sew, but that was enough for one night. It didn't need to be completed until Sunday, ready for her window change on Monday.

As much as she'd told herself that she'd taken enough of a step out of her comfort zone for one day, she lay in bed thinking about Sebastian, of all people. Aside from the fact that she'd thought he was a bit of a wide-boy, whatever Matt and Oliver said to defend him, there was something about him. If she'd met him at the coffee house, or he'd been at the date-with-a-book club — not that she imagined he'd be interested in that for a minute — she might have felt differently about him. If she ever had a type, he was it. She'd have swiped right if she was still on Tinder. He might have been verging on unkempt, with his hair giving off a distinct bedhead vibe despite whatever he'd bunged on the quiff at the front, but he had a lived-in look that Jess liked. He looked comfortable. And somehow, the image he'd been portraying tonight didn't seem like it went with everything else about him. That was what bothered her. It also bothered her that she was looking forward to seeing him again. She exhaled loudly, annoyed with herself for acknowledging that when he'd been so cocky. But when he'd first walked in, she'd seen something in his face, or thought she had. It was so fleeting she might have been mistaken. He'd looked vulnerable. And that tugged at her heart. Maybe next time they met, now that he was going to be offered the contract, he might be more relaxed, and she'd see the real Sebastian. The one she hoped was there.

She drifted off to sleep and dreamed of going to a festival on a Greek island and this time, unlike the many other dreams she'd had in the same place, she wasn't frantically looking for Jon.

10

The next traders' meeting was arranged for Wednesday night and had another good turnout. Being able to introduce Sebastian had helped enormously and Jess had to admit he came across very well, patiently answering lots of questions about logistics, costs and timelines as best he could. There were definitely fewer traders with folded arms and stern looks on their faces than there had been at the last meeting.

'Thanks very much Sebastian,' said Oliver, who was chairing the meeting. 'Can we have a show of hands if you're happy to appoint Sebastian Thorne as our event organiser?'

Almost every hand went up, much to Oliver and Jess's relief. Oliver had explained to Sebastian that they'd need sign-off from the traders before they went ahead, and he was confident they'd get it, but you could never be too sure.

'Great, that's a majority,' he said to Jess, who had agreed to minute the meeting as it would probably be the first one where there would be big decisions made. 'Now Toby Trentham will explain what he's found out about how we can legally structure ourselves as a company.'

Toby stood up and gave a brief presentation, recommending that they set up a Community Interest Company. He explained the advantages and disadvantages and told them about other ways they could do it and why he'd discounted those as unsuitable. He answered a few questions at the end and then handed back to Oliver.

'Can we have a show of hands for who agrees we will set up as a CIC?' Oliver said. 'And that's a majority,' he said with a huge grin. 'So by the next meeting we'll need to have decided on directors for the company. If anyone feels they'd like to join me and Jess on the committee, please stay behind afterwards and we can have a chat about that. I'll put that out on the WhatsApp group too for anyone who couldn't make it tonight.'

A few of the traders came over to say thank you, that they were behind the project and would be keen to help closer to the time, but weren't able to join the committee. Jen from the Courtyard Café, Rob from the music shop, and Hilary, who had recently opened a homewares shop, all stayed behind.

'Obviously I'm new to the town, so if you think I'm being a bit pushy coming onto the committee, please say. I won't be offended. But I do like to be busy and something like this is also a very quick way to get to know the town,' Hilary said.

'We need all the help we can get, and a fresh pair of eyes is always great,' Jess said, reassuringly. 'I love your shop, it's a brilliant addition to the town. I haven't managed to pop in yet, but your windows make it look very tempting.'

'Thank you!' Hilary said. 'I used to do merchandising for a big store in London, but after my marriage ended I fancied a change of pace.'

'Do you live in Croftwood?'

'Yes, actually Toby and I bumped into each other on the way over here and it turns out he's a close neighbour of mine. I moved about a month ago but I've been so busy with getting the shop up and running, I've barely had time to unpack.'

Jess remembered going through almost exactly the same. 'I

moved here and opened my shop at the same time, too. I wondered how I'd managed it once I had chance to take a breath.'

Hilary laughed. 'I'm not quite at the point of taking a breath yet, but I'll let you know.'

Jess interrupted Oliver and Jen, who were deep in a discussion about coffee blends. 'Guys, do you know Hilary? She owns Candles and Cushions.' They all introduced themselves.

'Let's arrange a meeting with Toby to get the paperwork sorted out. That's probably the next step,' said Oliver.

They called Toby over from where he'd been chatting with Sebastian and a couple of the traders, then they all pulled out their phones and came up with a date that worked for everyone.

'Great, thanks for stepping up, guys,' Oliver said to Jen and Hilary. 'I think it's going to be brilliant fun.'

'I'm really looking forward to getting stuck in,' said Hilary.

'Me too,' Jen said. 'I feel more comfortable with the whole idea now you've got a professional involved.' She nodded towards Sebastian, who was laughing with Rob from the music shop.

Sebastian had seemed more genuine tonight, Jess thought. Perhaps now he knew he'd won the business he wasn't having to try so hard, if that's what he'd been doing, because she hadn't noticed any arrogance while he'd been speaking. He'd come across as reassuring, confident and as someone who knew their field. There was something quite attractive about that. He was almost masterful.

'Jess?'

She realised she'd been staring at Sebastian and must have been daydreaming. 'Sorry, I was miles away.'

'Toby was suggesting meeting at his house?' Jen said.

'Oh, great,' Jess said.

'Should we ask Sebastian?' Oliver suggested.

'I don't think there's any need at this point,' said Toby. 'It's probably a good idea to keep a professional distance between the events management and the business side of things. You may go with someone else next year. We don't know how it's going to work out yet.'

'That makes sense,' said Hilary. 'We don't want to get into conflict of interests territory.'

'Exactly,' said Toby, smiling at her. 'And we will have some formalities to go through since you're all going to be directors.'

'That sounds quite intense,' Jess said.

'It's important you're aware of your obligations. But don't panic, it's nothing onerous at all.'

'Right, let's get tidied up so we can get out of here. I'm supposed to be taking Lois out for dinner tonight,' said Oliver.

The following day was Purl at the Pictures at Croftwood Cinema. It was a morning showing of One Fine Day with George Clooney and Michelle Pfeiffer and would be shown with the lights on just enough so that people could knit while they watched. It had been the brainchild of Patsy, who was a keen knitter, and she'd encouraged Jess to come along when it had started, to spread the word about The Croftwood Haberdashery. People travelled surprising distances for the opportunity to knit at the cinema and it had become a bit of a hit. Jess had soon realised that it could be lucrative to offer sewing up needles, knitting needles, crochet hooks and other bits and pieces people tended to forget when they brought their project with them. Patsy had agreed that she could set up her wares on the end of the bar that was in the cinema foyer, and that had happened for the past two or three months.

Jess kept a box of supplies in the same cupboard as her workshop sewing machines, and she arrived early so that she had a chance to set up before anyone else arrived. The door to the cinema was unlocked, so she let herself in and called out to see who else was there.

'Morning, Jess,' said Patsy, emerging from the ladies' toilets with a caddy of cleaning things and sporting some pink Marigolds.

'Morning. Do you need a hand before I set up?'

'No, luckily for you, I've just finished,' Patsy said with a grin. 'So I hear you're the director of the Croftwood Festival.'

Jess rolled her eyes. 'Honestly, I don't know how it's gone from me suggesting a big date-with-a-book club meeting to Lois, to being the director of a new annual festival.'

'You hadn't accounted for the Oliver effect. Do you think I planned to be the co-owner of a cinema? I was pretty happy being the best barista in the world.'

Jess laughed. 'Oh, really? Everything changed for you because you got dragged into renovating this place.'

'Exactly,' she said. 'It was the best thing that could have happened. Made me realise I'd been hiding out, scared of the past, when there was all this possibility out there.'

Patsy didn't know anything about Jess's past with Jon. No-one did, so it was scary how close her recounting of her own experience mirrored how Jess had realised her own life was playing out. But Patsy did know that Jess skipped around the edge of everything, relationships in particular. And as much as Jess pretended to her friend that she wasn't ready to settle down, or hadn't found Mr Right, it was no wonder that Patsy was suspicious of Jess's situation when there were so many parallels with her own. Jess was running from the past, that much they had in common, but Patsy had literally been hiding from an abusive ex-husband, whereas Jess was hiding from…what?

'It's different. Oliver could see you needed something to bring you back to life, Patsy. Look at you now, you've never been happier, and he knew you well enough to see that you'd flourish given the chance.'

'Okay, so I'm not saying you're not living your best life, Jess, but this might give you a chance to fly by the seat of your pants for a change. There's nothing like stepping outside of your comfort zone to really make you feel alive.'

Jess tried not to be offended by the idea that Patsy thought her life was boring, predictable, and not fulfilled by her business when that wasn't true.

'But I love the haberdashery. It's literally the dream job for me.'

'Jess, it's not a criticism. No-one is saying that you're doing anything wrong but just like I couldn't see how taking on the cinema project could bring me a whole new life that I didn't think I'd ever have, the festival might open some new doors for you.'

On the defensive, Jess said, 'Well, I've been offered the chance to teach sewing workshops on a cruise.' Okay, so not entirely true, but it could be.

'Wow! That's amazing! And are you going to take it up?'

She didn't want to lie to Patsy. But admitting that she wasn't sure was the same as admitting that maybe Patsy was right, that she was firmly stuck in her comfort zone. 'I'm waiting to hear the details, but it sounds amazing.' Not a lie.

'Good for you! See? That's what I'm talking about. A new challenge can make all the difference to everything.'

The first customers arrived, and Jess was relieved that the conversation was over. As soon as she started chatting to people, she fell into her happy place, talking about the shop and asking people about what they were working on.

'Go in and watch if you want to,' Patsy said. 'Is Penny in

the shop?'

She nodded. 'Thanks, I might just do that. I love this film.'

Jess sat at the back of the stalls so she could help anyone who needed emergency haberdashery and pulled her crochet out of her bag. She was teaching herself to crochet granny squares and had thankfully got to the stage of knowing what she was doing, so she could get into a bit of a rhythm with it. She didn't care what it looked like. It was just practice, and it was nice to have something to do while she watched the film.

Perhaps Patsy was right. Being involved in the festival might seem daunting, especially since she seemed to be a director now, but maybe it would help her get used to doing something different. Then maybe the idea of the sewing cruise might not seem like such a leap into the unknown. And maybe it was time to acknowledge that she needed to let herself come to terms with losing Jon. That shutting that part of her past out was holding her back. Why did so many things seem inextricably linked to that summer with Jon when there was no reason for them to be?

After the film, Jess stayed behind to help Patsy tidy up.

'You're right,' she said. 'I've been hiding in Croftwood ever since I came here.'

Patsy leant her dustpan and brush against a chair and sat down, patting the chair next to her. 'What from?'

Jess took a deep breath, not sure how to say any of it, because she never had before. 'I came here because I lost my boyfriend.' She couldn't say it any other way, and she hoped her eyes would convey to Patsy that "lost" meant so much more than that.

'I had no idea,' Patsy said, reaching out to take Jess's hand. 'I'm so sorry.'

'Thanks. It's a long time ago.'

'I'm not sure it matters how long it's been. Time doesn't heal everything.'

Jess took some comfort from the fact that Patsy understood that.

'No, it doesn't, but after almost ten years, and a fresh start, I was hoping it would have helped.' She smiled. It wasn't as hard to talk about now that she'd started.

'I know it's not the same, but for me, the fresh start was always because of what'd happened before, and was always kind of tainted by that.'

It made so much sense. 'That's it exactly. I think I've only just begun to realise that.' She paused. 'Jon and I grew up together. We'd been in love since we were old enough to know what that was. I haven't been home much since because I'm scared everything will remind me of him and it'll hurt too much, even now.'

'All I know is that facing the things you think you can't face makes you stronger in the end.' Patsy said. 'You think you're still the person who left ten years ago, but you're not, Jess. You're stronger. Going back won't change that.'

Jess wiped at her eyes. 'I've been thinking about going back for a visit. It might be the only way to move on. I loved moving here because it felt like I'd left all of that behind, but you don't really leave it behind because the memories are inside me, not in bloody Dorset.'

Patsy laughed. 'That's it exactly. But knowing that's true doesn't make it any easier to go back to where those memories were made.'

'Or any easier to think about doing stuff that might remind you of things you've tried not to think about. The sewing cruise I told you about?' Patsy nodded. 'Straight away, it took me back to me and Jon in the Greek islands. I mean, it's not even going to be in the Greek islands!'

'No, but there's an association, isn't there? Have you been anywhere since you moved to Croftwood? Since you lost Jon?' Patsy asked gently.

'Not really. In the beginning, it was too sad to think about being on holiday without him, so I stopped thinking about holidays or anything like that. And now, when this is a work thing, it's like my mind thinks: it's a cruise, it's a holiday. And that's it, I'm fighting against all the memories again.' Jess sighed and leant back in the chair, closing her eyes for a second. It was exhausting letting all of this out. She'd said none of it out loud before and somehow, already, she felt lighter for it.

'I think you're answering all your own questions here,' Patsy said. 'What are you going to do?'

'I'm going to go to Dorset for a couple of days before my life gets taken over by this festival. Maybe if I go back and it's not as bad as I'm expecting, it might help me feel less anxious about everything else.'

Because she *was* anxious, she realised now. She'd loved the idea of the festival, but being so heavily involved in the organising of it was worrying her, and there was nothing at stake for her personally, other than spending precious time on something that might not pay off. But that was the worst thing that could happen, wasn't it?

'Thanks for listening, Patsy. I appreciate it.'

'Anytime. And if you need me to tell Ollie to back off over the festival, I'd be glad to. Anytime,' she grinned.

Patsy began sweeping again while Jess straightened the chairs back into the formation they'd been in before the knitters gathered them into clusters.

'It's not Oliver that worries me. Have you met that guy Sebastian Thorne yet?'

'No, but Ollie mentioned you'd decided to give him the contract.'

'Mmm.'

Patsy raised her eyebrows. 'Why? What's wrong with him?'

That was a good question. Was there anything wrong with him? He was confident, good-looking in a dishevelled kind of way, and when he smiled at her, it made her wish she hadn't taken against him. Because she'd quite like him to smile at her again.

'I don't know. Matt knows him from before and he trusts him.'

Patsy shrugged. 'I don't think they're friends or anything, but I think Matt's a good judge of character.'

'I know, so why do I feel like Sebastian's hiding something?'

'Like what?'

'I don't know. Maybe I'm reading too much into it.'

'You have a lot going on. It's not your job to get to the bottom of everything by yourself. If you're worried, talk to Ollie. He'll take anything you say seriously, you know that.'

What would she even say? That she had a 'feeling' he was hiding something? It was hardly grounds to withdraw the contract from him. Besides, she hadn't felt the same way yesterday at the traders' meeting.

'Ignore me. I need to take a breath, that's all. I'm sure he's fine. I need to give him a chance, after all, he's already done plenty to help us out and we haven't paid him a penny yet.'

'That's got to be a good sign.'

After she'd packed up her wares, Jess wandered back through the park to the haberdashery. She noticed the cherry trees and a couple of magnolias beginning to show signs of blossoming. She smiled. It felt like a sign. She would go to Dorset. Allow herself to be open to the memories in the hope that she could move on. It was time.

11

Sebastian was still on a high from winning the Croftwood Festival contract. There was a lot of work to do, especially considering how little he personally was likely to make from it, but as long as he could pay the rent on the unit and feed himself, that was enough for now.

He'd spent the morning checking out a handful of potential festival sites. It was the main thing he needed to pin down before he could start writing the Event Management Plan. The traders had put forward various suggestions, ranging from a farm that was closer to Worcester than it was to Croftwood, to a piece of land that was perfect apart from being ninety-five percent covered in trees.

In his mind, there were two contenders. The first, and his preference, was to have the main festival site in Croftwood Park. It was easy to fence off, it belonged to the Council so hopefully it would be easy to get permission, and it was close enough to the town that they could have some fringe events in the town centre. It was almost perfect, apart from not being immediately obvious where they'd be able to have a campsite. An important detail, but Sebastian wasn't in the habit of letting things like that put a stop to a good idea. The other option was Croftwood Court. It was an old estate on the edge of town, and he'd been told by more than one person that Lord Harrington might be open to the idea. It was in second place since it was that bit too far from the town to be within walking distance for everyone, but it might end up being the only viable option, so Sebastian was on his way to meet the Estate Manager.

From his brief internet research, he knew that Croftwood Court itself was surrounded by fields and still farmed by tenant farmers. He'd emailed via the estate website and had made an appointment.

The wrought-iron gates were already open, and judging by the grass growing around the gateposts, perhaps they always were. The house wasn't visible from the road and even as Sebastian reached the estate office after only a minute or so, it still couldn't be seen. It was a good sign that there was plenty of room for a festival and that it wouldn't necessarily disturb the lord of the manor.

He pulled up outside the offices, which were in the least dilapidated of three stable blocks that surrounded a central courtyard. Everything looked run down; the guttering was broken and hanging down in multiple places and there were quite a few tiles broken or missing on the roofs. If this place was any indication of the state of repair of the wider estate, they might welcome the money they could charge for hosting a festival.

As he got out of his truck, a dog came out to investigate him. It was a border collie. Perhaps she'd been a sheepdog, although with her black patches greying, and a sedate way about her, she was probably retired.

A man about the same age as Sebastian, although looking older than his mid-thirties since he was dressed in tweed, emerged from the office and strode towards him with his hand out. 'Hi there, I'm Archie Harrington. You must be Sebastian?'

'Yes, good to meet you. I appreciate you agreeing to meet me on such short notice.'

Archie bent down and patted the dog before flinging his hand out, gesturing for her to head back inside. 'Come on Tatty, inside.'

'Tatty?' Sebastian couldn't help himself.

'Tatiana. Named by my younger sister when she was having a Russian literature phase. No good for a working dog, so we compromised.'

Tatty led the way inside to what at first glance looked like a highly disorganised office, and settled herself in front of the fire. There were two desks that faced each other, the point where they butted together impossible to see due to the pile of paperwork and other paraphernalia that was acting almost like a privacy screen.

Archie sat behind one of the desks and gestured for Sebastian to take a seat in a shabby old armchair across the other side of the room, but thankfully close to the fire.

'So, you're interested in renting some land?'

It had felt safer to be vague. Getting the face-to-face meeting was the goal. He knew that blurting out that he wanted to organise a festival would result in rejection because most people equated festivals with Glastonbury.

'Yes. I don't know if you've heard of the book club that Croftwood Library runs?' Sebastian had a fair idea that even if Archie hadn't, it sounded respectable enough for him to be heard out.

'Ah yes, I know a chap whose wife had something to do with that. She uses the mobile library and they were impressed that a book club was on offer, even to those customers.'

Sebastian had no idea about that, but nodded as if he did. 'Hugely successful. The Croftwood Traders' Association, along with the library, are hoping to host a huge meeting of the same book club in the summer. Potentially invite people from all over the country to join in.'

Archie was nodding thoughtfully as Sebastian spoke. It could only be a good sign.

'As discussions have gone on, we've come to realise that we may need to provide other entertainment at the same time. I mean, there is only so long one can spend talking about books.'

'Hah!' Archie blasted, making Sebastian jump. 'I was just thinking the same!'

'So we'd need to provide some food, drink, and possibly a little entertainment. And camping.'

Archie frowned. 'Camping? You mean a festival?'

'We're not talking about Glastonbury,' Sebastian said with a wide smile. 'Very different demographic.'

'Right.' Archie still looked uncertain. 'I'm going to stop you there. It's going to be a no, I'm afraid. There's no question about holding anything of that nature on the estate itself. You might not be aware, but the majority of the estate land is managed by a trust. It is not a straightforward arrangement and would involve gaining all sorts of permissions. Besides, my mother still lives in the Court and while she might enjoy the odd book, she certainly would not appreciate the influx of…' He seemed to be grasping for the right word. 'Campers.' He almost shuddered.

Sebastian suddenly made the connection; Archie Harrington was the Lord of the Manor himself. Lord and Estate Manager by the looks of things.

'It was a bit of a shot in the dark, to be honest, because what we'd prefer is to keep the festival within the town. It's possible to run everything from Croftwood Park, but we're stuck for where to situate the… camping.' Sebastian almost struggled to say the word himself this time, knowing the reaction it had caused.

'Ah, well, my friend, I might be able to help you with that.'

By the time Sebastian headed back to the unit, he had a plan, thanks to Lord Harrington. With his biggest problem as good as solved, his mood was buoyant until he returned to the unit, to the prospect of another night spent alone in the cold.

While he sat, nursing a generous measure of whisky that evening, as much for its ability to warm him from the inside as for taking the edge off, he wondered, as he did most evenings, whether he was being stubborn. He could pick up the phone, call his father, and most of his problems would be solved within a few days. But it felt like a failure. His father would see it like that, as well as seeing it as his victory. Charles Thorne was not a supportive father.

After Sebastian's mother died, Charles didn't enjoy being a single father, and shipped Seb off to boarding school while he quickly moved on, marrying a much younger woman who preferred living her life without a ready-made son being part of it. But keeping Sebastian at arm's length didn't stop Charles from having strong opinions about what his only son ought to be doing when he left school. So, instead of going to university as Charles was insisting he did, Seb got a job as a stage-hand in a theatre and had stood on his own two feet ever since.

If Charles had mellowed in his old age, or ever tried to reconcile, then Seb might have found it easy to ask for some interim financial support while he built the business up again. But he knew that wasn't the case. If he asked for help, there would be strings attached, and after being independent for so long, it was hard to imagine being beholden to anyone, especially his father. Charles would be thrilled to be proven right, that's how Seb knew he'd see it, even after all this time. He wouldn't want to acknowledge that Seb *had* been a success. Until now. So yet again, Seb came to the conclusion that he had no choice but to stick it out, hope for things to turn around and do everything he could to make that happen.

12

The following Monday morning, before the shop opened, Jess picked up two coffees from Oliver's and headed to Croftwood Library. It was the one morning a week when Lois arrived early so that she could get a lift to town with Oliver, and a while ago, she had offered Jess the chance to browse the library shelves before opening time, since it wasn't always easy for Jess to find time when the library was open.

She texted Lois as she left the coffee house and by the time she'd walked along the high street to the library, Lois was waiting to let her in.

'Oh, you're a lifesaver, thanks,' she said as Jess handed her the coffee. 'I forgot to get some milk, so I had to settle for a cup of black tea.'

'Don't you just love Mondays?'

Lois laughed. 'Come in.' She held the heavy wooden door open for Jess and then dropped the latch once they were both inside.

'Have you decided on the books for the next date-with-a-book club?' Jess asked as she made a beeline for her favourite place in the library: a display unit where all the latest romance books to arrive at the library came before they ended up on the shelves.

'Yes, they're in the usual place.' Lois headed over to the big reading table that was in the middle of the library and took a seat, pulling the top off her coffee cup. 'I hear you've found a festival venue?'

'Have we?' Jess said, not paying too much attention as she read the back cover of the latest Jilly Cooper novel.

'Oliver said Sebastian's made some kind of deal with Lord Harrington.'

'Lord Harrington?'

'He owns Croftwood Court.'

Jess was paying attention now. 'But that's not what we planned at all. It's supposed to be in the town, not in some fields in the middle of nowhere. We want people to feel like they're coming to Croftwood to the date-with-a-book club, where it all started.'

'I might have got the wrong end of the stick,' Lois said, trying to backtrack. 'Oliver mentioned something about the park too, so perhaps I've got it wrong. It's hard to keep up with everything. He's so enthusiastic, it can be a bit wearing sometimes.'

Jess couldn't help but laugh. 'I'm sorry. I shouldn't be cross. It's not as if we don't need to find a venue. If he's already done that, it's great. He knew what we were after and I'm sure he's run it past Oliver.'

But why hadn't he run it past her? Was this what it was going to be like? That even being a director was not going to elevate her to the same level as Oliver in the eyes of Sebastian. For whatever reason, he was going to bypass her, just the same as when he couldn't meet her eye in that first meeting at the coffee house.

'Talk to Oliver, Jess. He really values the fact that you and the others have stepped up. He wouldn't do anything without you knowing.'

Jess picked up the Jilly Cooper and chose the Dictionary of

Lost Words as her book club read.

'It's not strictly a romance,' said Lois, 'but I loved it and I think it'll be a great book for people to talk about.'

'That's the whole point, after all,' Jess smiled. 'I think I might need a palate cleanser, anyway. Too much romance isn't good for me.'

'Oh, come on. Doesn't it give you hope that you might find a lovely man, just like the ones you're reading about? Perhaps not Rupert Campbell-Black,' she said nodding at the Jilly Cooper, 'But maybe, I don't know, someone like lovely Atlas from Colleen Hoover's It Ends With Us.' They'd both read the TikTok sensation a few months back and had agreed that Atlas might just be the perfect man.

'I don't know. I'm starting to think that those sort of men don't exist in real life, or if they do, they're all taken by now. Anyway, you know me, I'm not really that interested.'

Lois looked at her as other people did when she said that kind of thing to them. They wanted to ask why. But all Lois said was, 'Good for you.' And if she suspected there was more to it, she also respected the fact that Jess would have told her if she'd wanted to, and that made Lois a very good friend indeed.

'Thanks for the books. I'll see you soon.'

'Thanks for the coffee. And make sure you talk to Oliver. You might need to rein in this Sebastian chap if he really is doing things without your say so.'

'I will.' But she already knew that she had, again, thought the worst of Sebastian before she knew the facts and was glad that she'd spoken to Lois before she found out from Oliver or Sebastian himself. She might have flown off the handle and made a fool of herself.

Jess was back at the haberdashery and ready to open at nine-thirty sharp. She pottered around picking stock for a handful of internet orders, then flicked through some fabric samples that had arrived in yesterday's post. What Lois had said was bothering her, but without Penny helping in the shop today, she had no chance to pop out and talk to Oliver.

It was window-changing day. Jess chose Mondays for the job because aside from the odd customer who had run out of sewing thread or wool over the weekend, it was usually quiet enough for her to get on, even if she was in the shop by herself. The quilted jacket had turned out perfectly, and she knew it was going to be a draw. It looked like something you'd buy from Oliver Bonas, but you could make it for a fraction of the price.

The first job was to empty the window of what was already there. Jess systematically removed balls of wool, pattern books, sewing patterns and bolts of fabric, laying them on the counter before she'd put them back into stock. She was gazing out of the window while she folded a length of tweed fabric, when she saw Sebastian on the other side of the road.

Before she'd even thought about what she was going to say, she was out of the door.

'Sebastian!' she yelled across the road, unwilling to cross over just in case the shop got looted while she was away.

He looked surprised and turned, scanning for who had called his name.

'Sebastian!' She waved to grab his attention.

His face broke into a grin, which had the surprising effect of making her heart flutter, and he looked both ways before crossing over the road.

'Hi, how are you?' He was still smiling, looking just like someone who hadn't done a deal on a venue for the festival without having agreed it first.

But the smile was disarming. And attractive.

'I hear you may have found a venue for the festival.'

He moved around her to keep out of the way of people who were walking past, and she caught a whiff of aftershave.

It was her weakness and her stomach did an involuntary flip, which only annoyed her more.

'Oh, yeah, I was just on my way to see Oliver—'

'Right, so you've arranged something with Croftwood Court?'

His smile disappeared and his eyes narrowed. 'Yes. How did you —'

'Brilliant. You do know that's too far out of town, completely wrong for what we wanted and you didn't even have the decency to run it past *all* of us, *all* the directors,' she emphasised, 'before you went ahead.'

'Went ahead? What do you mean?'

He was playing dumb to take the wind out of her sails. Although he was looking puzzled now. Had she got the wrong end of the stick?

'I heard you made a deal with Lord Harrington.'

'That's true,' he said.

His face had relaxed, and Jess found herself staring into his eyes. They were the deepest brown with green flecks in and her mind leapt back to the first time she'd seen eyes like that.

'Jess?'

'Sorry.' With some effort, she dragged herself back, remembering that she was in the middle of tackling Sebastian about whatever was going on with Lord Harrington. 'So you admit it?'

'Look, I think there's some crossed wires here. Have you got time for a coffee? Maybe we ought to have a chat.'

'No, I haven't got time. I'm in the shop on my own today.' She was finding it hard to keep up this level of impatience when now he was looking at her with a concerned look, and she wasn't sure why.

'Are you alright?'

She wanted to laugh it off, but suddenly she knew her laugh was about to come out as a sob. What was wrong with her? 'Fine, tell Oliver and I'll catch up with him later.' Before he could say anything else, and before she caught a glimpse of his eyes again, she turned and headed back into the shop.

'Oh, I'm sorry, I wasn't sure if you were open,' said the young woman, who was standing uncertainly just inside the door when Jess went back inside.

'I had to have a quick word with someone.' She put on her brightest smile. This stuff with Sebastian and the Festival had to wait until much later. She could hardly sit in the shop and sob for half an hour. 'Can I help you?'

An hour or so later, despite her vow not to think about any of it until the shop had closed, the lack of customers had taken away the distraction she was hoping for. She'd finished the window and was sat with a Cup-a-Soup and a banana at the table, beginning to feel like she'd made a fool of herself.

They had the same eyes. Sebastian had Jon's eyes. There was no other similarity between Jon and Sebastian whatsoever. If there was, she'd have noticed the first time they met. And a person's eyes were more about the bit around their eyes. The way the corners crinkled when they smiled, the way they might raise their eyebrows or frown. Things like that. Again, no similarity. But his eyes were exactly the same colour as Jon's, and all Jess had been able to do in that moment was stop while a movie played in her mind of the times she'd looked into Jon's eyes.

She heard the door open, snapping her out of her thoughts about eyes and all the feelings that went along with that. Tucking her banana skin into her empty mug, she headed towards the counter ready to greet her latest customer.

'Sebastian.'

'You should call me Seb,' he said, handing her one of the coffees he was carrying. His coat was slung over the top of his leather satchel, which he lifted from his shoulder and put on the floor.

'Thanks,' she said, trying not to brush his fingers with hers as she took the coffee. She'd all but admitted to herself that she'd been wrong to have a go at him based on a throwaway comment from Lois, and she'd been hoping she wouldn't have to see him again until she'd had time to get over how foolish she felt. The hour or two since she'd last seen him was not long enough at all.

He leant back against the counter, seemingly in no hurry to explain why he was here. His shirt sleeves were rolled up to the elbows and the cuffs of the long-sleeved t-shirt he was wearing underneath were pulled up just enough to display his impressive forearms. It was another of Jess's weaknesses. Unfortunately, Sebastian's were among the nicest she'd seen, with just the right amount of dark hair scattered from wrist to elbow and muscles that rippled attractively when he crossed his arms. Why was she noticing all these things today? It was as if he was deliberately presenting his full arsenal of redeeming features one after the other to throw her off.

'I wanted to apologise for earlier. I was worried I might have upset you.' He looked concerned, reminding Jess of the look that had been on his face earlier. She inwardly cringed again.

'So I got the wrong end of the stick? You haven't organised the festival to be at Croftwood Court?'

'No, I haven't.'

He was looking at her in a way he hadn't seemed able to the first time they'd met in Oliver's. If only he'd been like this that night, she might have felt differently about him from the start.

'I've been to see Lord Harrington though, so I can understand where the confusion's come from.'

Jess was well aware that he was trying to spare her embarrassment by pretending she hadn't over-reacted, but it was completely mortifying. Sebastian must think she was a complete nutter, accusing him of... what? Helping them? Doing his job?

'Okay, well, I'm sorry. Perhaps I overreacted.'

He laughed. 'Maybe.'

He was laughing at her. She'd just admitted she might have been wrong, and he was laughing. Her blood pressure climbed. Just as she'd been thinking she was wrong about him, he showed his true colours again.

'Do you know what? I might have overreacted, but it's only because you're not being up-front about what you're doing and it annoys me.'

He looked surprised but said nothing, so against her better judgement, she carried on.

'I can see you're only interested in working with Oliver. But I can tell you now, he doesn't operate like that. Whatever you think you're gaining by keeping me out of the loop, he'll include me anyway.'

'Jess, I'm sorry.' Cue the surprised look again. 'I'm not keeping anything from you. I only went to see Oliver to ask if we could get everyone together to discuss the options.'

'You laughed at me.' She hadn't meant to say that.

He looked down at the floor and gently shook his head. 'I wasn't laughing at you. It was relief that you realised you'd... got the wrong end of the stick. I wasn't laughing at you,' he said again. He turned his head to look at her, and Jess sucked in a breath. This time, she knew without a doubt that he was sincere. 'I want to work with you. With all of you.' He picked up his coffee and took a sip. 'It's good coffee.'

'It's great coffee. I'm sorry. Can we rewind to the part before I saw you walking past the shop? Let's pretend I waved through the window at you instead.'

'Okay. How did I end up here then? I don't need any knitting wool today.'

'You popped in to tell me about the venue idea. You told

Oliver while you were getting coffee and now you're going to see Rob, Hilary and Jen to tell them.'

He pushed himself up to standing and turned towards her, locking eyes with hers. 'I only bought one extra coffee, and that was for you.'

Jess felt her cheeks redden.

He took a step towards her. There were only inches between them, and the smell of his aftershave was intoxicating in the best way. Jess wanted to rub something against his face so that she would have the smell of him on her long after he left. She took a deep breath and attempted to get a grip.

'I will take one of these, though.' He reached past her to a tub of tape measures that were next to the till and picked one out. 'You can never have enough tape measures.'

'It's on the house,' Jess said, retreating behind the counter.

'You sure?'

She nodded. It felt like a peace offering.

'Thanks. So I guess I'll see you soon?'

She nodded and watched as he picked up his bag and pulled it onto his shoulder. He tucked his new tape measure in his pocket, picked up his coffee and left.

She stared at the door for a good while after he'd walked out of it, his aftershave lingering in his wake. It was an entirely unfamiliar feeling that she hadn't expected. Yes, she grudgingly admitted that despite his initial cockiness she'd thought Sebastian was attractive, but this was next level, something she hadn't ever experienced before. Never. Not even with Jon. And that was scary and exhilarating all at once.

13

Jess conceded that Sebastian had indeed managed to come up with the perfect solution to the question of where the Croftwood Festival would be held. Apparently, he'd been turned down by Lord Harrington for using Croftwood Court and Jess couldn't help thinking that if he hadn't been, is that where the festival would be? But actually, the irritation that Sebastian sparked within her had faded and now, she didn't believe he'd try to do anything underhand. After his visit to the shop, she'd decided to make a fresh start with him, if only to explore the way he made her feel in a little more detail. Having said that, she was pleased tonight was only a meeting of the directors: her, Oliver, Rob, Jen and Hilary.

Sebastian had sent an email, via Oliver, explaining what he'd agreed in principle with Lord Harrington. He had offered them use of some other land that he owned, which was a stone's throw away from the park. It was towards where Matt and Patsy lived and Jess, along with everyone else, had assumed it was common land and therefore off limits to them, when in fact it was part of the Croftwood Court Estate. It wasn't adjacent to the rest of the estate land, which is why it wasn't subject to the same rules as the land that was managed by the Trust. Sebastian was suggesting they hold the festival in the town, predominantly in the park, with the camping facilities and parking on Archie's land. They could hopefully arrange a walkway through the land between the park and the campsite. It was a mixture of scrubland and allotments that Sebastian had discovered was owned by the Council.

'It sounds brilliant,' said Hilary.

'Having the festival in the park is going to mean the town benefits directly,' said Oliver. 'It'll be much easier to get the other traders on board and means it'll be easier for all of us to get involved since it's not far from our normal places of business.'

'Can we use the cinema as part of the venue?' Rob asked. 'It'd be great to have some bands on in there, and would save hiring a temporary stage.'

'It's fine with me, Rob. I suppose it depends on licences. We're going to have to talk to the Council soon. At the moment, the cinema isn't licensed for live music, but we might be able to get a temporary licence as part of whatever permission we're going to need for using the park.'

'What's the next step then?' Hilary asked.

'We'll need the go ahead from the Council to use the park,' said Oliver. 'I'll see if Matt knows who we should talk to. He's got plenty of contacts in the planning department.'

'It was easy enough to get permission for the food festival last year,' said Jen. 'I've got all the info about what we had to do for that. I'll share it because I'm sure it'll be along similar lines, just on a smaller scale.'

'Great, thanks. Perhaps you could pass that over to Sebastian so he can incorporate it into the EMP.'

'But now that we have a venue, even if we don't have the Council on board yet, Sebastian can fine-tune the EMP,' Jess said. 'And once we have that, we'll know what our budget is.'

'That has to be a priority so that we can price the tickets

and start selling them,' said Rob.

'If we can use the cinema, perhaps we could have the date-with-a-book club meetings there in the daytime and then have music in the evenings?' Jess suggested.

'I thought we'd be having music all day,' Rob said, frowning. 'That's what festivals are all about.'

'This is a bit different to other festivals, though, isn't it?' Hilary began diplomatically. 'We do want music, but that's not the main draw. I think we all agreed at the start of this that the book club would be the driver and then we'd offer other things around that based on what we can offer from our own businesses. That's what's going to make it unique and truly a Croftwood Festival.'

Jess grinned. Hilary had nailed it. That was exactly how she'd imagined it.

'I didn't agree to anything of the sort,' said Rob. 'A festival isn't a festival without music.'

'And we will have music,' Oliver said patiently, 'but it's not a music festival. We need to be clear on that.'

Rob grunted in response, but didn't say anything else.

'So we're agreed that we're in favour of the venue that's been suggested,' Oliver said.

Everyone nodded their agreement.

'So actions. I'll talk to Matt about who we should contact at the Council. Rob, can you start putting together a proposal for a late-afternoon, early-evening music offer? Hilary, any chance you could speak to the traders about what they might want to do, whether it's having a stall or volunteering to help out with something else.'

'I'll enjoy that,' said Hilary. 'It'll be a good excuse to get round and meet the traders I haven't come across yet.'

'I'll start talking to food vendors,' said Jen.

'Shall I talk to Lois about the book club part, or do you want to do that?' Jess asked Oliver.

'She's got her hands full with the date-with-a-book club rollout, so if you have an idea of how it could work, I think she'll be happy for you to deal with it. Just run it by her.'

'Cool. I do have a plan. I'll see what she says.'

Jess drove home that night feeling excited again about the festival idea. They were managing to divide the work between them and now that they'd sorted out all the legalities with Toby a couple of weeks ago, she felt happy that there was nothing too onerous for her to deal with.

She hadn't seen Sebastian since he'd been to the shop earlier in the week and bizarrely, she was sorry he hadn't been there tonight. It would have been good to acknowledge in person that he'd come up with a great venue. It might help her to get some closure on the whole embarrassing episode.

And while she was thinking about closure, it also seemed like it could be a good time to start planning to go home to Dorset.

That evening, after she'd eaten, she picked up the scrapbook and laid it on her lap, running her fingers over the fabric cover. Tentatively, she opened it. There, on the first page, was a photo of her and Jon, arms around each other, tanned faces full of joy as the sea breeze tousled their hair. That day, they'd been on a boat trip to a sandy cove that could only be reached from the sea. They'd eaten Greek salad and drunk cold beer and spent the afternoon snorkelling and swimming in the clearest sea either of them had ever seen.

It was strange looking at the photograph after so long. In her mind, when she conjured up that image, she looked as she did now, not her twenty-one-year-old self. It was literally an illustration of the fact that she was a different person now. And a stark reminder that Jon hadn't changed at all. He was forever that twenty-one-year-old, gorgeous man who loved her.

Everyone aligned on festival site! - Oliver

It was a relief. After Jess's reaction, even though he knew now she'd only heard half of the story before she'd been so angry about it, he'd worried that everyone would think he'd made the wrong call by getting involved with Lord Harrington. It really was the perfect solution as far as he was concerned and easily the hardest thing to accomplish on his to-do list.

Though, saying that, the new hardest thing on his list was proving more difficult to overcome. He'd spent the day at the unit, poring over his laptop, trying to find an EMP that he'd saved from any event that bore a remote resemblance to the Croftwood festival. But there wasn't anything suitable. Most of his work before had involved him being a subcontractor to the main events company, so he hadn't been involved in that side of things, but with a meeting with the Croftwood Council Licensing Officer on the horizon, he was going to have to come up with something.

His phone buzzed, and he picked it up absent-mindedly, his eyes still on the laptop.

'Sebastian,'

Suddenly, he was transported back to his house in Cheltenham and was in the front room having an out-of-body experience as he watched the woman he thought had loved him leave. He vividly remembered feeling as if his heart was crumbling as he watched her get into a car with one of his friends and drive away.

'Maria.' He could barely say her name. His throat felt tight, along with his chest.

'How are you? I hear you sold the house.'

He wasn't about to tell her he lost the house and that what was left had been spent on loan repayments and paying off huge credit card debts. 'Yep.' He badly wanted to ask her what she wanted. Why was she calling him after three years with no contact?'

'I'm glad you're okay, Sebastian.'

Had he said he was okay? Or did she need to believe he was okay to assuage the guilt that he hoped had crippled her?

He cleared his throat. 'What can I do for you?'

'I just thought you should hear it from me.' She paused long enough for him to make a mental list of the very few things that he ought to hear from her, as if she'd bothered about sparing his feelings at all before now. 'Mark and I are getting married.'

What was he supposed to say to that? It's great? I'm so happy for you? At least you're marrying the man you left me for and it wasn't all for nothing? 'Good for you,' he settled on, trying to keep the worst of the bitterness out of his voice.

'Are you seeing anyone?' Her assumption that the only progress he might have made in the past three years was to be vaguely *seeing* someone was like a punch to the gut. This was why she'd left, because she had no respect for him. She didn't see him as worthy of finding anyone who he might mean something to, because he'd never meant enough to her. Why had he wasted his time mourning what he'd lost with her?

'I am. We're very happy,' he lied. Was it even lying to save face in front of someone whose expectations were so low of him?

'Well, that's great, Sebastian. No hard feelings then. Look, I'd better go.'

He hung up, stunned that she would actually bother to call and tell him that. He didn't have the same friends anymore. It had been too difficult for everyone to choose between him and Mark. Ultimately, it had been Sebastian, as the brokenhearted singleton, who lost out because Mark and Maria were a shiny new couple who fitted in with all the other couples better than him after that. No, he was sure she wanted him to know for some other reason that he couldn't fathom.

And now, even though he liked Jess, and felt like there was something bubbling between them since she'd stopped hating his guts, he had nothing to offer. Who wanted to date a man with barely a penny to his name who was to all intents and purposes living in an industrial unit?

He closed the laptop, unable to pull his concentration back to where it had been before the phone call from Maria, and poured himself a Scotch.

14

Jess's phone pinged with a notification. It was from the festival WhatsApp group. Oliver had put, 'Jess - suggested to Sebastian that you guys get together to go through the Event Management Plan before the meeting with the Council.'

Since she had the music plans from Rob and a list of what traders were interested in having stalls, and she'd spoken to Lois about the book club, she supposed it made sense. But she was a little nervous about a one-to-one meeting with Sebastian. Aside from the general mortifying humiliation she remembered from the day he'd visited the shop, she also remembered how he'd made her feel that day. It felt shallow to admit, even to herself, that she'd found his scent and his forearms ridiculously sexy, but she had. In all the dates she'd had in the past few years, she'd never met anyone who came close to making her feel like that. And what made it worse was that she'd found him so infuriating to begin with. It was almost like her emotions were betraying her by finding him attractive when she was trying quite hard to dislike him.

'No problem,' she replied.

'I'll tell him to call you to set something up.'

It was less than two minutes later that her phone rang. It must be him.

'Hello?'

'Jess, it's Seb.'

'Oh, hi,' she said. Seb. Somehow, it felt intimate that he referred to himself as Seb with her now.

'Can we set up a meeting? I need to finalise the floor-plan, so to speak. Oliver says you have all the requirements?'

'I've got lists of what we're doing, times and what kind of spaces, that's all.'

'That's all we need. How about tonight?'

'Tonight?' She wasn't doing anything, but hadn't expected it to be right away.

'It needs to be as soon as we can.'

She could hear the urgency in his voice, and there was no reason to delay.

'Sure, tonight's fine.'

'At Oliver's? After you close?'

'Okay, I can be there by six.'

'Great, see you later.'

He hung up, leaving Jess feeling entirely unprepared for reasons she couldn't begin to understand.

She locked up the shop just before six o'clock and headed to Oliver's. Jack was behind the counter.

'Latte? Sebastian's waiting upstairs.'

'Thanks Jack, that'd be great.'

She'd rather have had a gin and tonic to take the edge off the inexplicable nerves, but coffee was better than nothing. At least she was wearing one of her favourite dresses today, and she was having a good hair day.

She carried her latte upstairs to the flat and pushed the door open. Seb was sitting on one of the sofas, looking at some large sheets of paper on the coffee table.

'Hi,' she said, thinking he must not have heard her come in, since he hadn't looked up.

'Hi,' he said, not looking up.

Jess bristled with annoyance, then reminded herself to be more zen. She was going to have to get past this compulsion to find fault in everything he did. Despite the fact that she found him attractive, he did a good job of annoying her beyond belief at the same time.

'Is that a plan of the park?' She sat on the edge of the sofa and peered at the large sheet of paper.

'Yes, sorry. I was just checking the scale.' He was looking at her now, his eyes smiling in the same way they had before he'd crossed the road the other day. Before he'd stopped smiling because she'd had a go at him.

'Thanks for doing this, Jess. I think it'll be easier if we can go through this between us and then we can run it by the others. I need to finalise the EMP and get the bookings in for the tents and toilets, generators, lighting, all of that.'

'What have you got so far in the EMP?' She had to force herself not to raise an eyebrow of disbelief as she asked, because she was certain it was imaginary; part of his spiel to get the contract.

'I don't have it with me.'

'Oh, shame.'

He flicked a look at her, as if he knew she was testing him. 'There's nothing relevant to show you yet. We're in a bit of a chicken-and-egg situation at the moment. We need to see what we can fit in, what we *need* to fit in and that'll inform our best guess at capacity, and by extension, the EMP.'

'Then we can start selling tickets?' She made a mental note to speak to Patsy about setting up a website.

'Yes. I don't know that much about how festivals organise that side of things but I think you could do an early release at a price lower than you're intending to charge, maybe a couple of hundred tickets, just to get some cash in to pay deposits on things. You don't even need to know what your capacity is to do that.'

'That's true,' Jess said thoughtfully. 'I suppose I thought it'd be like a concert where you know how many seats you have and you know how much your costs are, and that's how you set the price. Where would we even start?'

Seb laughed, 'I know, right?'

Jess relaxed. They went through her lists and Seb, referring to a list of tent sizes from one of his suppliers, drew rough outlines in pencil on the scale drawing. Jess watched him as he concentrated on what he was doing. His hair had fallen across his eyes when he bent his head down and he was too engrossed to notice. It was endearing, watching him work so intently.

After an hour or so, the park part of the festival was pretty well organised.

'It's perfect,' said Jess. 'Having the book club meetings in the cinema is perfect. Then we only need one huge tent.'

'Which is just as well because with all the trees we need to negotiate, there probably wouldn't be room for two. I don't think we can rely on the cinema bar by itself. We'll put a bar in an open-sided tent over the other side of the park to spread things out.'

'So you think just the one bigger tent for alternatives to the book club? And do you think this one, or the other one for the shopping village?'

'You don't need to worry about that at this stage,' he said. 'This plan works from the point of view of the electrics and other things like that we need to consider. The finer details can come later.'

Jess had to defer to him because she had no better idea. 'Okay,' she shrugged.

'I've had a look at the plans Lord Harrington sent me of the fields he's given us for the campsite. I think we need to make some assumptions so that we can work out how many pitches we're going to cater for. And how many toilets and showers we need to hire.'

'Showers? Do you think anyone bothers at a festival?

Seb looked at her in surprise. 'You're the last person I thought would condone not showering for a whole weekend.'

'What do you mean?' She was genuinely curious. Not having been to a festival, but having heard stories of the queues for showers at Glastonbury, she assumed most people wouldn't bother.

'Well, I don't know,' he began, staring at the map again. 'You always look nice, like you shower every day.'

Unsure whether to thank him, because was that a compliment? Jess said, 'I might rely on baby wipes at a festival rather than brave the showers. It seems like a lot of trouble.'

'Fair enough,' he said.

'Anyway, I won't be camping. I'll commute.'

'Really?' Now he did look at her, swiping his hair back with one hand. 'But half the fun's the camping. You'll miss all the best bits if you don't.'

'Like what?'

'Like having a beer under the stars while you listen to someone playing their guitar from a couple of tents away. Walking to the loo across the dewy grass while most people are still asleep, apart from the early-risers who are quietly boiling some water for a peaceful cup of tea. And at a certain time in the morning, the smell of bacon wafts around the campsite and makes you wish you were as organised as the people with the bacon.'

He had a faraway look in his eyes as he spoke, clearly thinking about good times he'd had himself and hearing him talk about it, Jess could understand that those were the kinds of things that might erase memories of cold showers and unsavoury toilets.

Jess laughed softly. 'It doesn't sound that different from

having sleep-outs on the beach.'

'Do people actually do that?'

Jess smiled at him. 'I grew up by the sea and sleeping on the beach isn't encouraged, but a group of us did it at the height of summer a few times when it didn't get too cold at night. We had a fire on the beach and I'm pretty sure someone magicked a guitar up from somewhere.'

'Aren't those the best nights?' Sebastian said, his eyes shining as he sat back on the sofa and laid one arm across the top of the cushions.

'The best,' Jess agreed. And she found she could look back fondly on that memory without feeling the need to shut it away because it included Jon. Maybe it was because they hadn't been by themselves. Or maybe it was a sign that beginning to allow these thoughts of him in from time to time was getting less painful. 'Hanging around on the beach is what I did for most of my teenage years.'

'I lived in landlocked Wiltshire, but we were close enough to Somerset to have a few visits to the coast every year when I was small. I was always envious of people who lived there all the time.'

'It was an idyllic place to grow up, although I used to think it was boring. There wasn't much in the way of entertainment for teenagers.'

'Hence, the beach parties?'

'Exactly. Hey, we ought to make sure we have something at the festival that appeals to that kind of age group. I bet there could be parents out there who'd love to come as a family so they could do the book club.'

'Isn't there a kids' book club planned?' Seb scanned the list of plans that Jess had brought with her. 'Yes, look.'

'But that'll be for younger children. I'll talk to Lois about doing a separate one for teenagers. She set up a reading section for them at the library and it's really popular. We could do it at the same time as the kids one but on the balcony in the cinema, perhaps? It's dark and feels like the kind of place a teenager would feel at home. I bet they'd love that.'

'Great idea. You know what I saw at another festival I worked at? A retro gaming arcade.'

'Like Pacman?' It was the only arcade game Jess could ever remember playing.

'Yes! It was in a tent and they were free to play. They had one of those dancing games too, and it was full of teenagers all weekend.'

'Apart from you?' she teased.

'I was deprived of video games as a child, so I made up for it that weekend,' he laughed. 'I'll have to find out who owns it and see if we can book them.'

'I'd love to see you doing that dancing game.'

'Are you challenging me to a dance off?'

What was she getting herself into? 'If you book it, the challenge is on.'

He was looking at her as if she'd surprised him. Maybe she had; she'd surprised herself by actually having a normal conversation with him, not one where she was either cross or cringing with embarrassment.

'Maybe that's enough for tonight,' Seb said.

Part of her was disappointed. She'd just started to enjoy herself. But then, that wasn't why they were here. This was a business meeting.

'Okay. So you'll get started on the EMP. Let me know as soon as you have prices and I can plug it all in to my spreadsheet as we go.'

'Thanks, Jess.'

'No, thank you. We wouldn't have got as far as this if it wasn't for you speaking to Lord Harrington and finding out about his land. We'd be nowhere near thinking about booking tents and toilets.'

He laughed. 'Tents and toilets. I like that. Good name for a festival.'

'I'm not sure it's the right vibe for our festival, but it'd be a good name for something.'

They turned everything off in the flat and headed downstairs where Jack had locked up and was wiping down the tables.

'Thanks, Jack!' Jess called as they let themselves out.

'Can I walk you anywhere?' Seb asked. His truck was parked outside.

'I'm good, thanks. My car is only at the back of the church.'

They stood awkwardly for a few seconds.

'So I'll wait to hear from you guys about the next meeting,' he said, although still not showing any signs of getting into his truck.

'Okay. See you soon.' She smiled and turned away from him to cross the road. She could feel his eyes on her and was desperate to turn around. If he was standing there, as she imagined, staring at her, what did that mean?

She got to the point in the path that curved through the churchyard where she knew Seb would lose sight of her. A second after she'd passed it, she heard his truck door slam.

He'd been watching, she was sure of it. And that filled her with an inexplicable joy.

15

Seb watched Jess walk across the churchyard until she was out of sight. It was almost dark, and he wished he'd been more insistent about walking her to her car. Then he smiled; this was Croftwood. He probably had nothing to worry about on that score. But he'd have liked a few more minutes with her now that they finally seemed to be getting on. She'd looked fantastic in the dress she was wearing and her hair had been down, and was shiny and gently waving in a way that made him want to twist it around his fingers. He was sure she'd enjoyed the evening as much as he had and if he had been at a different stage in his life, he might be in a position to explore things with her. As it was, he had to accept that his priority was making a success of the festival because everything that happened after, depended on it.

It had been a relief to pin down the plans as far as they'd been able to. The Event Management Plan he'd promised was as good as written was far from it. He was desperate to present his first invoice, but knowing that they had no funding as yet, and with nothing to show them, it felt unfair. He had squeezed a couple of extra weeks' grace from the landlord of his industrial unit, after which time he would either have to pay up or get out. After tonight, he hoped he had planted the seed in Jess's mind about starting to sell early bird tickets. He knew from talking to Oliver that Rob and Toby were submitting grant applications to various places now that they'd formally registered as a Community Interest Company. A payment of some sort seemed like it was just around the corner.

He drove back to the unit, feeling the familiar dip in his mood the closer he got. Sleeping on the mezzanine and coping with a small WC and kitchen was only supposed to have been temporary, but he was yet to see the light at the end of the tunnel. It was impossible to get any work done; it was too cold to sit still for the kind of time required to write the Event Management Plan so he'd barely made any progress. Time was against him now, and until the weather became warmer, nothing about his situation was going to improve.

After he'd parked the truck in the designated parking space for his unit, he used the key fob to raise the roll-up door, ducked underneath as soon as there was enough space, and then lowered it back down. He shivered. It was icy cold. No insulation and a concrete floor did nothing to keep the heat in. The tiny office heated up quickly though, so after closing the door, he put the fan heater on for a couple of minutes in an attempt to keep the chill out of his bones while he made some notes.

Tomorrow he'd start contacting suppliers for quotes. It was a great excuse to reconnect with them and tap into the industry grapevine again. His other priority was to arrange a meeting with the Licensing Officer at Croftwood Council. It wasn't something he was looking forward to because he'd organised enough events to know that if you got on the wrong side of them, they could make or break you. Organising a meeting before they'd even seen the EMP was the worst thing he could do, although Jess and the others wouldn't know that.

Failing to impress the council would not make him look good and he didn't want to fall out with Jess. Again. After their rocky start, he felt as if he'd made some progress earlier in the week when he called in to her shop. He'd been surprised to see that it was a very modern, fashionable business and that he'd been seriously misled by the fact that it was called a haberdashery shop. An old-fashioned term, but everything came around to be trendy again at some point, he supposed. And what did he know about knitting or sewing?

She'd definitely begun to thaw on that day. He knew he wasn't looking his best; his hair needed a good cut, he needed a more thorough shave, and he was almost at the point where he'd worn all of his clean clothes and now was wearing things that hadn't seen the light of day since he was in his twenties. To compensate, he'd drowned himself in aftershave and hoped that would help with the overall impression. He desperately needed to pay a visit to a launderette. And a barber.

He cleaned his teeth and had a quick strip wash at the small sink, then dressed in the couple of layers of thermals he was using as pyjamas before he climbed the stairs to the mezzanine where he slept. It was supposed to be a storage area, and it was, because it had all his worldly possessions stacked in boxes around the edge of the space, with his bed in the middle. It helped to make it feel a bit more like a room, rather than the roof of the office that sat in the corner of the unit.

He lay in bed and thought back over the meeting with Jess. As well as achieving what they'd set out to do, they'd had a normal conversation. He knew a bit more about her, more than she knew about him, which was good, and he was beginning to think that they could be friends. If it wasn't for the fact that he was penniless and living in an industrial unit, he'd push for something more now that he knew she didn't completely detest him. He chuckled to himself at the idea that he could go from her yelling at him in the street on Monday to thinking there might be something more between them only a few days later. Ridiculous.

The following morning, he woke to the sounds of his neighbours opening up. He lay in bed, preparing himself for the chill that would envelope him once he threw the covers off, but risked sticking his hand out to grab his phone.

There was a message from his step-mother reminding him it was his father's birthday the following week. He sighed, wishing not for the first time that he had siblings. Someone who would be on his side, would understand how the difficulties of the past couldn't be brushed aside with no acknowledgement. He tapped out a message to say that he hadn't forgotten and left it at that. After so long, he didn't feel guilty about not making more of an effort. Anyway, it wasn't as if the cheque he received every year on his own birthday was the most thoughtful gift in the world.

Once he was up and the heater had warmed up the office, Seb got dressed in the last clean clothes he owned; some unfortunate baggy jeans which were a real last resort and a wool sweater that was riddled with moth holes, but with a dark shirt underneath, you couldn't see them. He hoped. At least he didn't think he'd be seeing Jess today. Somehow, today it seemed more important to make a good impression on her than it had yesterday. Was that because he'd seen a glimpse into her life last night, someone besides the owner of the haberdashery shop and his sort-of boss for the duration of the festival? Someone who'd grown up by the seaside. He imagined her wandering along the beach, carefree with the wind whipping her beautiful hair across her face before she turned her head and smiled at him.

He let out a small laugh. He was getting ahead of himself. She didn't hate him; he knew that much, and that was progress. Be happy with what you have. But actually, she was the only thing that brought any light into his life at the moment and he realised he needed it to stay that way. He'd tread carefully to nurture whatever this was, even if it ended up being friendship because christ, he needed a friend.

16

Sebastian had arranged for the Licensing Officer from the Council to meet them on Tuesday morning at Croftwood Cinema. Oliver had suggested all the committee be there but Hilary and Rob couldn't get staff to cover their shops and agreed to a debrief meeting that evening instead. Since it was Penny's usual day to work, Jess decided to go along, keen to hear what the officer thought of the plans she and Seb had agreed on last week.

Meeting in the cinema was a good idea, since it was raining and cold. Mist was clinging to the top of the nearby Malvern Hills in a way that told of the weather being set in for the day rather than a passing shower. Jess had met Oliver on the way and she huddled underneath his huge golf umbrella with the name of a coffee supplier emblazoned on it.

'Morning!' Patsy said brightly, as they arrived dripping and damp in the cinema's foyer. 'Matt's backstage getting coffee if you want to grab one.'

'Thanks Pats, I assume the others aren't here yet?' Oliver asked, with his arm stuck outside the door shaking the worst of the rain from the umbrella.

'No, you're first.'

'I'll wait with Patsy if you want to get a coffee,' said Jess.

'Latte for you?'

'Thanks, that'd be great.'

'I assume Matt's getting yours,' Oliver said to Patsy.

'He'd better be.'

Oliver propped the umbrella up in the corner behind the door and headed past the stalls to the backstage bar.

Patsy was watching him and as soon as he was out of earshot, she said, 'What's going on with you and Sebastian?'

'What do you mean?' Jess asked, taken aback.

'I was at Oliver's the other day and he came in saying you'd had a go at him in the street.'

Patsy was looking far too amused, and Jess blushed with shame as she remembered the whole awful episode.

'I wasn't having a go at him, I'd just jumped to a conclusion too quickly, that's all.'

'And didn't give him chance to explain.' She rolled her eyes and grinned. 'I love that! Keep them on their toes. Good for you.'

'God, no. It's mortifying. And then he came in the shop and…'

'And what?' Patsy's eyes were wide now. She was expecting something Jess wasn't sure she was ready to share, but which might nevertheless be true.

'I don't know. He was different. Less arrogant, more genuine, I suppose.' She didn't elaborate any further, or tell Patsy about the evening they'd spent planning the layout of the festival. She'd hardly admitted to herself that she found him more attractive every time she saw him, so wasn't quite ready to share that with anyone else.

'You're thinking he's not as much of an arse as you thought?'

Jess nodded slowly, trying not to look at Patsy for fear of giving herself away. 'He's not an arse all the time. That's true.'

The door opened and someone Jess assumed to be the Licensing Officer burst through, dripping wet. They stamped their feet and pulled the hood down on their parka.

'Oh, hi!' Jess said, recognising the woman as one of her customers.

The woman smiled once she saw Jess. 'Hi, I didn't know this was your event?'

'I'm on the committee. There are a few of us.'

'I'm Helena.'

'Jess.' It felt funny saying her name to this person who she'd met plenty of times before, but it was unusual to know her customers' names unless they told her for the purposes of ordering something or booking a workshop. 'We're just waiting for our events contractor.

'Speak of the devil,' Patsy said, raising her eyebrows at Jess as Sebastian walked in, closely followed by Jen from the Courtyard Café.

They were both as wet as Helena. Sebastian's parka looked particularly waterlogged.

'Lovely day for ducks,' he said, smiling at them all. 'I'm Sebastian Thorne.' He unzipped his coat and wiped his hand on his sweater before offering it to Helena.

'Nice to meet you. Helena.'

'Matt and Oliver are making coffee. Shall we head down to join them?' Jess suggested.

Sebastian and Helena followed Jess and Jen through the stalls to the backstage bar where Matt had handed over the coffee-making duties to Oliver.

Helena was introduced to them both, and once they all had a coffee, they sat on stools around one of the tall bistro tables to discuss the plan.

Helena pulled out a notebook and pen and started a fresh page with the heading, Croftwood Festival. 'First things first.

Do you have a date in mind?' she asked.

'We're planning on mid-August,' said Oliver.

'Next year?' Helena was giving Oliver a very stern look, as if saying anything other than yes would be the wrong answer.

'Um, no. This year.' It wasn't often that Jess saw Oliver thrown by anyone.

Helena exhaled loudly. 'I don't think you've sent in your Event Management Plan, so you've got no chance. It's already April.' She put her pen down and picked up her coffee.

Jess looked at Sebastian. He didn't seem phased at all.

'Is it because it'll take too long to get the licence?' Jess asked, hoping that the fact she already knew Helena might help soften her up a bit.

'No. I can tell you now, aside from the fact you've got next to no chance of procuring anything you need, without an EMP we can't go any further.'

They all looked at her mutely.

'Mr Thorne. You're contracted to run the event? Where is the EMP?'

They all turned to look at Sebastian.

He smiled, looking round at all of them, his gaze settling on Helena as he said, 'Obviously we have the EMP. I thought my assistant had submitted it. I'm so sorry. I'll make sure it's with you later today.'

Jess frowned. Why hadn't he shown it to them first? Surely they should have seen it to sign it off before it was sent anywhere? And it was the first time he'd mentioned an assistant.

'There are hundreds of festivals happening across the country from the spring through to the autumn,' Helena said. 'They will have submitted their EMPs and will have booked everything they need, and ninety-nine percent of those festivals will have deposits paid already. Where are you going to get your tents and toilets with only a four-month lead time?'

Jess couldn't help it. As soon as Helena said tents and toilets, she had to suppress a giggle. She did a good job of it and no-one noticed. Apart from Sebastian, who had instantly looked at her with mischief in his eyes when Helena had said tents and toilets. He smirked and chuckled, and the two of them shared a moment until Jess noticed Oliver looking at her incredulously while Helena glared at all of them.

'With respect,' Sebastian said, pulling his gaze from Jess, 'we know the timeline's tight, but we've got everything in place.'

'Oh, right,' Helena said, her expression falling. 'Well, in that case, let's get down to business.'

Jess looked at Sebastian. She was pretty sure he'd lied to Helena about the EMP, about having anything booked and about his supposed assistant. To give him the benefit of the doubt, she had to assume he was simply trying to stop Helena being judgy about them being late-starters in their planning for this year, but she didn't like being in the dark about anything and felt the old feelings of mistrust towards Sebastian creep back in.

As it was raining so hard, they didn't venture out into the park, but Oliver pulled back the huge wooden door that made up the back wall of the bar to reveal the park. In the summer, the door was open at every event they held at the cinema — apart from film showings themselves — making a fantastic indoor/outdoor space for parties. Today, the park was less inviting with the drizzle-soaked grass and bare trees, mist kissing their top branches. Still, they all knew the layout of the park, and with Sebastian's map as a reference, they were able to give Helena an overview of what they had planned.

'Obviously, all of this is subject to you receiving permission from the council to close the park to the public for a week or so,' Helena said.

'I've spoken to Gareth, and he doesn't think it'll be a problem,' said Matt, obviously dropping the name of someone he knew at the council. Someone senior to Helena by the look on her face.

'I can agree in principle,' she said reluctantly. 'It's subject to the usual checks and sign-offs. I'm sure you know all about those.' There was a sarcastic tone to her voice as she addressed the last part to Sebastian. 'In particular, the local Safety Advisory Group will need to look at it. You may be waiting some weeks until their next meeting before anything can happen.'

'Thank you, Helena,' said Oliver. 'We appreciate you taking the time to come and speak to us. We want to make this a success for the whole town, so it's important to us to work with the council and make sure everyone's happy.'

'It's no problem,' she said, thawing slightly in the face of Oliver's charm offensive. 'Perhaps once the weather's better, we can go and look at the route you're proposing to link the park and the campsite. We'll need to do some consultation with local residents well in advance of the event to address any legitimate concerns they may have.'

'Of course,' Oliver said, ushering her back towards the foyer.

'Well, that went well,' Matt said to Sebastian. 'We need her on side, mate.' He sounded exasperated, and Jess could see his point.

'Hopefully Oliver's buttered her up enough to make sure she still is,' said Jess. 'I think she had a point about the tight timeframe.'

'She does,' Sebastian admitted. 'And if you remember, that was a concern I had at our first meeting. But it doesn't mean she should assume we're total idiots who have nothing in place.'

'I think in her eyes that's exactly what you are,' Matt said.

Jess noticed Seb bristle as Matt directed that comment at him.

'Jess is right,' he continued. 'There's no point trying to pull the wool over Helena's eyes. It's her job to know what's going on and she'll find out eventually if we're leading her up the garden path.'

Matt said all of this with a smile on his face, but Jess knew he was telling Sebastian in no uncertain terms to lose the arrogance.

'There's nothing to stop us booking everything now, is there?' said Jess. 'Then there's nothing for her to complain about.'

'That Safety Advisory Group is no walk in the park. You must have come across them before, Sebastian?' Matt asked.

'Sure. It's nothing to worry about. We're a low-risk event. As long as we keep the capacity low and push the book-club angle, it'll sail through the SAG.'

'I'd like to have your confidence,' Matt said, sounding as if he was losing patience with Sebastian.

'One thing she was right about, we need to get those bookings firmed up. We need money to put down deposits,' Sebastian said.

'Right. You did say. I'll talk to Patsy about the website,' Jess said, trying not to think about the fact that Sebastian had as good as admitted he'd lied about having anything in place.

'It's your lucky day, Jess,' Patsy said, walking into the bar with Oliver and heading over to the coffee machine. 'I've just finished helping Hilary with her new website and I'm at a bit of a loose end in that department now. It's always nice to have a website project to while away the time when there's a film on. There's only so many times you can watch some of them.'

'Really?'

Patsy nodded. 'Of course. I know me and Matt aren't on the committee, but we're still in the festival gang.'

'Thanks,' said Jess. 'We need to get some early bird tickets up for sale as soon as we can, to get the money together for deposits on the stuff we need to hire.'

'Let me put something together, and in the meantime, you guys work out how many tickets and what the price points are. Then it'll just be a quick update once you've decided.'

It was that easy.

'I'll arrange a committee meeting and see if Toby can come along too,' said Oliver. 'We might need him to draft some terms and conditions for us.'

'Right, I'd better go,' said Sebastian. 'Actually, do you know where the nearest launderette is? My washing machine's on the blink.'

'It's on the Leigh Road, next to the Chinese takeaway. But it only takes coins.'

'Ah, okay. Does anyone ever carry cash these days?' he laughed, as he pulled his soaking coat back on.

Jess rummaged in her bag and found a handful of change. 'You're welcome to this. I've got no idea how much it costs these days.'

'You could use the washing machine in the flat,' said Oliver. 'There might even be some detergent under the sink. And it'd be good to do a couple of loads, keep it from seizing up now that no-one's using it.'

'You sure?'

'Yes, walk back with me and I'll let you in.'

'Thanks, and thanks for the offer of the change, Jess,' he said.

He and Oliver left, taking the umbrella, which Jess only realised when it was too late.

'How did that go?' Patsy asked. 'Oliver had the full charm switched on when he was seeing her out.'

'I'm not sure she was that impressed with us. Seb led her to believe that we had stuff organised which we don't, and Matt name dropped someone and that seemed to annoy her.'

Patsy laughed. 'Oh god, so it could all be over before it's begun? And it's Seb now, is it?'

'It's not funny!' Jess said, although she was laughing too. 'She thinks we've left it too late to get it off the ground for this year.'

'Have you?'

'Probably,' Jess admitted. 'I'm sure she knows better than anyone what needs to happen and how long it might take, but try telling that to the others. I need to get Hilary along to these meetings so that Jen and I don't get drowned out by the testosterone.'

'I love how you've artfully dodged my other question. Seb?'

Jess sighed. 'Sebastian,' she said, pointedly, 'is a total mystery to me. The other night I felt as if we had some kind of connection.' All thoughts of playing her cards close to her chest were gone. She thought she'd got the measure of Seb before this meeting, and now she wasn't sure she knew him at all.

'I knew it,' Patsy said. 'You don't have a fight with someone in the street unless there are some emotions involved.'

'It wasn't a fight. It was a discussion.' Jess ignored Patsy's knowing smile. 'And last night, he was totally Seb. He was warm, open and...'

'And you like him?'

'I do when he's like that. Sebastian this morning was an arrogant arse who was intent on covering his own—'

'Arse.'

'Exactly.'

Jess left Patsy to prepare for the matinee film and headed

back to the shop to cover Penny's lunch hour. The rain had turned to drizzle, thankfully light enough not to soak her through. Before she crossed the high street, she looked up and saw the light on in the flat over Oliver's. It crossed her mind to go up there and challenge Sebastian about misleading Helena, but it felt uncomfortably similar to when she'd confronted him in the street. The memory was too fresh, and it felt like a backward step in their fledgling friendship. She'd give him the benefit of the doubt. If he booked these things now and sent the EMP this afternoon like he'd said, it would have been a stretch of the truth rather than a lie. Wouldn't it?

17

'You should be making the most of your day off,' said Penny when Jess arrived back at the shop.

'You need a lunch hour,' Jess said.

'Phhhfff,' said Penny. 'I've got a sandwich with me. You get off and make something of the rest of the day.'

'Thanks, I will then. If you're sure?'

Penny as good as batted Jess towards the door. 'Go on. Oh, by the way, can you call Fi? She said it was urgent, but I didn't like to give her your personal number when it's about work.

'Thanks, I'll ring her when I get home.'

By the time Jess got home, it was lunchtime. She made a quick sandwich to keep her going so that she could spend the rest of the day sewing. It wasn't until she'd settled herself at the machine that she remembered about calling Fi back.

'Jess! I'm so glad you rang. I thought it was going to be too late.'

'Too late for what?'

'I'm doing workshops over the weekend and the person who's meant to be helping me has pulled out. They asked me to see if I could find a replacement, but they've given me until five o'clock today or they'll have to cancel the whole thing.'

Jess was confused. 'But I don't do workshops apart from at the shop. You must know someone better qualified?'

'They want a sewing person and honestly, everyone I know apart from you is a knitting tutor. Besides, I thought it could be a good opportunity for you to have a taster.'

The conversation was only getting more confusing. 'A taste of what?'

'The cruise workshops,' Fi said. 'Didn't I already say that?'

'A cruise for a weekend?'

'Yes, it's just a mini cruise for travel agents, so there's no pressure. It's from Southampton to Bruges and back, only two nights away. 'Before you say no, the pay is amazing. I'm sure it would cover the cost of you being away and don't forget what we were saying about it being great publicity for the shop. What do you say?'

Jess's heart began to pound. On the one hand, she loved the sound of it and Fi was right, if she was considering taking on a job on a longer cruise, it'd be stupid not to take this opportunity to try it out. Stupid.

'Could I think about it?'

'No, Jess! There's no time, just say yes!'

Fi's enthusiasm was infectious enough for Jess to find herself on the verge of agreeing. 'I can't. I'll have to call you back when I've spoken to Penny to see if she can look after the shop for a weekend.'

Jess fended off more pleading from Fi before she ended the call, all thoughts of her sewing pushed aside. Could she ask Penny to look after the shop for a weekend? And even if she did, and it went well, what would happen if she went on the actual cruise? That would presumably be for longer than a weekend. She needed to find out what Penny thought before she could make her mind up. It was such bad timing with everything that was going on with the festival planning as well. But it was only one weekend. And seriously tempting.

Throwing caution to the wind, she decided she was doing it. If it meant she had to close the shop for a couple of days, if Penny couldn't cover it, then so be it. It was an opportunity she had to take. It was out of her comfort zone, but isn't that just what she needed? If she dithered for any longer, she'd change her mind.

'Fi? Yes, I'm in,' Jess said, calling back before she thought any harder about it.

'That was quick! I'm so glad, Jess. We're going to have the best time.'

They spent a few minutes discussing the logistics of it all and what Jess would need to prepare in advance. Now that she'd committed, she felt much more excited about it. Even if it didn't lead to anything, a couple of days away was probably just what she needed.

She went downstairs and made herself a cup of tea, taking it into the lounge to enjoy. It was early, but since she was in for the rest of the day and it was miserable outside, she lit the fire and sat watching the flames lick around the pieces of wood until they were glowing with heat.

The scrapbook was still on the table. She hadn't picked it up again since she'd opened it to the first page and looked at the girl she'd been years before. In the days that followed, she'd been pleasantly surprised to find herself thinking of Jon in a much happier way. Cutting herself off from the wonderful memories had allowed worse ones to take root in her mind and seeing the old photo had helped her remember the inordinate amount of happy times they'd had together before the relatively tiny proportion that were simply dreadful.

She picked up the scrapbook and laid it on her lap, suddenly looking forward to revisiting that summer held forever within its pages. There were things she remembered as if they'd happened yesterday, like the day they'd spent in

Venice wandering along all the alleyways, diligently following the signs to the Rialto bridge only to never find it. The tiny cove they'd hiked to in Ibiza where the water was the clearest they'd ever seen and they'd spent the afternoon skinny dipping with total confidence that no-one was watching. There were other things that she'd totally forgotten. A photo of her sat in the back of the van with a towel on her head as if she were playing Mary in a nativity play, her hair in wet tendrils down her face. Had they got caught in the rain? Had she fallen into the sea or just come from having a shower? Then there was the photo that had been funny until they'd known what it meant.

Jon had thought he'd had an allergy to something towards the end of their trip. They'd been travelling through some wooded areas, so he'd thought it was a tree spore that had caused his eyelid to droop. They'd thought it was hilarious and took pictures of him, one of which Jess was looking at now. It had been one of the last times they'd laughed together because once they got home, Jon had been diagnosed with a brain tumour, and everything had changed.

She closed the book. She'd taken the first step today towards pushing the boundaries of her life. If things were going to change, she was going to have to start seeing her relationship with Jon as it had been: a few years of absolute joy. They'd had their ups and downs like anyone else, but she was happy to look back with rose-tinted glasses if it meant she could look back and not just remember the last few months of his life.

'Hey Penny, how's today been?'

'You do know what the definition of a day off is, don't you?' Penny said with amusement that Jess could hear down the phone line.

'Very funny. I have a favour to ask.'

'Ask away. I hope it's that you want some time off?'

'You're a mind reader. Fi's asked me to help out this weekend on a workshop she's running on a mini cruise and then as I'll be down in Southampton, I thought I'd go to Dorset before I head home to see my family for a couple of days. I know it's a lot to ask and I'm happy to close if you can't cover all of that, but — '

'Jess, it's no problem,' Penny said, interrupting her. 'You need me Saturday to Tuesday? Is that long enough?'

'That'd be amazing, thank you. I'll drive down on Friday after work and I'll be back to open on Wednesday morning.'

'You deserve a break. Not that it sounds particularly restful but you'll have fun doing workshops with Fi, and I can't remember the last time you went home to see your parents.'

Penny had only worked for Jess for the past couple of years, so she had no idea that Jess barely visited.

'It's been too long,' she said truthfully. 'But it's the right time.'

Even though she was only going to be gone for four days, Jess felt as if she was leaving at the worst possible time. Since the meeting with Helena, there was still no evidence that Seb had finalised and sent the Event Management Plan as he'd said he would. She was pretty sure that it didn't exist and she'd purposely avoided him all week because she didn't want to confront him about her suspicions.

On Wednesday, it was the regular knit and natter night that she hosted at the shop. As ever, Patsy was the first to arrive, and Jess was always glad because it meant she could potter around the shop while they chatted without feeling like she had to entertain her.

'How's Sebastian? I haven't seen you since the meeting at the cinema.'

Trust Patsy to launch straight in.

'I haven't seen him since then, either. He was supposed to

have sent our Event Management Plan to the Council before that meeting and hadn't. Then he said he'd send it straight after, but I don't know if he did.'

'Wouldn't he have copied one of you in on an email like that?' Patsy said, frowning.

'Exactly!' Jess dumped some skeins of yarn that had come undone on the table and began twisting them back into tidy spirals.

'And you think because he didn't copy you in, he hasn't done it?'

'Shouldn't we have sign-off on the EMP?'

'The big plan of the whole festival? You should absolutely have sign off. Have you spoken to Ollie about it? I know he gets carried away with things, but I'm sure he'd want to know everything was being done properly,' Patsy said.

'I've wondered whether to talk to him to try to get to the bottom of what's actually going on with him, because there's something. I don't know if he's hiding things or if it's something more sinister. Sorry, I'm sounding dramatic.'

Patsy came over and laid a hand on Jess's arm. 'It's important to listen to your gut. You know what I went through with Dan.'

Dan was Patsy's ex-husband. He'd been controlling to the point where she'd lost everything. Luckily, she'd got away from him, but that hadn't stopped him tracking her down. Based on the couple of dates Jess'd had with him while he was using her to get close to Patsy, she knew how easy it was for someone to portray themselves as something very different when they wanted to.

'I know. That's partly why I'm being so careful. The thing is, Matt worked with him before. That should be a sign that nothing weird is going on.'

Patsy shook her head. 'You can never tell. Look, I think Ollie's closing up tonight. Once we get started here, why don't you nip out and talk to him? He'll listen, and he'd want to know if you think something isn't right.'

Feeling reassured, Jess relaxed. The ladies arrived and once they were knitting, with fresh cups of tea and coffee on hand, Jess gave Patsy the nod and headed along the road to Oliver's.

There were a handful of customers in the coffee house and Oliver was busy making drinks for some people waiting at the counter. Jess loitered until he'd finished.

'Jess, Sebastian is upstairs if you wanted a word,' he said, turning to the coffee machine again.

That wasn't what she'd planned, but perhaps it was better to confront Seb about the EMP before she got Oliver involved. Perhaps he had sent it in and there was nothing to worry about. She climbed the stairs to the flat and opened the door, expecting to see him sat on the sofa as he had been the last time they'd met here, but he wasn't in the lounge. The washing machine was going. Maybe he'd nipped to the loo.

Jess sat on the sofa to wait. The minutes ticked by and he hadn't appeared. Out of boredom, she sifted through the paperwork on the coffee table. There was nothing of interest other than a printout of sheets from something called the Purple Guide. It was a lot of information about festival camping. It was reassuring to see, since hopefully it showed that such things had been considered and were covered in the elusive EMP.

A couple of minutes later, the bathroom door opened and Seb appeared in a cloud of steam, naked apart from a towel wrapped around his waist.

'Oh, god!' he said, his hands grasping the towel in just the spot they would be if he wasn't wearing it.

Jess leapt up. 'I'm so sorry! I had no idea you were in the shower.'

'Give me a minute,' he said, walking towards her and

snatching a pile of clothes from the arm of the sofa before disappearing into what Jess assumed was the bedroom.

What was he doing having a shower in Oliver's flat? It was one thing doing his washing, he'd at least asked Oliver about that but surely Oliver would have warned her if he thought she might be walking in on a half-naked man.

She was torn. Her instinct was to leave, but she also knew she needed to get to the bottom of everything before she went away for the weekend. So she sat down again and tried to distract herself by reading up on the suggested ratios of toilets to provide for various kinds of events, but all the time, the only thing in front of her eyes was the memory of Sebastian in a towel.

18

Jess hadn't thought about what she might find attractive in a man's body — the parts you don't usually see, at least — in a long time. Her attraction to Jon hadn't been particularly physical. In the beginning, she'd thought he was the funniest person she'd ever met, and he loved making her laugh. That was where the spark between them had come from. After that, the men she'd met from using dating apps had been the opposite. Without having met someone, it was hard to go on anything other than their profile photo and the bio, which would inevitably bear little relation to real-life in most cases. So a couple of dates was all it took for her to realise they weren't soul mates and she never really got as far as being properly physically attracted to any of them. And she was looking for more than that. After a while, she'd been convinced that she would never get beyond a few dates with anyone.

But with Seb, seeing him standing there, half-naked, that had aroused some feelings she'd thought had been buried with Jon. He actually had a six-pack. Again, something she didn't know she would find attractive before she'd seen it on display above the edge of Sebastian's towel.

She took a deep breath to bring herself back to reality. This was Sebastian. Annoying, irritating, potentially lying to them about god knows what. And how shallow was she to be swayed by a six-pack? She giggled, imagining what Patsy would say when she told her. Then she pulled herself together and tried to put the memory of Sebastian's toned, lithe body out of her mind.

When he emerged from the bedroom, he was fully dressed and looking sheepish.

'So your shower's on the blink as well as your washing machine?' said Jess.

'Something like that,' he said, collapsing into the corner of the sofa.

'Are you alright? You don't look very well.'

He was pale and sounded croaky. Then he coughed, confirming her suspicions. 'I'm fine,' he said.

'Well, obviously not. Is your boiler faulty or something? It won't do you any good being in a cold house if you're poorly.'

He laughed. 'My gran used to say poorly.' Then he coughed again.

'Seriously, Sebastian.' She fixed him with her best look, hoping to convey that he'd better tell her the truth.

'There's nothing wrong with my boiler.' He closed his eyes briefly, but for longer than a blink took, and Jess wondered for a second whether he'd fallen asleep.

'I came up to ask you about the EMP, but perhaps now's not the time. Look, you shouldn't drive home if you're feeling rough. I'm sure Oliver wouldn't mind if you stayed here. It's not as if he's using the flat.'

Before Sebastian could argue, Jess had headed downstairs to ask Oliver.

'Of course he can stay,' Oliver said, looking concerned. 'He sounded a bit rough when he came in earlier, but I was in the middle of the lunch rush.'

'He's been here since lunchtime?'

Oliver shrugged. 'I guess so. I hadn't thought about it. Anyway, it's kind of the festival office so he can come and go as he likes. You all can.'

Jess went back upstairs and found Seb asleep on the sofa. She turned off all the lights apart from a table lamp, went into the bedroom and fetched the duvet off the bed, laying it over him. He didn't stir. She stood for a long moment, watching him sleep, his dark lashes stark against his pale cheeks. Her heart ached for him, but she wasn't sure why. There was something that didn't add up.

She resisted the urge to drop a kiss on his forehead and left, closing the door behind her as quietly as she could.

'He's asleep. I'll be back in the morning,' she told Oliver on her way out.

'I'll leave him a note about how to lock up in case he wants to leave before I get back in the morning.'

'He's out for the count, but yes, good idea.'

She headed back to the shop where there was a lively discussion going on about the merits of keeping a pint of milk in the freezer for emergencies. Jess took the teapot from the table and went into the kitchen to make a fresh brew. She took her own knitting out from the bag it was shoved in between knit and natter meetings and tucked it under her arm before going back and taking a seat at the table.

'I'll be mother,' said Mary, standing up to pour everyone a fresh cup.

'Help yourselves if anyone wants coffee instead,' said Jess.

'You're not still knitting that shawl, are you?' Linda asked.

'I shouldn't have chosen something that I have to count,' Jess sighed. 'I end up unpicking everything I've knitted most weeks. And you know I'm not a natural knitter.'

'But you're persevering, that's the main thing,' said Mary.

'Do you know how many garments I've sewn since I

started this shawl? Knitting is the slowest way to make clothes.'

'But the most satisfying,' Patsy said, grinning. 'And it's the opposite for me. I reckon I could knit a cardigan or two in the space of time it'd take me to make a dress.'

'Jess is off gallivanting at the weekend. On a mini-cruise and to Dorset,' Penny announced when there was a lull in conversation.

It was notoriously hard to keep anything private with the knitting group. Jess found that both comforting and frustrating at times.

'Oh, I love a cruise,' said Mary. 'Where are you going?'

'It's only to Bruges. I'm doing a sewing workshop, so I expect it'll be over before it feels like it's started,' said Jess.

As expected, she was also quizzed about why she was going to Dorset, how long since she'd been, why it was so long since she'd been home and why wouldn't you visit more often given it was like going on a free holiday to the seaside? It would be easy to tell them about Jon. They'd understand and it would explain a lot of other things. But she'd known some of these ladies a long time and none of them knew. For the first time, it struck Jess as odd that these people, who were quite a big part of her life, didn't know about one of the biggest parts of it. If she told them, would they feel hurt that she'd not confided in them before?

'I love the seaside in the winter,' said Linda, wistfully. 'Walking on the beach with the wind blowing straight through you, waves crashing and the salt spray everywhere.'

'The salt spray making your hair puff to twice its usual size,' Patsy laughed.

'My parents live so close to the beach that when there was a big storm, the spray from the waves would splatter against the windows,' said Jess.

'How amazing to have grown up by the sea,' said Mary.

Jess was reminded of the similar conversation she'd had with Sebastian, but she didn't want to reminisce tonight. 'You take it for granted if that's all you know.'

'Like the Malvern Hills,' said Penny. 'People come on holiday to walk on those, and when's the last time any of us went up there?'

Jess giggled as they stopped knitting, almost in unison, to ponder when the last time had been and after that, it wasn't long before Penny packed up her knitting, signalling to the others that it was time to call it a night. Patsy hung on until everyone else had said goodnight and gone.

'So what did Oliver say?'

Jess was confused for a second, until she remembered that Patsy didn't know Sebastian had been at the coffee house too. 'Oliver was busy, but Seb was up in the flat, so I went up to see him instead.'

'Get it straight from the horse's mouth,' Patsy said, nodding.

'He was in the shower. Having a shower. In the flat.'

'What?' Patsy was open-mouthed. 'Did Oliver know?'

'I don't know. I didn't ask. But it's weird, isn't it?'

'Maybe there's some explanation.'

'I asked him whether his boiler had broken down and he said, "something like that". I mean, that's a rational explanation, but I think there's more to it.'

'Like what?' asked Patsy.

'I'm not sure. He's ill and when I saw him with just a towel around him, he looked too skinny.'

'You saw him in a towel?' Patsy was almost shouting, and her eyes would have popped out of her head if they'd got any wider.

Jess couldn't help but laugh. 'Yes!'

'And?'

'And… he has a nice body, I suppose. I wasn't looking on

purpose. He just came out of the bathroom and obviously wasn't expecting me to be there.'

'He could have not even bothered with the towel, thinking he was alone,' Patsy said. 'Imagine that.'

'No thank you,' said Jess, as primly as she could manage, although she couldn't deny that thought had crossed her mind. 'Anyway, the point is that he's ill and I'm not sure he has anywhere to go. I suggested that he stayed there tonight rather than drive home, so he's asleep on Oliver's sofa now. He didn't argue with me. Maybe he doesn't have anywhere to live at the moment.'

Patsy frowned. 'But he has his own business. He must be doing alright?'

'That's what I thought, but I wonder whether we're his only client. Matt said he'd had a hard time getting the business back on its feet after the pandemic. Perhaps he's in trouble?'

'I guess it's a possibility,' Patsy said. 'Do you know if he has a partner? Maybe they've had a row and he's left? I'm not sure he can actually be homeless, can he?'

'We don't know how many other people he might have been asking to use their washing machines and showers,' Jess said, not even sure whether Oliver knew he'd used the shower, not that he'd mind. 'If he is in trouble, we need to help him. We haven't paid him anything yet and that might be making things worse. If we know what's going on, at least we can try to do something.'

'I'll see whether Matt can put some feelers out.' Patsy pulled her coat on, followed by a beautifully delicate knitted shawl she was wearing as a scarf. 'He doesn't know Sebastian that well, but they might have a friend in common or something, back from when they worked together.'

'That'd be good.' Jess's imagination was working overtime, thinking about all the interactions she'd had with Sebastian, looking for signs.

'Hey, it'll be okay,' Patsy said. 'He's safe and warm for tonight. Try not to worry.'

Jess locked up and walked across the churchyard towards the car park. Before she turned the corner, she looked back at the windows of the flat. It looked like the lamp was still on, so he was probably still asleep. Perhaps she should have gone back before Oliver left for the night. She could have stayed in case Seb woke during the night. She was worried he'd think he shouldn't have fallen asleep there and would leave to go back to goodness knows where. But it was too late now. Oliver had left, the shop was locked up and Jess didn't have a key.

Even though it was late when she got home, she did some sewing. It was the only way she knew to take her mind off Seb, and she knew if she went straight to bed, she'd lie awake thinking about him. Once she'd decided to be at the coffee house for six in the morning, which is when she thought Oliver would arrive to open up, she began to relax.

Her current project was for her. A pair of trousers made from heavy cotton twill in a shade called Nordic Spruce. They were just what she needed for her break to Dorset. It was no use wearing dresses when she was planning on long walks on the beach, which would inevitably mean the odd moment of having to scramble across some rocks or sand dunes. It was also a way of preparing herself that she was actually going. Imagining herself walking from her parents' house, along to the farthest end of the beach where the old beach huts were, was also good preparation. The way she felt now that she'd realised her emotions around Jon's death weren't as heightened as they'd been the last time she'd allowed herself to think about it for any length of time, meant she felt more positive. Going home wouldn't be the gruelling trip down memory lane that she always feared. Looking at the scrapbook the other night had made her realise that the pain of remembering had softened a little and she was looking forward to seeing whether that feeling could translate if she came across places in the real world where they'd spent so much time together.

As she considered all of this while she was pinning the waistband onto her trousers, she realised she hadn't actually told her parents that she was visiting on Sunday and although it was late, sent her mum a quick WhatsApp asking if it would be okay. A reply came back almost immediately, saying that they couldn't wait to see her. So it was done. She was going to Dorset on Sunday.

19

Despite worrying about Sebastian, Jess had slept well and was on the doorstep of Oliver's bright and early at six am. It was still dark and even though it was halfway through April, it was cold enough for there to have been a slight frost on Madge's windscreen that morning. The light in the flat still looked as it had when she'd left last night, giving her hope that Seb would still be there.

'Morning,' said Oliver, surprised to see her. 'I'd have looked in on Sebastian, you know.'

'I know. I just... I think there's something else going on with him. I want to see if he'll talk to me.'

'Okay,' Oliver said, looking puzzled but not asking questions. He unlocked the door. 'I'll get the coffee machine warmed up and bring you a couple of lattes up.'

'Thanks. And thanks for letting him stay last night.'

They both raised their eyes to the ceiling as they heard the unmistakable sound of coughing.

'Blimey, that's some cough he's got for us to hear it down here,' Oliver said.

Jess headed upstairs, knocking gently at the door before going inside when she got no answer. Seb was still lying on the sofa and appeared to be asleep, although how anyone could cough like that and not wake up, Jess wasn't sure. But she didn't think it was a good sign.

'Hey, Seb,' she said softly as she went over and knelt next to him. He shifted slightly, but his eyes were still closed. She put her hand to his forehead and realised straightaway that he had a raging fever. 'Sebastian, wake up,' she said, loudly this time.

His eyes opened slowly, and he coughed and tried to push himself up to sitting. Jess pulled the duvet off, able to feel the heat coming off him.

'You've got a fever,' she said. She unbuttoned his shirt, pulling it apart to help cool him down. He didn't stop her, although at least he was awake now.

'Did I sleep here last night?' He sounded confused.

'Yes. You're not well and Oliver said it was fine.'

She went to the kitchen, found a cupboard with glasses in and ran the water until it was cold.

'Here. Drink this.'

He took the glass from her, sipped it, and then put it down on the coffee table. Jess rummaged around in her bag until she found a packet of paracetamol and popped two tablets out and handed them to him. She picked up the water he'd just discarded and gave it back to him.

'You need to take these and drink all of this.'

He frowned. 'You're so bossy,' he said, followed by a coughing fit.

Jess took the water from him while he was coughing. 'As I said last night, you're poorly.'

'I'm fine.' He attempted to push himself up from the sofa but was overtaken by another coughing fit.

'Would you rather stay here or go to bed in there?' Jess said, making sure she sounded like she meant business, even if it had sounded like she'd propositioned him.

'Um. Go home?'

'And where's that?' she said gently.

He said nothing.

'Come on, Oliver's fine with you staying here until you're feeling better.'

He nodded. 'I'll go in there,' he said, nodding to the bedroom.

At that moment, Oliver came upstairs with the coffees.

'I've told Seb it's fine with you if he stays a couple of days,' Jess said, knowing that Oliver wouldn't mind at all, hoping he realised he needed to present a united front to Sebastian.

'Sure. Would you be better off in bed?'

'He was just on his way.'

Seb swivelled himself around until his feet were on the floor, then he sat for a minute with his eyes closed.

Oliver looked at Jess, shrugged and gestured picking him up. She nodded, grateful that he was here to lend a hand.

'Come on buddy, lean on me. When you're ready.'

Jess watched as Oliver helped Seb to stand, and then slowly led him into the bedroom, turning sideways as they approached the door. By the time Jess went in with the duvet, he was already lying on the bed with his eyes closed.

'Do you think we need to call someone?' Oliver asked.

'I'll pop back at lunchtime and see how he is,' Jess said. 'If he's any worse, we'll decide what to do then.'

'Okay. Jack's working today, so I'll pop up at ten and give him some more pills.'

'Thanks, Oliver,' said Jess, feeling guilty about Oliver taking that on, even though it was no more her responsibility than it was his. As it was, she'd have to see if Penny was around to pop in at lunchtime and cover the shop.

As it happened, Penny was more than happy to help, and came in at midday. On Jess's way back to Oliver's, she popped into the pharmacy and bought more paracetamol and some Vick's VapoRub, since that was what she always wanted when she had a cough, or flu, or whatever it was that Seb had. She was hoping his temperature had gone down, since she wasn't sure what the next step was if it hadn't.

'How is he?' she asked Oliver on her way up to the flat. The coffee house was busy with the lunch rush and Oliver could only pause for a moment to tell her there was no change last time he went up, before he had to go back to frantically filling panini.

Jess climbed the stairs, and this time went inside without knocking. She headed for the bedroom and found Seb where they'd left him, but now with the duvet haphazardly pulled across his torso so that his head was buried in it but his jean-clad legs were uncovered. They should have helped him to undress. It couldn't be comfortable being in bed fully clothed.

She crept around the side of the bed so that she could feel his forehead. This time, he felt clammy but not as hot to the touch, which she took to be a good sign that the two doses of paracetamol were working. It was a couple of hours before he could have any more, so she decided to wait. If he woke up in the meantime, she could suggest he undress.

Jess sat in the lounge and, to pass the time, looked through what Seb had been doing yesterday. His laptop was on the table, closed. She picked up the Purple Guide that she'd flicked through last night while he was in the shower and noticed underneath it a printed-out sheaf of papers secured with a bull-dog clip. The front page read, 'Event Management Plan.' Ready to breathe a sigh of relief that here it was in the flesh, on turning the page it appeared to be a plan for another event entirely. A festival, but a very different one from theirs. Had Sebastian been using this as a template for their EMP? It wasn't quite the ready-to-go template he'd implied he had, and now Jess was just as doubtful that their EMP was finished, let alone submitted, if he'd still been referring to this other document yesterday.

Just before two o'clock, Jess pushed two paracetamol out of the foil pack, got a fresh glass of water, and went into the bedroom to wake him. She touched his forehead before she roused him, because she wasn't sure she'd feel able to do that if he was awake. It felt cooler.

Perching on the edge of the bed, she gently shook his shoulder until he stirred. He looked surprised to see her.

'Hey, you need to take these,' she said, holding her hand out.

He leant up on his elbow, took the pills and put them in his mouth and then gulped the water. He seemed much better than he had earlier that morning.

'What are you doing here?' he asked.

'I'm making sure you don't die of a raging fever.'

He tried to laugh, but coughed instead and lay back down. 'That's good to know,' he said, once he'd recovered.

'Also, I hate to ask when you're not well, but I wondered how you're getting on with the EMP?' She really did hate to ask but she was also mindful that they needed Helena on side and that having promised her the plan the same day as the meeting, it didn't look great that she still hadn't received it.

'I'm sorry.'

'It doesn't matter.' She batted away his apology, because there was nothing to be gained by recriminations at this point. They just needed to get it done. 'How far off is it from completion?'

'Not that far.'

Jess raised her eyebrows and fixed him with a look that she hoped gave him no option other than to tell the truth.

'Honestly,' he said, and she believed him.

'Give me your password and I'll finish it.'

He shook his head as he tried to sit up, causing him to cough violently enough for him to lie straight back down again.

'Look. I'm quite capable of using that other plan as a template, and I'll only add to what you've already done with anything that's absolutely necessary.'

He looked so sorry that Jess wanted to take him in her arms and hold him. Instead, she pulled the duvet back over him.

'I'll come back later and check on you.' She stood up to leave, but he caught her hand and she turned back.

'Thank you for looking after me,' he said. He dropped her hand and closed his eyes, leaving Jess breathless. Whether it was because it had been a long time since a man had touched her hand, or whether it was because it was Seb, she wasn't sure. But she'd felt a jolt of something at his touch. Something she'd never felt before. Something that she had an inkling was entirely to do with Seb and nothing to do with not being touched by a man for so long. Because of course she'd held hands on the odd occasion with a man. After the first date, but before the third or fourth, when she'd decided it was a non-starter. And none of them had ever made her feel like that. In fact, she didn't remember Jon making her feel like that, and that made her sad.

She walked back to the shop, thanked Penny for holding the fort and spent the rest of the afternoon coming to terms with the fact that she might be falling for Sebastian Thorne in all his irritating, cocky, vulnerable handsomeness. For the first time since Jon died, she found herself having a conversation with him in her head. She had to explain to him that she'd loved him more than she could ever love anything and that nothing would ever change that. And even though his touch hadn't sent a bolt of lightening through her when they were fourteen, it didn't matter because they had other things that made them special. Nothing with anyone else would be special in the same way.

So by the time she went back to the flat, after she'd closed up the haberdashery, she was feeling ready to accept that she had feelings for Sebastian. Not necessarily right now, because apart from her heart breaking for him since apparently he had no-one to look after him in his hour of need, he really needed a shower.

This time, she didn't need to wake him up. When she went into the flat, he was still in bed, but he stirred when she went into the bedroom.

'Back already?' he smiled.

'Yep. These are for you,' she said, handing him two more pills.

'Thanks,' he said, downing them with a gulp of water. 'I think I'm going to have a shower. Do you mind waiting, just in case?'

'No, not at all.' She almost made a joke about seeing him a towel again, but she had no idea whether he was thinking the same things as her. He may not have had a lightning-bolt moment and would have no idea of the effect that seeing him in a towel had on her.

While he was in the shower, she stripped the bed, finding clean sheets on a shelf in the wardrobe.

'You didn't need to do that,' he said, coming into the room with the towel around his waist, just as before. But this time Jess had been half expecting it and, aside from taking a gratuitous look at his six-pack, kept her eyes on his face.

'I don't mind. It's nice to have a fresh bed when you're feeling rough. I bought this for you.' She presented him with the pot of Vicks.

'I haven't seen that since I was a kid.'

'It's a bit old school, but I think it works.'

She went back out to the lounge so he could get dressed. When he came to find her, he'd left the towel around his waist and just put a t-shirt on.

'Let me show you this,' he said, opening his laptop. 'I

honestly don't know when I'll be able to get it finished because I think I might fall asleep mid-sentence. So if you're willing to make sure there's enough information there to send it to the Council, I'd be grateful.'

Jess nodded. 'I don't mind. We're in this together.'

'You're paying me to be in this with you, and I know that I should have done this before. I'm sorry, Jess. I have no excuse.'

Jess was pretty certain by now that he had a very good excuse. He'd been here in the flat for twenty-four hours and all the evidence was beginning to point to the fact that he had nowhere else to be, no-one to tell, and probably nowhere to live. No wonder he'd let this slide.

20

Seb sat next to Jess and logged her into his laptop, asking her to write down the password so that she could get into it again without him next to her, if needs be. Despite having slept all day, he could barely keep his eyes open. The effort of having a shower had taken it out of him and he'd been worried that he might keel over in the bathroom, which was why he'd asked Jess to stay.

Not the only reason he asked her. Seb was painfully aware that he owed Jess an explanation and an apology, but he didn't have the energy for either. He didn't have a great excuse for not having the Event Management Plan prepared before the meeting with the council, but he regretted pretending that he had it all in hand when that couldn't have been further from the truth.

The work that he and Jess had done to prepare for that meeting would inform most of the plan. It was just a matter of putting it together into one cohesive document. Except it wasn't. He'd underestimated how long it would take to do and had stayed up all hours in the freezing industrial unit that he called home until he realised how rough he was feeling and sought out a day's respite in Oliver's flat on the pretence of doing his washing. He hadn't counted on Jess coming to find him. Although now, he was grateful to her for looking out for him and even more grateful that she was going to finish the EMP for him because he'd never felt as ill as this before in his life. All he could think about was the desperate need he had to lie down and close his eyes.

'Are you sure you don't mind me using your laptop? I can email it to myself instead, if that's better?' she said.

He trusted her and anyway, there was nothing he needed to hide from her on there. 'It's okay. You may as well do it here. All the reference documents are there.' He nodded to the table, then regretted it when his head pounded. 'The document should be open,' he said, closing his eyes tightly against the pain.

Jess reached over and touched his forehead. It felt familiar, as if she might have done it before, and she didn't seem hesitant. 'How are you feeling?'

'I might lie down, if you don't mind. I'm sorry to leave you to it. Wake me if you need anything.'

'I won't,' she said smiling, but with concern in her eyes. 'Put some of that Vicks on before you fall asleep. It works miracles.'

He needed a miracle. If only he'd got the EMP sent off before his body had been overtaken by god knows what, no-one would be any the wiser and he definitely wouldn't be looking like a complete idiot in front of Jess.

'Thanks,' he said, standing slowly, unsure whether he would make it as far as the bed before he passed out.

'Night,' she said.

He pulled his towel off and got into bed. The sheets smelled fresh and felt cool against his skin. And he was much more comfortable without all of his clothes on. What had he been thinking? Still, at least Jess hadn't undressed him or anything embarrassing like that. He took the Vicks from the bedside table and slathered a good scoop all over the top of his chest. It brought back vivid memories of childhood that made him smile.

His mother used to sit on the side of his bed and rub this in for him, then she'd sit there and stroke his forehead until he fell asleep.

Jess was the only person since then who had made him feel as cared for as his mother. He turned over and was asleep within a minute.

The following morning, he awoke to the sounds of the coffee machine downstairs. He rolled onto his back and looked up at the ceiling, assessing himself. He felt better. He felt like getting up. Apart from the t-shirt he was wearing, his clothes were all in a clean pile in the lounge or in a dirty pile on the bathroom floor. He wandered out into the lounge, feeling hungry for the first time in a couple of days. When he went over to grab some clean clothes from his pile of fresh laundry, he saw Jess asleep in the corner of the sofa. He was butt-naked. Why hadn't he learned his lesson the other day after he'd come out of the shower?

He dressed as quickly and quietly as his stiff limbs would allow and checked the time. She'd be upset if she was late for work, but it was only seven am. He'd probably been woken by the sound of the first brew of the day. There was time to let her sleep. Goodness only knew how long she'd worked on the EMP. The laptop was still open but had powered down at some point. He switched it on and put the password in. The document was there and a quick scroll through it told him she'd completed all the information that had been missing. It was ready to send.

After a night on the sofa, she was probably in dire need of a coffee and something to eat, so he ventured downstairs and found Jack serving the first customers.

'Morning,' he said, once he had cleared his small queue of early birds, greeting Sebastian as if it was no surprise to see him emerge from the flat. 'What can I get you? It's on the house, Oliver insisted. He says there are no supplies upstairs.'

'Um, two lattes, please. And two pain au chocolates, if that's okay?'

'Feeling twice as hungry and thirsty this morning?' Jack said, laughing.

'Jess is upstairs too,' Sebastian said, realising when he saw Jack's eyebrows raise, how that sounded. 'She's been working on some festival stuff.'

'Riiiight,' said Jack in a way that meant he thought it was an excuse. It didn't matter to Sebastian, but he didn't want Jess to be embarrassed if Jack thought they'd spent the night together.

In the end, he just smiled because anything he said would probably make it worse. He carried it all upstairs on a tray without dropping it and put it down on top of some paperwork on the coffee table. He sat at the end of the sofa, next to Jess's feet, and took a deep breath, feeling as if he'd run 10k as well as gone downstairs for coffee. It might take a few days to get over this virus, or whatever it was. Jess still hadn't stirred, so he gently rubbed her leg and she shot bolt upright, gasping in shock.

'Oh my god!' Once she realised where she was, she relaxed and took a deep breath. 'Sorry. I wasn't expecting to wake up here.'

'It did look as if you'd dropped off mid-flow,' he said, nodding towards the open laptop. 'But you got it done. Thank you so much.' He hoped she knew how grateful he was.

'There wasn't much to do. It only needed tidying up and a few bits of information that I found in here.' She pointed to the Purple Guide. 'That's pretty useful.'

'It is,' he agreed. 'I'll send it off to Helena.'

'Why hadn't you already done that?' she asked. It wasn't

an accusation. She sounded curious.

He handed her a coffee and a pastry. Explaining, saying it all out loud was difficult. But he wanted to tell her, if only so that she'd know how much it meant to him that not only had she looked after him for the past two days when he had no idea what was going on, she'd saved this contract for him. At least he hoped that's how it would play out. For all he knew, she might have decided he'd broken their deal by not producing the plan and he'd get the sack. But somehow, he didn't think she'd have stayed up all night to finish it for him if that was the case.

'Honestly, I underestimated how hard it would be to produce the EMP when so many of the plans were still up in the air. Then time got away with me until the meeting with Helena.' He paused, taking a moment to prepare himself. 'To tell you the truth, this is the only contract I've ever had where I've been responsible for producing the EMP. Someone else has always done it. I should have known and I'm sorry I let you all down.'

'Then why did you give yourself the impossible deadline of saying to Helena that you'd send it after the meeting?'

It was a reasonable question with an answer that was highly embarrassing to have to say out loud. 'I didn't want to look like an idiot in front of everybody.'

Jess snorted out a laugh. 'That didn't work out too well, did it?'

He was almost shocked that she'd basically just called him an idiot, but then he laughed too. 'Christ, no, it didn't. What was I thinking?'

'That you could pull off a miracle?'

'I mean, all the detail was all in my head. I suppose I thought I'd just blurt it all out onto the laptop, use that other EMP as a template.'

'But it was for a very different kind of event,' Jess said,

hitting the nail on the head.

'I know. Idiot, as you said.'

'I think you said that.' She smiled, and he felt a surge of affection towards her.

'Thank you. You didn't have to do this. Any of this. If it wasn't for you…' He'd have hypothermia in an industrial unit and no-one would know, and he'd still have an EMP to finish when that was the last thing he felt like doing.

'You're welcome. It was no trouble. I did wonder whether there was anyone we should have called for you?'

He shook his head. 'I'm not close to my family. My mother died when I was young, and my father and I don't see eye-to-eye.'

She was looking at him, a question still there.

'And I've been single for a while.' He didn't want to get into his whole backstory now. He didn't need pity.

'I'm sorry.' That wasn't pity, it was understanding. 'You know, if you need a few more days here until you're properly feeling better, I'm sure Oliver wouldn't mind.'

Did she know he had nowhere to live? He had a feeling she did, but he wasn't ready to admit that to anyone.

'Thanks, I'll see if I can catch him in the coffee shop later. I'd better make sure.'

'It's a coffee house,' she said.

'I know.'

'You said coffee shop. Oliver's very particular that it has to be a coffee house. I'm only saying, just in case it comes up.'

'Thanks for the warning.' How weird was Oliver. Coffee house? 'Anything else I ought to know?'

She dropped her gaze to the empty plate on her lap. 'Just that you're in the gang now. We look out for each other. You don't have to hide anything from us. If you're having trouble with anything, just because we're paying you, or we will be soon, it doesn't mean you have to shoulder everything on your own.'

Sebastian looked at her. How was it possible that she'd picked up the pieces for him and was still willing to offer him more than he deserved? He moved along the sofa towards her and put his arms around her. Without hesitation, she accepted his embrace, wrapping her arms underneath his, rubbing his back with her palms. It was a long time since he'd been held by anyone. It felt good. Especially because it was Jess. Whether he felt differently because he couldn't believe she was so kind to have kept an eye on him, made him stay here the other night when he'd felt like death, or whether it was something else; that he actually had feelings for her. He suspected that he might.

She pulled back, but her hand rested on his forearm and it was all he could think about.

'I'm going away for the weekend,' she said, 'a mixture of work and seeing family. Are you going to be okay? Do you have anyone who could pop in and feed you paracetamol?'

He briefly thought about Maria, because she was the last person who'd been in his life who might have cared enough once. But he didn't think she'd have cared as much as Jess, even back then. He smiled and shook his head. 'I'm okay now. I can see to myself.'

That's how it always was and why these past days, with Jess watching over him, had warmed his heart in a way that surprised him. It had been nice to have someone around to lean on a little. He'd been more honest with her about, well, not everything, but as much as he felt he could be at this point and it felt good. He felt unburdened after backing himself into a corner and not being able to see a way out. And she didn't look at him as if he was hiding something anymore.

'Well, you have Oliver downstairs if you need anything.'

'I'll miss you,' he said, noticing how her gaze shot to meet

his. Did that mean she felt the same?
'Me too.'

21

By the time Jess closed the haberdashery on Friday afternoon, she was ready for her trip to Dorset via Southampton. In some ways it had been a difficult week but now that the EMP was finally in Helena's hands, they could concentrate on pulling all the elements of the festival together, until the council held the next Safety Advisory Group meeting where all the local representatives of the fire service, police and anyone else with a vested interest would decide the fate of the festival. For now, all they could do was get bookings in for everything they needed, which Sebastian had promised he was doing, and applying for a licence for the park which Oliver and Matt had offered to sort. Rob had a list of bands and musicians who were keen to provide some evening entertainment and gentle music during the day and he was taking care of auditioning them and putting a programme together. Hilary was liaising with the traders about stalls they might want to have and Jen was co-ordinating anyone who wanted to be a food vendor at the festival. Jess's main job was the book club, and that wasn't quite so time-critical.

With all of that in hand, and now that Seb was on the mend and hopefully staying in the flat for the moment, there was nothing weighing her down. Now, she was looking forward to the break in Dorset, bracing walks on the beach and catching up with her family. All that stood in her way was the mini-cruise. She'd hardly had time to think about how nervous she was. She'd spent the day prepping her kits for the workshops; she planned to teach English Paper Piecing patchwork and some embellishment quilting methods, so she felt confident in being ready for the workshop. It was work, not a holiday. It was nothing her brain ought to relate to anything that she'd done with Jon. They'd never been to Southampton or Bruges together. Or on a cruise, for that matter.

She'd packed the night before, carefully folding her new trousers into her holdall along with a selection of her usual dresses for the cruise, and in case she got dragged out to eat while she was at her parents' or they went to the pub for a drink. Almost as an afterthought, she packed the scrapbook. It might be nice to look through it back at home. She was ready to bring a bit of closure to that part of her life. It had always felt unresolved, somehow, and until now she'd resisted anything that might make her think too hard about everything that had happened back then. But now, something had shifted. Maybe it was because being involved with the festival was bringing her out of her comfort zone. Or maybe it was because of Sebastian Thorne.

He'd said he'd miss her. It was a sign that things had shifted between them over the past week. She liked to think that she'd be just as heartbroken for anyone who was helpless and alone with no-one to look after them in their hour of need, but deep down, she knew those feelings were particular to Seb. He wasn't someone she felt the need to brush off after a couple of dates, not that there had been any dates. Yet. If anything, that's what she wanted. To explore whatever this was. To spend time with him, especially now that he'd admitted he'd messed up with the EMP. Hopefully, the person she was seeing now was the real Sebastian emerging from the image he'd tried to present.

Jess walked to the car park where she'd left Madge with her luggage safely stowed in the boot. It would be the longest journey Madge had made in a long while and Jess had had her serviced in preparation. The car was the equivalent of an octogenarian in car years, so preparation was everything. Once night fell, it was cold, so Jess had laid a homemade quilt and a wool blanket on the back seat and had a bag of snacks and a flask of hot tea that she'd made before she left the shop, just in case. She had Now That's What I Call Music 20 in the tape-player, purely for its longevity so she wouldn't have to change it so regularly, and she had her favourite fingerless gloves on, a knitted gift from Penny. It might be late April, but Madge's heater wasn't the best. Madge herself was raring to go and Jess made good time getting down to the south coast in a little under three and a half hours.

The cruise ship was nothing like Jess had imagined. It was vast, luxurious, and didn't bear any resemblance to any kind of boat she'd been on before. When they set sail on Saturday morning, the seas were calm and engrossed as she was in teaching her workshop to a series of travel agents and holiday company bigwigs, she barely noticed the voyage itself.

In the evening, with the boat alongside in Bruges, she and Fi had a fun evening together wandering the streets of the picturesque town, stopping here and there for drinks and food.

'I'm so glad I said yes. Thanks for asking me,' said Jess, her arm looped through Fi's as they wandered back to the ship.

'I knew you'd love it and you've done a brilliant job. The patchwork project is genius for this taster cruise because people can spend as much or as little time as they like having a go.'

'And I can sit and do it while I'm chatting to them, so it's win win. I lost count of how many people asked about the shop. I gave some cards out. I hope that's okay.'

'Of course it is. The whole point of doing something like this is to spread the word about your business.'

But for Jess, the whole point had been to see if she could do something she'd almost turned down out of fear of the unknown. And the fear of memories from the past overwhelming her. Neither had happened; she'd not even thought about Jon, and she felt more prepared now to face the visit to Dorset knowing that she'd achieved this. It was just two days away. To anyone else it would seem ridiculous to place so much importance on being able to get through two days on a mini-cruise, but it meant everything to Jess that she hadn't been crippled by grief, or guilt, or anything else. All she had done was enjoy herself, and she couldn't wait to do it again. She resolved to email the company and put her name down for any work that might come up in the future. If anything came of it, she could worry about the shop then.

The streets near her parents' house were unchanged and Jess took comfort from the familiar because her insides were churning, despite having left Southampton hoping that she wouldn't feel like this. She always felt like this when she came here, but it was just because she hadn't been that often since she'd said goodbye to Jon. Visiting once in a blue moon wasn't going to normalise it anytime soon. But it felt like a step forward to realise that. To be coming here knowing this time that she needed to allow herself to move on.

Her parents' house faced the sea with a wide road and a strip of grass and sand dunes between the house and the beach. Jess parked up on the road outside the house, climbed out of the car, and stretched her arms above her head. She was tired after the crazy pace of the cruise, but she could smell the sea on the breeze and couldn't help but smile. It was one of her favourite places in the world. Why hadn't she realised before that it was part of her? Even though it had seemed safer to stay away, it might have helped her heal. She took a deep breath. There was no point in wishing she'd done things differently. The important thing was to take stock and forge ahead on a different path from now on.

She closed the driver's door, then opened the boot and unloaded her bags. The moment she slammed it closed, the front door opened and her mum stood there waving to her.

'Do you need a hand?' she called.

'No, I can manage.' Jess pulled her holdall onto her shoulder, picked up her handbag, and headed up the path.

'Oooh, I've missed you!' her mum, Clare, said, wrapping her in a hug before Jess had got inside or put her bags down.

'Shut the door!' Her dad said, coming out of the lounge. He sounded cross, but he wasn't, and his face broke into a smile as soon as he'd shut the front door and taken Jess in his arms as well. 'Your mother costs me a fortune, letting all the bloody heat out.'

'Oh, shut up, Joe,' Clare said, wrapping her arms around her husband as soon as he'd let Jess go. 'You wouldn't have it any other way.'

'Pffftt!' he huffed, pecking her on the cheek.

'Am I in my room?' Jess asked, keen to end the awkward parental display of affection.

'Yes, love. Let Dad take your bags up.'

'Christ alive, woman, are you trying to kill me?' Joe said. 'She's thirty years younger than me. I think she can carry her own bags.'

Jess laughed. Nothing changed.

Although they all referred to Jess's room as hers, it was nothing like it had been when she'd lived at home. One of the built-in cupboards was still given over to storing all the bits and pieces that she never got around to taking with her, but apart from that there was no trace of her life in this room anymore. It was a lovely guest room, though. It was at the front corner of the house and had two windows, one at the front and one at the side, so there was a fantastic view of the beach for as far as you could see, right until it disappeared at the headland. Jess used to love watching the sea during a storm and eventually her dad had built a bench seat into the corner underneath the windows so that she could sit there for as long as she wanted. It was still her favourite place in the house and was even better than before since it had been upgraded and piled high with scatter cushions to match the fancy bedding.

Jess pulled her trousers and dresses out of the bag and hung them in the wardrobe, then sat in the window, drinking in the view, even though all she could really see at this time of night was the reflection of the moon on the waves.

'Do you want something to eat, Jessie?' Clare called up the stairs.

'Coming!' She pulled the curtains to keep the warmth in and looked forward to revisiting the view in the morning.

Joe was watching football in the lounge, so Clare and Jess sat at the kitchen table eating toast and marmite.

'Are you sure that's enough? I don't mind putting some pasta on.'

'No, it's too late to eat a proper meal. This is great. Anyway, I had a big lunch on the boat, so I'm not starving.'

'That sounded so exciting. Fancy working on a cruise ship.'

'It was brilliant.' She didn't know how to explain to her mum why it had been a big step. On some level, she probably knew.

'What brought this visit on, then?' Clare was straight to the point and Jess admired her for not beating around the bush. After all, having barely visited since she moved to

Croftwood, it was bound to seem out of character.

Jess exhaled, readying herself to explain. Where would she start? But Clare took it as a sign that Jess didn't want to talk about it.

'You don't have to tell me, Jessie. I'm glad you're here, that's all.'

'It's not that I don't want to tell you. I suppose I'm not sure myself what's made me feel different about it.' She took another piece of toast and spread more butter on it than she normally would because it felt like a treat, and she was on holiday. Kind of. 'I've been thinking about Jon a lot lately. I tried not to for a long time because it was easier to forget. I've realised that I need to get some closure on things and it felt like I needed to come here to do that.'

'That's good,' Clare said reassuringly. 'Do you think something's happened to trigger this?'

Jess shrugged. 'I almost turned down the cruise job. I didn't want to, but since Jon died, I haven't been anywhere because everywhere I'd been before was with him. I thought it would be too much, bring back all the memories of that summer. I've spent the last ten years keeping my life totally separate from all of that and suddenly it felt like those two parts of my life were intersecting and it felt wrong. That makes no sense at all,' she said, shaking her head.

Clare put her hand on top of Jess's. 'It makes total sense. Moving to Croftwood was an escape for you when you were still grieving. It was survival, Jessie. It's not surprising that you felt as if you'd be threatening that safety net you built for yourself by introducing something that feels linked to Jon.'

'That's it, Mum. And I realised I can't let that happen. I had to try to deal with it and this feels like the right way to do it. Try to face the past, or something.'

'And it was okay?'

Jess laughed. 'I can't believe now that I'd equated any kind of holiday with Jon. It seems so bizarre now. But I didn't know that until this weekend. I guess I had to push myself out of my comfort zone to realise it was going to be okay. And coming back here is kind of the same thing.'

'So what are you going to do?'

'I'm going to the beach huts. I think that'd be a good start.'

Clare smiled. 'There's only a couple left now. You might not even get inside them anymore. I'm surprised the council hasn't cleared them away altogether. Still, they're too ramshackle for even the local kids to want to hang out there anymore. That's probably why they haven't bothered. They're no risk to anyone, just becoming a bit of an eyesore.'

'Lucky I've come to my senses before they disappeared then.'

'Don't be too hard on yourself. That was a huge thing to go through, losing Jon so suddenly and having to cope with that enormous grief at such a young age. It was always going to be difficult to move past that. But you've built a wonderful life in Croftwood, and you're doing exactly the right thing by making sure you don't let the past hold you back.'

Jess almost told her mum about Seb, but she wasn't sure what to say. Instead, she told her about their plans for the festival and mentioned that they had a contractor called Sebastian. It felt like a gentle introduction to someone she wasn't sure was anyone she'd need to tell her mum anything more about in the end, anyway. Who knew what was going on? But Jess hoped that after this weekend she would feel able to pursue something with Seb if that's where things headed, without the ghost of Jon holding her back.

22

Even though she'd only had a moment to take in the sea air when she'd arrived last night, Jess was sure that was the reason she'd slept so well. As much as she loved her little cottage on the hill, the chill in the air was never far away, even at this time of the year. It was a relief to wake up feeling enveloped in warmth for a change. She was pretty sure her mum and dad would have been passively aggressively altering the thermostat up and down since she'd arrived. The thought made her smile. She also thought about Seb waking up in the flat in Croftwood. It must be a relief for him to know he had somewhere reliable to stay while the weather was still making its mind up whether it was spring yet. It was a relief for her too. She still didn't quite understand why he hadn't shared exactly what his situation was. It wasn't any of her business, she knew that, but she still wanted to know, so that she could know him.

She climbed out of bed and drew the curtains back to find a bright, windy day outside. The waves were sparkling in the sunshine and had white foam tops thanks to the wind whipping the water. She couldn't wait to get out there. Pulling on a pair of soft jersey trousers and a hideous fuchsia super-chunky knit cardigan that she'd made with Patsy's help, she headed downstairs. The cardigan had been an early attempt by Patsy to get Jess addicted to knitting. The idea was that the wool was so thick, it would knit up in a few hours, encouraging her to keep knitting as the results were so fast. It hadn't quite worked out like that because there were some inexplicable holes that even Patsy couldn't fathom out how to sort out without unpicking the whole thing, and Jess had refused to let her, insisting that it was a learning exercise. So it looked awful, too bad to wear in front of anyone usually, but Jess loved it because she made it, and it was very cosy.

'Morning, love,' her mum said, immediately filling the kettle to make a fresh pot of tea. 'Did you sleep alright?'

'Yes, like a log. I always forget how that happens here.'

'Want some eggy bread for breakfast?'

'Yes, please.' It had been years since Jess had had her mum's eggy bread and another wave of nostalgia swept over her. 'I never think about making it at home, and anyway it'd never be the same as yours.'

'What are you up to today?' Clare asked. 'Because your dad and I have taken the day off and he's keen to go for a pub lunch at the Woodsman.'

'That sounds great. I'm going to wander along the beach to the headland this morning so maybe I should meet you there to save coming back here.' The pub was about a mile along the road, not too far to walk to which meant they could all have a drink.

'Good idea. I'll ring and book a table for one o'clock.'

After breakfast, Jess dressed in her new green trousers, layered a couple of tops underneath her hand-knitted fairisle jumper that she'd found in a charity shop a few years ago, then added a hat and gloves along with her coat. Although it was sunny and fairly warm, the wind would put a chill in the air.

She left the house, stopping off to grab her sunglasses from

Madge's glove box before she headed across the road and over the grassy dunes to the beach. The tide was out and once she'd battled through the soft sand, the ground was firm beneath her feet as she headed straight for the water. It looked inviting, the clear shallows glistening in the sunshine, but Jess knew it'd be icy cold if she dipped her toes in. There was no chance of that this weekend. She let the waves reach the tips of her boots before she stepped back, playing chicken with them, loving the feeling of having nothing to do apart from making it to the pub in a few hours.

The beach was deserted; not that surprising for a Monday morning at this time of year in a sleepy seaside village away from the tourist hotspots. Jess headed to the right, keeping close to the waves, but not so close that they'd reach her. Until the tide began to turn, then she'd have to watch out.

About half the distance along to the main headland there was a rocky outcrop which she could skirt around because the tide was low, but at high tide, it separated the beach into two distinct coves. This was where they used to hang out when they were at school. It was out of sight of the village and had no houses overlooking it since the road took a turn further inland at this point. At the far end, nestled into the gently sloping cliff of the headland were the handful of council-owned beach huts that had been gradually battered by the sea enough times that it had been generally accepted that this beach was never going to be the kind of place where the price of a beach hut could be more than you'd pay for a house. The council had stopped maintaining them, then had to stop offering them for hire, and that's when the local teenagers had moved in to claim them as their own. When Jess had been in that tribe, there had only been a couple of huts that you could call usable. Most of them were missing parts of their roofs, or a front panel, making them more vulnerable to the persistent battering of the sea in the winter.

Now, as she walked closer, most of them had been dismantled and the debris taken away by the council or by the sea. Only two remained and you couldn't call those intact. She would guess that by next summer the sea and sand would reclaim the beach as their own and the huts would be gone forever.

It was hard to know after all this time, and without all of the huts as a reference point, which one had been their favourite. Was it one that was still standing, or not? Against her better judgement, Jess stepped onto the weathered decking at the front of one of the huts. Even now, with the little windows missing and the door hanging off its hinges, it would still be a lovely sheltered spot to sit on a windy day in the summer. Perhaps that's why the council had left them for so long.

She pushed at the door with her foot and it scraped against the floor and opened further. There was a small hole in the roof and the floor was covered in drifts of sand. It didn't look as if anyone had been inside for a long time. Certainly there were no signs that anyone used it regularly like they had back in the day. They'd always left the odd clue that they'd been there; a half-drunk bottle of fizzy drink, the odd cigarette butt, a couple of candles, their bottoms melted onto a flat piece of rock.

It suddenly felt like it could have been yesterday that she'd last been here with Jon. Jess sat down on a bank of sand that had piled up in the back corner of the hut and looped her arms around her knees. She could see the sea out of the door. Was it this view that she remembered? Did they ever look at the view, or were they only looking at each other? She took a deep breath. After a few moments, she began to feel more rooted. Those memories didn't feel as close as they had when she'd walked in. When she remembered being here with Jon, she was different. She was young, sure that he was the one for her forever, and even though she'd still thought that when he died, she knew now that there was room for love in her future with someone else.

Jon was gone. Obviously, she knew that, but she'd thought that coming back here would hurt. She'd expected to sit here and imagine that he might walk through the door of this beach hut as if he'd never been gone. But now she was here, she couldn't imagine it. If he walked in now, they'd have a shared past from so long ago that they'd be virtual strangers. Strangers who'd loved each other with the fierce love that only youth, naivety and inexperience can fuel. But there would be a distance between them now because of a life lived apart, and Jess hadn't appreciated that until she'd sat on the floor of this beach hut and allowed herself to think.

Being in Croftwood for so long had made it easy to forget. The physical distance between here and there was breathing space that she'd needed to begin with, but that had become a barrier to moving on in the end. Jess saw it all with sudden clarity. This was the place she'd needed to come to understand the difference between cherishing the memory of Jon and the brief life they'd shared, and the value of moving on. The value of living a life that he couldn't be part of, but would hopefully be proud of.

Jess didn't know how long she'd been sitting there, but when she stood up, it felt like the right time to go. There was a lightness to her that felt almost palpable and a fizz of energy about what was to come that she'd wished she'd had in her life before now, but better now than never. Pulling the door closed behind her was pointless since it no longer fitted into the doorframe, but it felt necessary. It felt like a physical embodiment of the closure she'd got from coming here.

The sea had travelled further up the beach and Jess knew it was time to go before she missed the chance to take a shortcut to the pub around the rocks instead of having to hike over the rocks and along the road. As it was, she had to play chicken with the waves until she could run around the rocks without getting her feet wet. She laughed, loving reliving the same thing she'd done so many times, so many years earlier.

By the time she got to the pub, her dad was halfway down his first pint and her mum was sipping a glass of red wine.

'Sorry I'm late,' she said, taking off a few layers since the log fire was giving out some serious heat.

'There's no such thing,' said Joe. 'There's all the time in the world.'

'Well, the kitchen closes at three, so not all the time,' said Clare, passing out the menus.

'What are you drinking, Jessie?' her dad asked.

'I'll have a glass of wine, whatever Mum's got.'

'Have you been to the huts?' Clare asked her as soon as Joe had gone to the bar.

She nodded. 'I thought it would be hard, but it wasn't.'

Clare nodded. 'It's easy to play these things out, how you think something's going to go, and then it's a surprise when it's not like that at all. And how can you really know how you'll feel until it happens?'

'Yes, exactly. I think I was coming at it as if it would be me from ten years ago walking into that beach hut. I thought it would feel raw and take me back to feeling like I did back then, when Jon died. But I'm not that person anymore. I left her behind without even noticing.'

'You've moved on, Jessie.' Clare said gently. 'That's a good thing. It just took you a while to realise it because you had no markers in your life to measure it against.'

'I should have come back sooner.' She tried not to live with regrets about anything. It was better to see the things that you wished you'd done differently as leading you to a path you'd never have taken otherwise. But this felt like something she would regret. She'd wasted ten years thinking she wasn't over Jon. And worse, she'd spent years deliberately not allowing herself to think about him, trying to keep her heart safe from the hurt and grief, and all that time, she'd been healing.

'No, you weren't ready before. Even when you came back for Christmases, you could have been anywhere. You never left the house from the moment you arrived to the moment you left. I'm not sure you even went on the beach.'

Jess nodded. It had been hard, but had felt like self-preservation. 'I thought I'd see Jon everywhere.'

'I know. And there was no point me or your dad saying anything, because you have to live through something like that. There are no shortcuts with grief.'

'I think I could have shaved a couple of years off,' Jess said, smiling at her mum.

'I'm just glad you're back. Maybe we'll see more of you now.'

Joe came back to the table with a glass of wine for Jess and another round for him and Clare. 'Otherwise we'll be ready for another in the middle of our lunch,' he said, when Clare raised her eyebrows.

'I thought you were trying to get me squiffy, Joe Taylor.'

Joe rolled his eyes and smiled. 'You're already squiffy, my love,' he said. 'But it's not often we get to have a pub lunch with our girl. It feels like a celebration.'

After lunch, they all walked along the beach back to the house. Joe put the kettle on, and Jess went upstairs to fetch the scrapbook.

'I don't know if I ever showed you this,' she said, sitting down on the sofa next to her mum.

'No, I don't remember seeing it,' said Clare, taking it and opening it carefully. 'Oh my goodness, Jess. Look at you both!'

It was lovely to share the memories of the holiday with

someone after so long trying not to think about it. Clare chatted about other things she remembered from when Jess and Jon had still been living in Corfe Bay. Once they'd flipped through the holiday scrapbook, Clare went to the sideboard and pulled old photo albums out of the cupboard.

'Oh no, look what you've started now,' Joe groaned.

Jess laughed. 'Come on, Dad, it's fun looking back at the old pictures.'

'Old pictures make me feel old, Jessie.' But he sat down on the other side of Jess and the three of them spent the rest of the afternoon reminiscing.

When she went up to bed that night, Jess felt so happy. It had been an incredible day. She felt like she'd come so far and she definitely wasn't that girl from ten years ago. She was a woman who'd been shaped by what had happened to that girl, but not a woman who would allow herself to be defined by that any longer.

23

The following day was bright and breezy, beckoning Jess out onto the beach again. This time, she planned to head in the opposite direction towards the edge of Corfe Bay before it turned into the Purbeck peninsula, the next town being Swanage. It was at least a couple of hours' walk to Swanage along the beach and it was only possible to do when the tide was on its way out.

Joe had set off early for work. He was an engineer for a company that built super-yachts in Poole. Clare was a practice nurse for one of the local GP surgeries and worked every morning until one o'clock, so she and Jess arranged to meet for lunch at a café in Swanage.

'Are you sure you can remember how far it is?' Clare asked. 'Why don't you get the bus?'

'I've got all morning and I fancy a long walk. I'll be fine.'

Jess layered up again, thinking that she should have made another pair of trousers since it looked as if her dresses weren't going to see the light of day for the whole visit. She chose a lighter jumper today, a sweatshirt that she'd made out of some striped jersey fabric. It always felt great to be wearing an entire outfit that she'd made herself.

Today, she took a more leisurely pace, sticking to the high

tide line so that she could keep an eye out for sea glass and pretty shells. There wasn't much to be had, unless she wanted to sift through the strands of seaweed that denoted where the sea had come up to earlier that morning. But once she'd started looking, it was hard to draw her eyes away from the sand, just in case she missed something. The coloured glass, the bottle green or even more rarely blue, was easy to spot, and it wasn't long before Jess found a piece of green that had all its rough edges smoothed by the sea. She put it in her pocket and kept her gaze down, bolstered by her find. It was a lovely way to spend a couple of hours; quite mindful. Her thoughts wandered, as much as her feet, with her mind not settling on anything for long enough to give it much consideration at all. It was a wonderfully freeing feeling. In Croftwood, she went from work to home, where sewing was therapeutic most of the time, but also amounted to work most of the time. Until now, she'd hardly allowed herself any downtime to do nothing. Maybe she'd been scared to think about anything too deeply. But now, since the beach hut, since coming here, since the cruise, she knew things would be different. Okay, maybe she wouldn't be tramping up the Malvern Hills every day being mindful, but she would certainly take time away from the shop to do something other than sewing because as much as she loved it, she was loving this feeling of giving herself time, with no agenda, just as much.

After an hour, or maybe it was longer, the outskirts of Swanage came into view. The Victorian seaside town had barely changed since the last time Jess had done this walk more than ten years ago. She left the beach at Peveril Point and walked along the road, with the sea to her right, looking ahead to the old quayside where the colourful boats were pulled up onto the sand, before the town proper began. Looking at her watch, she still had an hour before she needed to meet her mum. More than enough time to stroll along the promenade towards the other end of Swanage beach, past the beach huts and the Victorian guest houses that sat along the sea road. Before she went back down to the beach, she popped into the fish and chip shop and bought a mushy pea fritter. It was one of her favourite things in the world and she'd never seen it anywhere else. One ball of crispy pea loveliness wasn't really enough, but she didn't want to be full up before she'd even met her mum. She knew she'd be back sometime soon, anyway.

All the beach huts were still boarded up for the winter to help them weather the worst of the battering they'd get from the sea. Jess had always wished they could have hired a beach hut for a week in the summer when she was younger, and she and her sister had begged their parents. They found it amusing and said, quite rightly, what would be the point when they lived a stone's throw from the beach. It was better, they said, to let families who weren't as lucky to be living by the seaside have the chance to enjoy them. But even now, they held a special magic that Jess felt like she was missing out on. Perhaps one day, she'd hire one for herself. It didn't need to be in the height of summer, early in the season would still be lovely. She'd sit inside and watch the world go by, punctuated by some reading, or hand-stitching and plenty of cups of tea, and she'd be the one who people envied when they walked past, wondering what it would be like to be one of those people who had the sea on their doorstep for a week.

When she walked past the information board next to the beach huts, she snapped a picture of it just in case she ever actually got round to taking herself seriously. Although, she suspected there might be nicer spots to have a beach hut, somewhere more secluded, where the world wasn't traipsing past your door all the time.

'Jess?'

She jumped, lost in her thoughts and not expecting anyone to say her name. It took her a moment to realise who the man was, staring at her, looking slightly puzzled.

'Zac.'

'It is you.' He pulled her into a hug. 'Oh my god, Jess, you look just the same.'

'You too.'

Zac was Jon's younger brother, but they could have been twins. He was older now than Jon had ever been, but Jess caught a glimpse in Zac of how Jon might have aged and it tugged at her heart.

'What are you doing here? I mean, I know your folks still live in the bay, but I haven't seen you since…'

'I moved to Worcestershire. I've been there almost ten years now. I run my own business, so I don't get back that often.'

'Have you got time for a chat?' He gestured to a bench a few strides away from them.

Jess checked her phone. 'I have a few minutes. I'm meeting my mum for lunch.' She kept the timings deliberately vague, so she'd have an excuse to leave if it all got too much. Her heart was racing. It was strange that yesterday she had been feeling a huge sense of closure whereas now, the past was staring her right in the face.

They walked along to the bench and sat at either end, looking out to sea. At least that was something. They could talk without having to look at each other, which always made things easier.

'I've wanted to say sorry for ever, Jess.'

She looked at him in confusion. What did he have to be sorry for? She smiled and shook her head. 'There's nothing to apologise to me for, Zac.'

'There is. I'm ashamed of how my family treated you.'

It was as if a stone had thudded into the pit of Jess's

stomach. She thought for a second that she might see the pea fritter again, but took a deep breath and looked at the sea to centre herself.

'Jon loved you, and my parents took him away from you. They panicked when they knew they were going to lose him. It's not an excuse, but that's why.'

It was hard to think back. It had been the darkest time in her life. She'd lost him before he'd died because his parents had cosseted him away, unwilling to share what little time they had left with anyone else. And there had been nothing she could do to change their minds. Her grieving had begun before Jon had died, knowing that she would never see him again. It had hurt that his family, despite knowing how he felt about her, had thought she was unimportant. That their relationship was somehow less meaningful than the family connection that they had with him. And by then, once the doctors had told them that there was no hope, as if they couldn't already see that for themselves, it didn't matter what Jon wanted because he was too weak to fight.

Jess had been angry and bitter for a long time. Leaving Corfe Bay was the only way she could escape the hurt. And she'd been frightened to come back for all this time.

'It took me a long time to stop regretting those last few weeks before he died. I should have fought harder to be with him.' All the feelings of hurt and resentment came flooding back, and Jess choked back a sob. 'I felt as if he'd died thinking I didn't want to be with him, that I couldn't go through it with him. It was devastating not being able to explain to him that I wanted to be with him every step of the way. All of the way.'

Zac reached over and took her hand. 'He knew, Jess. You might not have been next to him, but he knew why. He didn't want to fight against what mum and dad thought they were doing for the best. He knew that he was breaking their hearts and the only thing he could do to help was let them care for him in the way they needed to.'

Jess sniffed and fished in her pocket for a tissue. 'They didn't let me say goodbye.'

'I know. And I'm truly sorry. Towards the end, none of us knew which conversation was going to be our last with him. I hadn't said goodbye, because I couldn't. I didn't want to think that any of those last days I spent with him were going to be the last, and I know you didn't have that chance like I did, but Jess, you had the best of him. I don't think he'd have wanted you to watch him die.'

Zac had tears running down his cheeks when Jess turned to look at him. She pulled him towards her and they sobbed into each other's shoulders for a minute or two.

'I didn't expect today to turn out like this,' he said, laughing and wiping his eyes.

'Neither did I.' She squeezed his hand. 'Thank you, Zac.'

He shrugged. 'I wanted to say all of that before but I haven't seen hide nor hair of you for years, and it wasn't until a long time afterwards that I realised what had actually happened.'

'Better late than never,' she said, leaning into him and smiling. 'But honestly, thank you. It means a lot that you've said all of that.' She didn't ask whether his parents regretted the way it had all played out. Whether they wished they'd allowed their son to be with the woman that he'd loved for the last moments of his life. It was better not to know. It didn't matter anymore.

'Have you had a pea fritter yet?'

She laughed. 'I'd just finished one when I bumped into you. They still taste the same.'

'Remember when Mum used to make Jon pick me up from school and I'd have to hang around with you two? He used to buy pea fritters for all of us and make me sit on the quayside to eat it so you could two snog on the bench behind without me seeing.'

'And you used to threaten to tell on us for sneaking out to meet each other unless he bought you a chocolate milkshake from the café on the front.'

'I used to get a lot of milkshakes out of him,' said Zac, throwing his head back and laughing. 'Good times, hey?'

'Good times,' she agreed. 'So you still live down here?'

'Not in Corfe Bay anymore. I live in Sandbanks, not on the water, obviously, but I'm doing okay.' Sandbanks was one of the most expensive places to live in the country. Even away from the waterside.

'What do you do?'

'Tech stuff. It's too boring to go into but I'm good at it,' he grinned.

'Blimey, good for you.'

'How about you? You said you have your own business.'

'It's a sewing shop.'

'I can totally see you doing that. You used to make some really weird clothes when we were kids.'

'Original creations, you mean.'

'They were definitely that.'

They sat in silence for a couple of minutes, remembering.

'I must go and meet my mum,' Jess said, eventually.

They stood up, and Zac pulled her into a hug again.

'It's been great to see you, Jess.'

'You too.' She wanted Zac to understand how much it meant to her to hear him acknowledge, even though it hadn't been down to him, that it had been wrong to keep her from Jon at the end of his life. 'I came back to try and get a bit of closure on everything. I've only recently realised that what happened back then might have stopped me from moving on.'

'With someone else?'

She nodded. 'But with everything, really. I've barely been back except for fleeting visits at Christmas. I thought it would be hard to face this place without Jon. But actually, I've felt close to him in a way that's made me realise that I have moved on. Running into you today feels like fate, as if you knew I had unfinished business here today.'

'I didn't,' he said. 'I had something to pick up from the boatyard.'

'Don't spoil it!' Jess said, laughing, walking backwards away from him.

'You take care. Live your best life, Jess, for both of you!'

24

Submitting the Event Management Plan gave Seb a bit of breathing space. The worst of the admin was over, thanks to Jess, meaning he could concentrate on the things he was good at. Or at least the things he used to be good at. He'd come to an arrangement with Oliver so that he could stay in the flat above the coffee house on a rolling contract at a ridiculously cheap rent. He knew Oliver was doing him a favour and Oliver knew he wouldn't want to accept the flat for free. There was no way he could find somewhere else to site the festival office and was lowering the rent to reflect the inconvenience of that. Seb was desperate not to have to go back to living in the industrial unit, so his pride allowed him to accept Oliver's offer.

Although he was still feeling tired after his bout of sickness, living somewhere warm and comfortable lifted his mood enough to make him feel as if he'd bounced back better than before. He was ready to take on the festival and all the challenges they'd identified along with those the council would inevitably flag once they'd reviewed the EMP. The quotes he'd half-heartedly been working on needed completing, and he spent the next two days negotiating the best prices he could for the tents, toilets, and everything else they'd need. It was exhausting and hard to keep track of everything as he went along, but by the time the coffee house closed on Tuesday evening, he was sure he had ticked everything off his list of things he needed to hire.

There was a committee meeting the following evening, on Wednesday. Jess would be back by then so he could update them all with his progress, and he was looking forward to that. It would be a great feeling to tell Jess, and the others, what he'd achieved. They finally had a rough cost of setting up the infrastructure, so they could prepare a proper budget and set a ticket price. That meant they could start selling tickets almost immediately because he knew Patsy had finished a first draft of the website. They could add more information to it all the time, but he knew that advertising the dates, and that it was a festival to do with the date-with-a-book club, would be enough to start the sales coming in. He hoped they could agree on a price at the meeting on Wednesday so that he could present his first invoice, knowing that they'd be able to pay him. It was still touch-and-go whether it would be in time for him to pay his rent, but at last it was a distinct possibility.

There was a knock at the door. Oliver sometimes popped his head in before he left for the day, but it was his day off. He opened the door to find Jess.

'I didn't think you were back until tomorrow,' he said, surprised by how pleased he was to see her.

'I'm back in the shop tomorrow so I travelled back this afternoon to give myself a chance to relax tonight.'

'And yet, you're here,' he grinned, standing aside to let her in.

'I just wanted to make sure you hadn't had a relapse. You look better.'

'I feel great,' he said. 'Do you want a cup of tea or something?' He wished he had more than a few quid to stock the cupboards so that he could offer her a glass of wine, or a beer, but all he could offer was tea or water.

'Tea would be great, thanks.'

While he put the kettle on, he noticed Jess looking at the paperwork on the coffee table. It was a mess since he'd had everything out to cross-reference and keep track of his progress with suppliers. Computers were all very well, but he preferred a visual overview of his notes, plans, and lists while he worked. The plan of the park that he and Jess had put together was now highly colourful, and he could see her looking at it, trying to work out why.

'I've been colour-coding everything on there according to what the area is going to be for. See, the cinema is in green because it's the main venue, it's partly covered by a license already, and I don't have to hire anything to get that set up.'

'Green for go?' Jess said, drily.

'Yes.' Her expression made him smile. 'Simple and easy to remember.'

'But that's the only green thing on the map.'

'At the moment it's the only thing that we could say is sorted. Everything that needs to happen at the cinema is down to Patsy as the person technically hiring the venue out to the festival.'

'Right.' Jess sat down on the sofa and pointed to a couple of blue areas. 'What are these?'

'That's the toilet block and the other blue things are where we'll have the wheelie bins. Those are things we need to hire — that I *have* hired,' he added, 'and which don't need anything else doing. Whereas the orange things are things we need to hire that also need installation.'

'Like the festival lighting,' she said, catching on, 'which is why there are orange lines everywhere.'

'Exactly!'

'It looks like you've made a lot of progress in the last few days,' she said.

Her words of praise were like a warmth that enveloped him. It mattered to him what she thought. Not because he was trying to impress her, although, maybe he was, but it had begun with a need to show her she hadn't been right about him. That he could pull off what he'd promised he would, despite the bump in the road that had been the last couple of weeks.

'I needed to. Helena was right. We're up against it trying to pull this off in a few short months. If you hadn't got the EMP done the other day…' The familiar guilt crept in.

'Seb, don't worry,' she said softly. 'No-one thinks any less of you for not getting it done.' She paused and looked at him in such a way that he could tell there was something she wanted to say, but wasn't sure whether to. He had a fair idea what it was. It was the same thing he'd been wondering whether to tell her.

'I want to be honest with you because you stood by me when I didn't deserve it. No, please, let me finish,' he said, when she opened her mouth with what he knew would be reassurances he wasn't worthy of. 'I needed this contract, Jess. I've been struggling to keep my head above water since the pandemic. I had to furlough my staff and by the time the industry got back on its feet, they'd moved on. I couldn't bid for the kind of contracts that were my bread and butter because I couldn't afford to hire more staff without having a contract in the bag. It was a vicious circle that I couldn't get out of, then before I knew it, I owed payments on the bounce back loans when I hadn't bounced back enough to pay them, and I still had nothing substantial work-wise to get the business back up and running. I had to sell my house to clear everything, and that's all gone. I don't have the debt anymore, but I don't have anywhere to live either.'

Jess gasped, which surprised him because he'd been sure

she'd already guessed that he was as good as homeless.

'And you've been doing this work for us without having been paid a penny yet,' she said. 'Why didn't you say? We could have got some money together sooner. I'm so sorry.'

He shook his head. 'No, it's business, Jess. I can't present an invoice just to aid my cash flow. That's not how it works.'

Jess huffed and stood up. 'Don't tell me how it works.' She was angry. 'I've run my business for long enough to know how it works. You made yourself ill, living god knows where rather than ask for payment for work you were doing for us.'

'I didn't even produce the EMP. You did.'

'You found a site for us. You sweet-talked the traders into getting behind it. We'd never have got anything off the ground if you hadn't done those two things. Anyway, why you would do anything without some payment up front is beyond me,' she carried on. 'I thought it was because you were mates with Matt, not because you were too proud or whatever other bloody nonsense stopped you from asking. Christ.'

Seb wasn't sure what to say. He couldn't take his eyes off her. If he'd found her attractive before, he was drawn to her like a magnet now. Even though she was having a go at him, it was highly arousing. She was almost quivering with rage, and glaring at him, waiting for him to say whatever he was going to say. She wanted him to justify himself, argue his corner. But he already knew she was right. It was pride that had stopped him.

'So now you know.' He stood up to face her, loving the anger flashing in her eyes but hoping to diffuse it because he didn't want to kiss Angry Jess, especially when she was angry with him.

But he did want to kiss her, of that he was absolutely certain.

He looked down to where her hands were clenched in fists

at her sides, reached out and cupped a fist into his palm, rubbing his thumb gently on the back of her hand. She looked at him, the anger turning to surprise, but she didn't pull away.

'I'm sorry,' she said, her expression softening.

Why he felt so confident about what he was going to do next, Seb had no idea. But he leant towards her and kissed her, half expecting to have his ego dented when she pulled away.

Except she didn't.

He could feel her relaxing, giving herself up to the kiss. Her hands found his, their fingers intertwining as they continued. Jess was leaning into him, and it wasn't long before he had to bring his arms around her to stop them both toppling over. The change in his stance broke the spell, and she pulled back, her eyes still glinting, but this time there was a smile on her face and he knew she was feeling the same way as him.

'Okay?' He needed to be sure that she hadn't got carried away on a tide of pity and sympathy.

'Mmm.' She put her hands on his cheeks and drew his face towards hers for another kiss.

It felt so good to be touched. He couldn't remember the last time someone had been tender towards him. It was a long time since he'd had any kind of relationship with a woman, especially not the kind where anyone's feelings were involved. After Maria had left him, his world and his confidence had shrunk to the point where all he had left was work, and he hadn't moved past that. In any aspect of his life.

He'd never imagined, the first time he'd met Jess in the coffee house, that he'd end up feeling something for the woman who had looked at him with nothing but disdain. It made him smile, and she pulled back.

'What?' She was smiling too.

'I was just thinking that, based on the first time we met, I'd never have thought this would be happening between us,' he murmured.

She laughed softly. 'Me neither. I thought you were a bit of an arse. Sucking up to Matt and Oliver and barely looking at me.'

'You could see right through me.' He remembered trying to avoid her gaze. 'You could see the desperation.'

'There's nothing wrong with knowing what you want and going all out for it,' she said.

He loved that she was willing to spin the whole thing to sound as if he had come into that meeting with ambition and confidence instead of barely concealed despair at it being the last chance to save his livelihood.

'Thank you. Shall we get back to what we were doing?' He took her hand and led her to the sofa. When they started kissing again, he gently pushed her down, so that they were lying side by side. He felt like a teenager, although he was on high alert for any signs that she might not want what he hoped was going to happen next. But her hands were searching for the hem of his shirt and then tugging the bottom of his t-shirt out from the waistband of his jeans. He took a deep breath when her fingers found the skin on his lower back. Her touch was like electricity and he wanted all of her. In a flash of emotion, it suddenly felt essential to his very survival.

She was incredible.

And she wanted him too.

That was more than incredible. It was like they were already at the happy-ever-after in a fairytale.

25

Jess was torn between staying wrapped in Seb's arms for another couple of hours, and going home to freshen up before she had to open the shop. As tempting as it was to stay in his bed, she was keen to avoid the walk of shame in front of Oliver or Jack, and she needed to go home to shower and change since she'd come straight to Seb's on her way back from Dorset.

She turned onto her side. He didn't stir. He looked peaceful, happy even. She gently swiped a lock of hair aside where it had fallen over his eyes before shifting out of his embrace.

'Hey.' His eyes were still half-closed, but he was smiling and had grabbed her arm before she had managed to leave the bed entirely. It was all she needed to be persuaded to stay.

'Hey.' She snuggled back into his chest and felt his arms around her again. This was so hard. How was she ever going to leave? At this rate, she'd be opening the shop looking exactly like she'd spent the whole night having amazing sex.

With Sebastian.

It almost surprised her, even though she was still here in his arms. Where had this come from? She'd definitely softened towards him over the past week or so, and she'd begun to find him more attractive the more she got to know him, but she wasn't sure she'd have predicted this so soon. It couldn't be because of her trip to Dorset. It was one thing to have gained some closure around Jon, but surely the change in her wasn't as instantaneous as leaving one relationship behind on the same day as starting another. Then doubt crept in. What if Seb didn't think this was the start of a relationship? What if this was a one-night stand?

In all the years she'd been single, apart from the very odd night with a man she'd thought she might have some chemistry with, Jess hadn't had sex. Not in a meaningful way. Not like last night. It had almost become something she thought she could live without. She'd been as resigned to the fact that she might never have sex again as she was to believing she would never find love again. Not that this was love.

This time she scooted out of the bed before he could catch her and instead he watched her disappear into the bathroom, greeting her with a lopsided smile when she came back into the bedroom. Until she started putting her clothes on.

He sat up. 'Are you leaving?'

'I need to open the shop in a couple of hours and I have to move my car before the parking restrictions start. And I need to shower and change.'

He rolled out of bed and walked over to her in all his glory. Jess sucked in a breath. She hadn't seen the full nakedness of him last night, and he'd just made it a lot more difficult to leave.

'I'm not ready to let you go.' He scooped her up and carried her back to the bed.

'Sebastian! Seriously,' she said, although she was laughing, so no wonder he wasn't listening to her half-hearted pleading. 'I have to go. We can see each other later.' She escaped his clutches and began dressing again while he sat on the edge of the bed. Naked.

'Really? We can do this all again tonight?'

She nodded because it was all she wanted to do right now, let alone have to wait all those hours until she closed the shop. And now, seeing his forlorn expression, she knew it hadn't been a one-night stand.

'You know there's a meeting tonight,' he groaned, his head in his hands.

'We could skip it.'

'Jess, you might be trying to make out that you're a bad girl, but I know you'd never miss a meeting. And I can't because they're paying me.'

'We haven't paid you yet. Perhaps this is the time to make a stand.'

He sat, watching her finish getting dressed. Then he went over to her, his nakedness a tantalising contrast. She kissed him, then pulled him towards her and they stood for a moment, their heads leaning against each other's.

'After the meeting, then,' she whispered.

'I don't know how I'll get through the day,' he murmured into her ear. 'God, Jess. You're…' He took a deep breath and pulled away. 'Go on,' he smiled. 'Before Oliver gets here.'

Jess skipped down the stairs, unable to believe that she'd just spent the night with Sebastian. She let herself out of the back door to the coffee house and went around the side of the shop where she found Madge, exactly where she'd left her last night, thinking she'd only be a few minutes.

It was still dark and there was no-one around. She looked up at the window of the flat and could see the light was off. Seb must have gone back to bed. If it wasn't for having to open the shop, she'd have stayed. It had crossed her mind to ask Penny to cover the morning, but she couldn't do that when she'd already done her such a big favour by covering her trips to Southampton and Dorset. It was too much to ask, just so that she could stay in Seb's arms for a few more hours. No, she had to get her mind focused on today. She could think about Seb later.

The haberdashery was busy enough to keep her from thinking too much about anything. She had customers waiting on the doorstep at nine o'clock and plenty of web orders to pick and pack. When Patsy came in at ten-thirty with coffee and pastries for them both, it was the first drink Jess'd had since she'd left the house, apart from a few gulps of water between customers.

'Oliver tipped me off,' Patsy said, handing a coffee to Jess with mischief in her eyes.

'Thanks. About what?'

'He saw you driving off this morning. Early.'

Jess's mind whipped from one excuse to the other, all equally implausible, before she realised that there was no actual need to lie. 'I thought I'd left early enough,' she said, feebly.

Patsy's eyes widened. 'You spent the night with Sebastian!'

'Shhh!' Jess led Patsy over to the table away from the customer who was choosing sewing thread at the end of the counter and didn't need to hear the details of her love life.

'I thought you were in Dorset.'

'I got back last night and popped in to see how he was.'

'And how long did that take?'

Jess gave Patsy her best unimpressed face. 'Very funny.' She pulled a pain au chocolat out of the paper bag Patsy had plonked on the table and took a bite.

'Jess! I need details.'

'No, you don't. But something happened.' She couldn't help smiling.

'Oh my god! You like him.'

'Well, obviously.'

'Um, not obvious. I thought you hated him.'

Jess frowned. 'I never hated him. I didn't trust him for a while but that's not the same.'

'And you can trust him now?'

'Yes.' She was certain. 'All of the things I thought he was being cagey about? I understand what was behind all of that now.'

'I'm glad. Ever since you got sucked into the drama with Dan, I've worried that might have put you off dating.'

Oddly enough, Jess hadn't found that experience nearly as traumatic as Patsy. Perhaps it was because all the dates she'd had since she'd moved to Croftwood had been with men she'd kept at arm's length. Looking back, none of those men stood out in her mind. Whether that was because she had never intended the dates to be a way of finding a meaningful relationship, or whether she'd felt no connection with any of them anyway, what she did know was that this thing with Sebastian was different.

'I never thought I'd find someone that would make me feel like Jon did. But with Seb, it's different to how I felt about Jon, anyway. Maybe that's why I didn't see it coming.'

'I suppose every relationship's different, isn't it? Like Dan and Matt are polar opposites. Even when I met Dan, on some level, I knew he was a bad boy and at the time that was exciting, but we know how that ended.'

'And you and Matt didn't fall for each other instantly, did you?' Jess remembered Patsy being exasperated by Matt's fixation on health and safety rules when they'd been working on the cinema's refurbishment.

'Not at all,' she laughed. 'But if I'd never had the relationship with Dan, I might not have known what good would look like. Matt might seem staid and boring in comparison with someone else, but he puts me and his kids first. He's considerate, kind and he loves me and that's what I love about him. I don't want to be with someone who's keeping secrets from me, or using me for their own ends. That's not love.'

'Until I went to Dorset, I thought Jon was still with me. That he'd kind of travelled along with me and we were both still the same people that we'd been then. But something's changed now. I can feel that I'm different and that I've moved on without him. And thank god, I feel okay about that.'

'That's why you feel open to seeing Sebastian.' Patsy said triumphantly.

'I think that's something to do with it,' said Jess, standing up and going over to take the money from her customer for the thread. She thanked her and said goodbye, then went back to sit with Patsy. 'Anyway. I feel rejuvenated and ready to get stuck into the festival now.'

'That's what good sex will do for you.'

'Oh, shut up!' Jess laughed. 'We've got a meeting tonight and I need to have a plan for the book club part of the festival. I might go and see Lois after work.'

'It's their late night, so I'm sure she'll be there. Oliver's worried about her though, thinks she's taken on too much with the British Library thing.'

'He's a fine one to talk about taking on too much. He's the king of spinning any plate he can lay his hands on.'

'I know! I have told him not to be such a hypocrite.'

'Anyway, I could do with running a couple of ideas past her.'

'I already know she's had a blinder of an idea to share with you.'

'Really? What?'

'No, I'm not spoiling the surprise, but she'll be your new favourite person. Guaranteed.'

Jess closed the shop on the stroke of five o'clock and headed along the high street to the library. Organising the book club for the festival was something she'd been looking forward to making a start on and it was only now that Seb was across the bigger picture that she felt certain enough that it was all going to happen, to allow herself to get excited about it.

The heavy wooden doors opened automatically for her as she approached them and the unique library smell enveloped her as she walked inside. Croftwood Library had missed out on being modernised at some point in its past and still operated with the front desk in the middle of the foyer so that you almost had to announce yourself to gain entry. Jess knew Lois had tried to work around this by having the turnstile open all the time, but people were still in the habit of presenting their library card for inspection when they arrived.

Today, Rosemary was behind the desk. Jess smiled and pulled her library card out because she knew Rosemary was finding it difficult to adapt to Lois's updates.

'Thank you Jess,' Rosemary said, peering at the card. 'You know where to find the book club choices.'

'Actually, I'm here to see Lois if she's around?'

'She's in the office, if you want to go through. Is it about…?' Rosemary's eyebrows raised as she left her question hanging, forcing Jess to say what she was here for.

'It's about the festival.' She turned towards the office, hoping that would be the end of the conversation, but of course, this was Rosemary.

'Oh, yes. I haven't seen a call for volunteers yet.'

'We haven't quite got that far,' Jess called over her shoulder.

She knocked on the office door and went in before Lois could say anything, so that she could escape from Rosemary and the risk she'd end up agreeing to something she'd regret.

'Sorry. Rosemary was about to breach my defences.'

'It's fine,' said Lois, laughing. 'Do you fancy a cup of tea?'

'That'd be great, thanks. I know you've got a lot on, but can I run a couple of ideas past you for the festival?'

'Definitely. I think I've had a brainwave,' Lois began as she made two cups of tea at the makeshift kitchen, which sat on top of a cupboard. 'You remember Bill from Steph's mobile library gang?'

'Wasn't he the one who was in that old film they showed at the cinema?'

'Yes! And he got together with another of Steph's customers at the date-with-a-book club.'

'Eunice.'

'Yes!' Lois's enthusiasm was growing by the second. 'Well, he has just finished writing his autobiography with the help of a ghostwriter. The book will be out in time for the festival, so I wondered about seeing if he could do a talk for you.'

'That'd be amazing. We could have that book as the non-fiction choice for the festival book club.'

'That's what I thought. If you're interested, he can put you in touch with his publisher. He thinks they might do a deal with us to sell signed copies over the festival weekend, something like that.' Lois put the tea down on her desk and pushed one over to Jess before she sat down.

'Thanks, Lois. Having talks is a great idea. It means we're offering something other than just a huge book club.'

'Have you got anyone else in mind?'

'I was wondering about approaching a local author for exactly the same reason. I thought they might be willing to come and sign books, but now I'll see if they'd be up for doing a talk as well. It'd be like a mini Hay Festival if we do that.'

'But more accessible for your average reader, which is what the date-with-a-book club was all about in the first place.'

They discussed some other ideas for the children's book club choice and Jess mooted her idea about one for teenagers, which Lois thought was brilliant, promising to come up with some book suggestions.

Jess downed her tea, realising that it was almost time for the festival committee meeting back at Oliver's, or more accurately, Seb's.

'I must go. We've got a committee meeting.'

'I know. Oliver's coming to pick me up afterwards so I can get a lift home with him. Let me walk you out so Rosemary doesn't have chance to pounce on you.'

It was all coming together, Jess thought as she walked back up the high street. She'd been so preoccupied all day with being busy at work and then thinking about the book club that she'd hardly had the chance to look forward to seeing Seb again. Her stomach did a flip as thoughts of the night before came to mind. Hopefully, there would be more of that to come later on.

26

Because she was late, there was no chance to talk to Seb before the meeting. Rob, Jen and Hilary had already arrived and the three of them, with Oliver, had taken over the sofas. Jess pulled up a dining chair. Seb was standing, ready to start talking, but before he did, they exchanged a brief longing look, silently wishing for the end of the meeting so that they could fall onto each other again. Or at least that was how it felt.

Seb gave everyone an update on what had been finalised in the Event Management Plan and submitted to the council. He showed them a very detailed Gantt chart which he explained was a project management tool that listed every single thing that needed sorting out from big things like booking tents to smaller things like checking the weather forecast, and where all of those things fitted into the timeline.

'As you can see, we are up against it time wise. Some of these things we shouldn't strictly be doing until we've got the sign off from the Licensing Officer, but if we wait, we'll literally run out of time,' he explained.

'What's the risk, financially?' Oliver asked. 'Are we potentially paying deposits that could be lost if we don't get the go ahead?'

'Honestly, yes. It's about ten thousand at the moment.' There was a collective gasp. 'But I've spoken to Toby, and he's sorted out some insurance to cover as much of that as we can. The excess is around a grand. We've had some grant money come through which will cover those deposits until we get the tickets sales going.'

'When can we start selling tickets?' Rob asked. 'I'm happy to sell them in the shop.' Everyone else agreed they could do the same.

'The website is up and running. It's just a matter of deciding on a price. Patsy can update that, and we can start selling tomorrow if we want to,' said Oliver.

'I've done a budget based on everything we know so far,' Seb said, pulling up another spreadsheet on his laptop. 'I've worked out that we can sell a couple of hundred tickets at an early bird price which would cover the deposits.'

'And would mean you could invoice us for your first payment,' said Jess, keen that everyone remember Seb hadn't been paid anything yet.

'Yes, that too.' He smiled at her across the heads of the others, who were busy looking at the figures on the screen. Then he winked as well and that just about finished her off. How she stopped herself from leaning over and kissing him, she didn't know. The fact that no-one else in the room knew what they were hiding made the thought of being with him all the more tantalising. Thinking about what they'd done on that very sofa the night before...

God, no.

She dragged her thoughts back to the festival. It wasn't right to be thinking about that when she was here with the others.

'I think we ought to go for it. Test the water, if nothing else,' said Hilary.

Jess briefly wondered what she was talking about, then

remembered they'd been discussing ticket sales before Seb had winked at her and almost sent her over the edge.

They settled on an early bird price and agreed to ask Patsy to put the site live.

'We'll have to do some serious promotion. Those tickets won't sell themselves,' said Rob.

'Patsy's also designed some posters that are ready to go. We can post them online and get some printed too. She's done it so that we can have the basics on there and as we add more and more to the programme, we can update them.'

'That sounds great,' said Jess. 'I've got a lead on a brilliant speaker for the book club. Bill, well, William Templeton, has written an autobiography. Lois has spoken to him, and he's keen to do something for us.'

'How amazing,' said Hilary. 'I'm not sure what kind of books you do at the book club, but I know a local author. She comes in the shop sometimes, she's quite well known, Alexis Diamond.'

'No way!' Jess couldn't help herself. 'She lives around here? I love her books!'

Hilary laughed. 'She's a very unassuming woman. I don't think her real name is Alexis Diamond. Would you like me to ask her if she'd be willing to be involved?'

'Oh my god, yes please! If she says yes, we've got two out of three of our book club books sorted already.'

'What else do you need?' Seb asked.

'Ideally a crime or thriller book. Alexis is a romance novelist,' Jess explained. 'We usually have a romance, a thriller and a non-fiction choice. If we're staying true to the date-with-a-book club concept, that's what we need to go with.'

'My cousin's ex-wife is an author. I could see if she'd be interested,' said Seb.

Jess didn't want to have to say no in front of everyone, but now that they'd potentially got William Templeton and Alexis Diamond, they needed someone of equal stature for the thriller or crime book. It was the most popular choice in the club most months.

'That'd be great, thanks,' she said, resolving to grill him in more detail later.

'Who's your cousin's wife?' Jen asked.

'Her name's Fliss Thorne. At least I think that's what she writes under. They're divorced now, so I guess it's possible she'd changed her name.'

'FL Thorne is your cousin?' Jess said, not able to get her head around how they were organising a book-related festival and only now, Seb was revealing that he knew *the* current chart-topping crime writer of the moment.

'No, she's my cousin's ex-wife,' he said patiently, seemingly unaware that he'd just helped complete the trifecta of book club line-ups. 'I haven't spoken to her since they got divorced, but we always got on so I don't see any reason why I can't ask her.'

'I read in some music magazine that she's dating an Icelandic musician. Something to do with Ned Nokes from that boy band,' Rob said, surprising everyone with having some celebrity gossip at his fingertips.

'Ned Nokes is going out with a woman who he sang to in a snowstorm in London. I remember seeing it in Hey! Magazine,' said Jess.

'Right. Ned Nokes aside, shall we see what's next on the to-do list?' Oliver put an end to the celebrity chit-chat and suggested they assign tasks from Seb's Gantt chart to themselves. It was pretty easy since they'd informally adopted their roles already, but it made clear where there were things not being covered by anybody, which was the whole point of the exercise.

'I'll speak to Mo about the book stall,' Jess said. 'I meant to do it before, but at least now we know what we're aiming for, she can tell us whether she's interested in being involved.'

'I did pop in and see her on my rounds, keeping all the traders up to date,' said Hilary. 'She didn't seem interested to be honest, even when I offered her a stall for free if she was willing to sell the book club books on there.'

'I wonder whether the library could run the book stall as a fundraiser,' said Oliver. 'It might be a good way to link the library with the festival. I'm sure Linda and Rosemary would love to set that up.'

Jess grinned. 'Rosemary was only saying to me today that she's keen to volunteer. That might be just the thing to keep her busy.'

'Brilliant,' said Oliver, giving Jess a knowing look. They all loved Rosemary on some level, but on all the other levels she could be quite wearing if there was something she wanted. 'You'll be doing Lois a favour if you suggest that. Rosemary's been on at her about helping with the British Library social media campaign. She sees herself as the face of the date-with-a-book club.'

'That's so funny,' Jess said. 'I thought she'd tried to distance herself from the fact it even has "date" in the name.'

'Yep. That woman is full of contradictions.'

They agreed to call a full traders' meeting for the following week. Sebastian was going to try to meet Helena to go through the EMP and perhaps pre-empt any questions she might have before it went in front of the Safety Advisory Group. They all felt it would be good to find out how the application had been received.

'I'd better make a move,' said Oliver. 'I need to pick Lois up shortly. Anything else you need from us in the next couple of days, Sebastian?'

'No, thank you all. I'll let you know how I get on with the council,' Seb said. 'Jess, if you stay behind for a sec, I can give you Fliss's email address.'

Rob and Hilary left at the same time as Oliver and Jen, and were too busy discussing the merits of the various local bands that Rob was hoping to approach to notice that Jess and Sebastian were ready to pounce on each other as soon as they were out of earshot.

'I thought that meeting was never going to end,' he said, closing the door behind them and dropping the latch. He stood there for a moment, with his back to the door and mischief in his eyes.

'So, I'd better get that email address.' Jess bit her lip and smiled.

'Do you have somewhere to be?'

'I have a lot of admin to get to.'

He began slowly walking towards her and she almost stopped breathing as his gaze told her exactly what he wanted to do next. When he reached her, he leant in and gently kissed her. That was all it took to unleash a much less restrained kiss from her. She ran her fingers around the waistband of his jeans, easing them underneath his shirt until she was touching his bare skin. She felt him gasp against her cheek when her hand tucked inside again to undo his button fly.

'God, Jess,' he murmured. 'They're probably not even out of the building yet.'

'Are you worried about getting caught?' she whispered in a taunting tone that came from who knew where. It was as if she was a different person when she and Seb were like this. Someone very sexual, the kind of person who thought nothing of being walked in on when they were having sex and might even make eye contact with the person who was watching while they carried on.

With his jeans around his knees and his shirt half off, Seb evened things up by helping Jess pull off her cardigan before he unzipped her dress as slowly as possible, making her groan in anticipation of his touch. All she wanted was to feel his hands moving across her skin, exploring every last part of her, and waiting for that to happen was excruciating.

'Seb, please...' she breathed, grabbing his behind with both hands to ease some of her rapidly building sexual frustration.

'Be patient.' He ran a single finger down her back, his touch featherlight. She tried to concentrate on that, to drink it in, thinking of what it was going to lead to, wishing she was less needy and more able to savour every second of this, instead of wishing it away.

It was too much for her. She pulled away and pushed him backwards onto the sofa. His eyes widened in surprise. 'You're taking charge,' he said in a tone that told her he was impressed.

'You're a tease.'

She pulled off her boots, her favourite black brogue boots that looked fabulous with a dress, and put them neatly by the door, bending over just enough that she was sure Seb could glimpse what was there waiting for him underneath her skirt. He groaned, as well he might. She'd worn stay-up stockings instead of tights in anticipation of this very moment. And now that Seb had seen, she was in control, tantalising him, and she loved it.

He was lying in the corner of the sofa, his arms out, beckoning her to lie down on top of him.

'No touching,' she said, trying to adopt a serious tone. She rested her foot on the edge of the sofa next to him, batting his hand away when he went to touch her leg. 'What did I say?'

'Sorry,' he said, sheepishly, with a lopsided grin.

Jess ran her own hands up her leg, with the kind of touch she was sure would have Sebastian wishing with all his heart that his hands were there instead. As she lifted her skirt, revealing the lace tops of her stockings, he closed his eyes and groaned.

'I'm going to explode if I can't touch you. How are you doing this to me?'

Jess loved that she was doing this to him. She'd never done anything like this in her whole life, so there were no comparisons going on in her mind. This was new, fresh, and absolutely amazing.

27

Jess spent the next two nights with Seb at the flat, getting hardly any sleep. By Saturday she was so tired she could barely get through a single sentence without yawning and realised that she needed a break.

'It's not that I don't want to spend the night with you, but there's no point until I've actually had some sleep,' she said, when he called in to the shop on Saturday afternoon just as she was cashing up. 'I can't keep my eyes open. And I'm behind on my shop admin. I need a day at home.'

He looked at her with a puppy-dog expression, then he sighed and grinned. 'Okay. That's fair. If you're comatose in the bed next to me, I can't vouch for how long I'd be able to let you sleep.'

'Okay. But Penny is working on Tuesday, so Monday night I'm all yours.'

'Shall I come round to yours?'

Jess had never had a man back to her house, and it took her a moment to get her head around what that might mean. She realised quite quickly that it didn't particularly mean anything, except that she'd never had a relationship where she'd wanted to invite anyone round until now. At least she had some notice. She'd have to do a bit of cleaning, change the sheets and what have you. 'Yes, great.'

'Sure?'

She loved that he already knew her well enough to have noticed the moment of doubt flash across her face. 'Definitely.' She went around the other side of the counter to where he was lolling in one of the chairs she kept there for people who had to wait for an enthusiastic knitting or sewing friend to make a decision. She straddled his legs, and he sat up straighter and drew her up onto his lap so that they were facing each other.

'What am I going to do with myself for two days?' he said with a sigh.

'Pine for me? Come on, you must have something you've been putting on hold while we've been…getting to know each other?'

'Mmm. I guess so.'

'Remember what we did last night?' she said, stifling a yawn. 'That's what you can look forward to on Monday night. But it'll be even better because I won't be half asleep.'

His eyes twinkled, and he grinned. 'I can wait forever if I know that's going to happen again.'

Once Jess got home, lit the fire and made some poached eggs on toast for her dinner, she felt relaxed rather than exhausted. She was looking forward to a day of sewing on Sunday, needing to finish something new to put in the window on Monday. It was hard to believe it was only a week since she'd been to Dorset. Because of everything that had happened with Seb, it felt like a lifetime ago.

The scrapbook was on the side. Jess picked it up and opened it, looking at the picture of her and Jon, briefly touching it before she put it back in the cupboard. It felt okay to do that.

It didn't take long for tiredness to take hold again, but before it did, she emailed Lois's colleague Steph. They'd met a couple of times at book club meetings. Steph ran the mobile library and sometimes brought some of her regular customers along to book club meetings so that they could join in and feel part of the library community. Steph was the person who could put her in contact with Bill. Jess thought that would be better than going straight to his publisher. She'd like to ask him first what his thoughts were about doing a talk and maybe a book signing. Hopefully, they might come to an arrangement with his publisher to take some of his books on a sale or return basis, and if Bill was willing to put in a good word, so much the better.

She was just about to close the lid on her laptop and finally go to bed for some much-needed sleep when she saw Steph had replied, inviting her out on the mobile library on Tuesday when she'd be paying a visit to Hawthorn Lane, the stop Bill lived near with his partner Eunice. Steph said they never missed a visit, so even though she couldn't guarantee it, she was as confident as she could be that it wouldn't be a wasted journey. She offered to pick Jess up from Croftwood Library at eight-thirty on Tuesday morning if she was up for it.

Of course she was, even though it meant that she'd have to curtail her lie in with Seb, and if this week was anything to go by, she almost certainly would not have had enough sleep. Still, she knew from Lois's stories that it would be fun to tag along and hopefully it would be a chance to get on top of some festival book club arrangements at the same time.

Seb hadn't actually given Jess Fliss Thorne's email address in the end; they'd had other priorities over the past few days. But since he hadn't spoken to Fliss since she split up with his cousin, Duncan, he thought he ought to get in touch before he encouraged Jess to, just in case the whole family had been tarnished by Duncan's misdemeanours.

'Fliss? Hi, it's Sebastian Thorne, Duncan's cousin.'

'Seb, this is a surprise!' Her voice was warm, which was a relief. They'd only met a handful of times at various family get-togethers but had got on well.

'How are you? I hear your books are all anyone's talking about in Iceland.'

'Oh, god, I know. How mad is that?' she laughed. 'Luckily, that was a wake-up call for my publisher to get behind them, so I'm a full-time author now.'

'Wow, that's brilliant news.' At least Duncan hadn't ruined her life. 'And the kids are okay?'

'Yes, Josh is at uni and Emma's not far behind.' She paused. 'So what can I do for you, Seb?'

'I hope you don't mind me running this past you. Please tell me to bugger off if you're not interested, I won't be offended.' Although it would break his heart to tell Jess that she'd said no. She'd been so excited. 'I'm helping to organise a book festival in August. The organisers need three books that people read before the festival and then on the festival weekend, they meet up with others who have read the books and, you know, talk about them.' He wished he'd listened harder when Jess had explained how the date-with-a-book club worked. He was sure there was more to it than what he'd just explained. 'And we were hoping to choose one of your books and wondered whether you'd like to come to the festival and give a talk or something?'

'That sounds like something they've started at my local library. They're doing something to do with dating a book, but there are three choices just like you said.'

'I think that's the same thing,' Seb said. 'It started at Croftwood Library and it's been rolled out to other libraries. That's partly how we're hoping to get some interest in the festival.'

'What are the odds?' Fliss said, laughing. 'I'd love to get

involved in that. What do I need to do?'

'I'll get my friend Jess to email you with the details. She's organising that side of things, but I wanted you to know what was going on before I suggested you, just in case.'

'Brilliant, tell her I'm definitely interested. And how are things? It's good to hear you've got some work again after the pandemic. I wasn't sure whether things had picked up for you. It must have been so difficult.'

Fliss was guessing based on the industry he worked in, because even his closest family didn't know the extent of the problems he was having. 'It was tough but this project has got things back on track. I'm living in Croftwood now.'

'Do you know, I have no idea where Croftwood is.'

'It's near Worcester. A small town at the foot of the Malvern Hills.'

'Oh, I do know. I remember going through there on the train to visit Josh in Bristol.'

'Yep, that's it.'

'I bet it's lovely.'

'It has quite a lot going for it,' Seb said, thinking of Jess. 'Look, I hope we can catch up if this all works out and you can come to the festival.'

'I'd love that. I might need to bring Emma with me, depending on what's going on.'

'No problem, she might enjoy it.'

'She might!' Fliss laughed again in a way that suggested Emma wouldn't want to come to Croftwood Festival if it was the last place on earth.

Seb said goodbye and ended the call feeling pleased with himself. It would be lovely to see Jess tomorrow night and be able to tell her he'd as good as booked FL Thorne.

He didn't have long to revel in the feeling of accomplishment. A text came through from the landlord of his industrial unit to say that they were evicting him. It wasn't exactly a surprise. They'd been more than patient and he'd had a hunch for a while that beginning to sell the festival tickets was going to come too late for him to invoice anything in time to pay his rent. He texted back to ask when he needed to have everything out. He had a week.

Just as he'd got back on track, this had thrown a bit of a spanner in the works. Yes, it had been inevitable, but he'd given no thought to finding a home for everything that was in the unit. And it was literally everything he owned. One thing he knew was that he had to act quickly. If he wasn't out within the timeframe, the landlord was well within his right to seize anything left in the unit. Seb counted himself lucky that they hadn't resorted to calling the bailiffs in, purely because they knew he was struggling and didn't want to strip him of the things he needed to start his business again. He owned a lot of kit that they'd need for the festival so he had to make sure that that at least was out otherwise it would increase the costs by having to rent things like generators, stakes and rope for marking out boundaries, smaller tents that could be used for things like the ticket office, security lights, and all kinds of other paraphernalia that was useful. As for his own possessions, most of which were still in the boxes he'd packed when he moved out of his house, he hoped Oliver wouldn't mind if he stacked them in the corner of the lounge at the flat.

'It's just temporary,' he explained when he popped down to the coffee house on Monday morning to check. 'I need to be out of my unit this week.' He hoped Oliver wouldn't ask too many questions because although he didn't mind people knowing that he'd been homeless and was now at risk of losing all of his assets as well, it put him in the awkward position of Oliver knowing that he'd misrepresented his situation in the beginning. He regretted that now, knowing that he could probably have got the contract anyway by being honest. Not everyone was as judgmental as he'd assumed. But his only motivation had been desperate survival, and that had clouded his judgment.

'It's no problem at all. It's your flat to do with what you want while you're staying there,' Oliver said. 'What about the other stuff?'

Seb didn't know the answer yet, so didn't answer.

Oliver assumed he hadn't thought about it, so embellished. 'I guess if you have a unit it's probably full of stuff you need to find a home for? Things that won't fit in the corner of the flat.'

'Yep, that's next on my to-do list. I have a couple of options.' Oliver had already been more generous than he needed to be, and Seb wasn't about to ask him for a solution to this part of the problem as well. Although he had no idea what he was going to do, he needed to figure it out on his own.

'Well, if there's anything I can do.'

'Thanks. I appreciate it.'

Ahead of the next traders' meeting that week, one of Seb's jobs was to meet with Lord Harrington so that he could sign the agreement for the use of his land for the campsite. Toby had insisted on drawing up a simple contract. The sum of money involved was tiny because Archie wanted to show his support for the town, but Toby was still insistent that they needed to have the proper documentation to protect everybody involved.

Seb pulled up outside the estate office and climbed out of his truck to be greeted by Tatty, the dog. He gave her some fuss and then followed her to the office, the door ajar as it had been the last time he visited. He rapped on it and called out hello before he went inside finding Archie in the middle of a phone call.

'Sorry,' he mouthed before beginning to back out of the

office until Archie shook his head and waved him in.

He sat in the chair near the fire, boldly throwing a fresh log on from the considerable pile stacked next to it.

Archie finished his call, which sounded like it was something to do with cows, and turned to give Seb his full attention.

'Sorry to drop in unannounced,' Seb said apologetically. 'I've got some paperwork for you to sign about the campsite for the festival.'

'Ah, yes, wonderful,' said Archie. 'Got time for a cup of tea? You can get me up to speed on your plans.'

'That'd be great, thanks. You sound like you're busy?'

'Middle of calving,' said Archie over the sound of the kettle coming back to the boil. 'Bloody nightmare for a few weeks, lots of admin.' He gestured to the desk, which seemed just as chaotic as the last time Seb had visited, when presumably it wasn't calving time.

Seb waited for the kettle to click off before he resumed the conversation. 'We've made a lot of progress on the festival. We've submitted our plan to the council, so we're waiting to hear their thoughts on that.'

'Any problems on that front, let me know,' said Archie, pointing a teaspoon at Seb. 'I have a bit of sway there if you need it.'

It seemed highly unlikely that Helena would succumb to pressure from the local gentry, but Seb thanked him and said he'd bear it in mind.

'My mother is very keen on this book club idea. Said she's seen it on Instagram.'

Seb stopped himself from laughing at the thought of the Dowager Countess scrolling through social media. 'Actually, we're hoping to have William Templeton as one of the guest speakers.' Seb thought it was a good bet that Archie would know who Bill was, and he was right.

'Good lord, Mother's going to be thrilled to hear that. I expect she'll rope me into taking her to see him.'

'We'd love to have her. We can organise some VIP treatment.'

'Wonderful, that's very kind. Right, what do you need me to scrawl on today?'

Seb presented the simple document that Toby had prepared and sat quietly while Archie read it thoroughly.

'Best to check the small print,' he said, grinning.

'Absolutely,' said Seb. He gazed out of the window, taking in the other couple of dilapidated stable buildings that fronted onto the gravelled courtyard. 'What do you use the other buildings for?'

'Unfortunately, the roofs leak like a sieve so we have to keep them empty. The hope is at some point that we'll have the funds to repair them, but there are always other priorities with the big house to maintain.'

Seb nodded and noted the fact Archie wasn't making much out of the Croftwood Festival, when perhaps he couldn't afford to be quite so philanthropic.

'I don't suppose you'd be open to me using them?'

Archie's eyebrows raised, his interest piqued. 'You can see the state they're in. If you think you can use them, I'm all ears.'

28

By the time Jess heard Seb pull up outside in his truck, she had a pot of bolognaise sauce simmering on the hob smelling delicious, if she said so herself, and had eased her nerves by having a small glass of wine when she'd opened it to add some to the sauce. The fire was lit, and she'd tidied the lounge so that there was somewhere for him to sit; she had a tendency to leave things lying around on any surface, including chairs, since she always sat in her favourite one.

'Hey, come in,' she said when she opened the front door. Straight away, she noticed that he hadn't got anything with him other than a bottle of wine and she loved that despite them both knowing he would end up staying, he had been careful not to assume that by appearing with an overnight bag.

'Something smells amazing,' he said, kissing her chastely on the cheek before handing her the wine and shrugging off his coat.

'Thanks. It's almost the only thing I can cook successfully that feeds more than one person. Spag bol,' she added, leading the way through the lounge into the kitchen.

She'd laid the small kitchen table with cutlery, napkins, wine glasses and a candle. It looked welcoming and cosy.

'Shall I?' Seb asked, picking up the wine that was already open on the table.

'Yes. It's almost ready. Just the pasta to cook.'

'How did it go today? Did you get the window changed?'

Jess told him all about it, loving that he was interested, while she pottered around with dishing the dinner up and by the time she laid the steaming bowls of pasta on the table, any awkwardness that she might have felt at Seb being in her house had melted away, and she felt as if this was something they did all the time.

'This is delicious,' he said, rolling his eyes to emphasise his point.

'Thanks.' It was nice to see him enjoying what she'd cooked. She so rarely cooked for anyone, she'd forgotten how satisfying it was.

'I meant to say, I rang Fliss to make sure she was still speaking to me after my cousin did the dirty on her.'

'And was she?'

'Yes, and she was interested in the festival. I'm not sure I explained it very well, but she's come across the date-with-a-book club at her local library and she sounds like a fan.'

'Oh, brilliant, thank you.'

'You're welcome.' He paused before scooping up the next forkful and looked at Jess for a moment. 'I've been given notice on my industrial unit.'

'Oh, no. Why?' As soon as she asked, she knew what the answer was.

'I'm behind on the rent.'

'I think you should put an invoice in. We've started selling the tickets.'

He shook his head. 'It's too late for that now. But it's okay. Archie Harrington is letting me use one of his stable blocks for now, to store some stuff until I get something else sorted.'

'I feel terrible that you're in this position because we

haven't paid you.'

'That's not why, Jess.' He reached across the table and took her hand in his. 'All of this was happening way before I started working on the festival. It was always going to end like this. At least thanks to Oliver, I only needed to find a place to put some of my kit. I'm not completely homeless and I can't tell you how grateful I am for that.'

'You were living there? Over the winter?' She'd guessed he must have been doing something like that, but to realise that actually was the case was sobering. It was shocking that someone could end up with nothing, seemingly so easily.

'Only since January. I had to be out of my house the first week of January.'

Jess wanted to ask why he hadn't stayed with friends or family. But she also knew that if either of those things had been an option, he would have taken them rather than end up in an industrial unit in the middle of winter with virtual hypothermia.

'That's awful.'

'It's an opportunity for a fresh start. That's how I'm trying to see it. I don't have any ties now.'

Jess's heart constricted slightly when he said that. Their relationship was far too new to be considering each other in any decisions, but she'd hoped they were heading down a path that might lead to that.

'No, well, it's important to make the most of that. It's great that you're so positive about how it's all turned out.'

'I don't think I would have been, except for you.' He dropped his eyes to the table.

Jess's heart constricted again for entirely different reasons. 'I haven't done anything,' she said softly. 'Don't forget, I thought you were an arse when we first met.'

He grinned and laughed. 'Okay, keep reminding me what a cocky bugger I was. Thanks!'

'You've pulled it back recently,' she said, taking in the smile in his eyes.

'You've been giving me that impression.'

He pulled on her hand, and she slipped out of her seat and onto his lap.

'And the thing is, if all of this crap hadn't happened, I wouldn't have met you.' He cupped his hands around Jess's cheeks and drew her gently towards him, pausing briefly before he kissed her to look at her intently. 'Could we move this to the sofa?'

'Or the bedroom?' What was the point of pretending?

'I didn't want to —'

'I know.' She shushed him with another kiss before she led him upstairs, while he followed with the rest of the bottle of wine and their glasses.

'This place is cool,' he said, making Jess wish she'd given him the grand tour before they got to this point, because her instinct was to answer him with all the things that made it not as cool as it seemed. Instead, she said nothing and distracted him by removing the wine and glasses from his hands before pushing him backwards onto the bed and beginning to undress very slowly in front of him while he watched and groaned. Jess didn't think she'd ever love anything more than watching the effect she had on this man. It was empowering, amazing and absolutely addictive and she hoped with all of her heart that she might be able to forge a tie to him so that she wouldn't be left behind when he picked up the pieces of his life and started again.

The following morning, Seb gave Jess a lift into Croftwood so she could leave Madge at home. They both knew that they'd be spending the night together one way or another, so it made sense. They were both a little sex-drunk, and Jess loved that look on Seb. She'd done that to him.

He parked the truck at the back of the coffee house and they spent a few minutes kissing like teenagers as they said goodbye to each other before Jess had to leave, for fear of getting left behind by Steph.

The mobile library van was already parked in front of the library on the small area of hardstanding between the building's entrance and the gardens that ran up to the road. Since the library had won the national Library of the Year award, some money had been spent on the neglected grounds and these days it looked smart, with new planting and some benches dotted here and there for people to sit and read or have a quiet coffee.

The side door of the van was open and Steph was inside, pulling books off the shelves and loading them into a box.

'Morning!' Jess said, brightly. 'Do you need a hand?'

'Hi, Jess. Perfect timing,' said Steph brightly. 'I need to switch out these for another box which Lois has put together for me. Last-minute snafu with loading up yesterday.'

'I'll go in and fetch the box, shall I?'

'Great, thanks.'

Jess went into the library. It was strange going inside when it wasn't open. Only the lights in the centre of the building were on, and the dark corners seemed eerie. The silence was deafening.

'Lois?' Jess headed towards the office and as she approached the door, Lois flung it open, making her jump.

'Oh my god!'

'Sorry,' Lois said, laughing. 'I didn't mean to scare you. Have you seen Steph?'

'Yes, she's after a box of books?'

'It's over here.' Lois went behind the desk and hauled the box up onto the counter. 'Can we carry it out between us?'

They took two corners of the box each and shuffled out to

the mobile library.

'How close are you?' Lois asked Steph. 'You know you need to be gone before we open.'

I'm meant to be halfway to Hawthorn Lane by the time you open,' Steph grumbled. 'Come on, let's be having you.'

Jess and Lois heaved the box onto the floor of the van.

'Can you start unpacking?' Steph said. 'It should be obvious where to shelve them.'

Steph and Lois took the box of rejected books inside, and Jess sat cross-legged on the floor and flipped through the titles in the box. She picked out all the children's books which were destined for the shelves at the very back of the van where there was a colourful mat for kids to sit on while they chose. After that, it was harder. Was the whole van alphabetical or was it divided by genre as well? Luckily, that was a question Jess didn't need an immediate answer to because Steph came back, closed the side door, and announced that they were off.

'This festival book-club sounds brilliant,' said Steph, while she expertly did a three-point turn in front of the library in a space Jess would have been hard pressed to turn a car.

'I hope so. I want it to feel like an extension of the date-with-a-book club, but I'm not sure we'll pull it off.'

'You will,' Steph said with confidence. 'It's not that different to the set up we had for involving the mobile library customers. You need to publicise the books you're going to have for the festival so people have chance to read them beforehand. If I was going, I'd read all of them to get the best out of the weekend. I bet other people will do that too.'

'That's a good point. I suppose I assumed people would just pick one, but the way we're setting it up, hopefully with the author talks and book signings, you could read all three books and get to go to a book club date about each one.'

'Exactly! You ought to encourage people to borrow the

books from their local library, in the spirit of the original book club, then you're more likely to make sales over the weekend if you're doing book signings.'

'What happens to the mobile library at the weekends?'

'It's parked up at the Hive.' The Hive was in Worcester, the main county library that was also the library for Worcester University. 'Why? What are you thinking?'

'I'm thinking it might be cool to have the mobile library at the event as the festival bookshop. Could we empty it and do that, or is it too much work?'

Steph mulled it over for a minute. 'It's an enormous job to empty it completely. We only do it once a year normally, between Christmas and New Year and I do it by myself over a few days. If we had a little army of volunteers, it would be doable.' She had a glint in her eye. Jess could tell she was up for it.

'Would you be willing to ask whoever you need to? See if it's a goer?'

'Definitely. If it's to do with the date-with-a-book club, you can pretty much guarantee that County Libraries will say yes. Actually, I might get Lois to ask.'

'Great, thanks.' It all seemed to be coming together. Now she just had to hope that William Templeton would be at the Hawthorn Lane stop.

'I think we're going to be about five minutes late,' Steph said. 'At least it's not raining.'

'Will they wait if we're not there?'

'Eunice is always first and I'm hardly ever late, but she'll definitely wait. Dottie usually comes a bit later with her son. He's a handful, and she's got another on the way.'

'So you have proper regulars?'

'Yes, there are a few in every place I go, apart from the Red Lion. Since Bill moved in with Eunice, I've lost him from that stop and for some reason, it's completely random who turns up. I don't really know any of them. I know I shouldn't have favourites, but this is my favourite stop. I wish I could come more often than every few weeks. Right, here we are,' she said, pulling to a stop in a lay-by where an elderly couple were standing at the side of the road. 'And there are Bill and Eunice.'

Steph opened the side door of the van, dropped the steps down, and put the handrails in place. 'Come on in, you two. We've got a visitor to share our tea and biscuits with today.'

They climbed inside and Jess introduced herself and explained about the book club festival while Steph pulled some flasks and a tin of biscuits out of a cupboard.

'A book festival sounds marvellous,' said Eunice, taking a seat on a stool and choosing a biscuit while Bill folded their coats and laid them on the passenger seat out of the way. 'Bill's written a book.'

'I had some help, my love,' he said, smiling at Eunice.

'Actually, Bill, I was wondering whether you'd be willing to come to the festival and talk about your book? We'd like to promote it as the non-fiction choice for the book club festival and I wondered whether you'd be interested in doing a book signing and perhaps an interview? It's all happening at Croftwood Cinema.'

'It would be my pleasure,' Bill said graciously, taking a seat next to Eunice. 'I'll ask my agent to put in a word with the publishers, see if we can do something about discounting some copies for the book signing. It's a completely new world to me. I don't know how these things work.'

Bill was utterly charming and Jess could immediately see that he'd still got the film star charisma that had made him a household name in the fifties.

'Thank you so much. It's especially brilliant because you've been involved in the book club from the beginning.'

'Do you know who the other authors are yet?' Steph asked,

pouring tea from the flask into four takeaway cups.

'We're hoping for FL Thorne. She writes crime books.'

'Set in Iceland,' said Steph. 'Tom loves those books.'

'And Alexis Diamond, the romance author.'

'Oh my goodness, her books are racier than Jilly Cooper,' said Eunice. 'What a wonderful selection. And you're hoping to arrange talks with both of them?'

'Fingers crossed,' said Jess, helping herself to a custard cream and wondering if it would be bad form to dip it in her tea.

'Well, count us in,' said Eunice, 'although we won't be camping.'

'That's half the fun,' Steph said.

'Not at our age,' Bill grinned.

'No Dottie today?' Steph asked Eunice when it was almost time for them to go.

'Oh, I forgot to say, she messaged to say that she had a midwife appointment. She thinks the baby is going to be early.'

'I hope everything's okay,' said Steph.

'Nothing to worry about at all, she said. I expect she's been doing too much. It's difficult for her dealing with Bert on her own when Alex is away during the week.'

Jess tidied away the tea things while Steph checked out the books that Bill and Eunice had chosen, then they waved them off and set off for the next stop.

'I can't believe he said yes,' Jess said, thrilled that she could tell Patsy to add Bill to the official line-up on the website.

'I knew he would. Those two love getting involved in things like that.'

'And he's so charming. He'll be perfect for someone to interview.'

'Yep, a proper old-school film star.'

By the time Steph dropped Jess back in Croftwood, it was

late afternoon.

'Thanks, Steph. I've had a great time,' Jess said, as she climbed out of the van.

'Anytime! And I'll be in touch about using the van for the festival.'

Jess strolled up the high street to Oliver's, looking forward to seeing Seb. She walked past the haberdashery and noticed that Penny had made a new sign advertising the next raft of workshops. It had been on Jess's to-do list for a couple of weeks, but time had got away from her. She loved that Penny felt she could get on and do these things without needing to ask permission. She resolved to see if Penny would like to do the mini-haberdashery at the cinema the following week for Purl at the Pictures. Jess felt as if she'd hardly spent any time at the shop lately and she may as well pay Penny to do that, she'd love sitting and knitting when the film was on. With the festival and Seb and having her shop, life was suddenly feeling very full. In all the best ways.

29

Seb had organised a meeting with Helena from the council for Wednesday morning, the day of the traders' meeting. He'd already found out that the Safety Advisory Group wasn't due to meet again until the end of June, and that made him uncomfortable. By then, it might be too late to change something that transpired to be a fundamental problem, so he hoped that the meeting today would be a chance to get ahead of that.

'Frankly, the timescale you're working to is borderline irresponsible if you want to run a successful event,' Helena began almost as soon as they'd greeted each other. 'And sending the EMP in late hasn't helped.'

'Look, I want to apologise for that. It was unprofessional and my only defence is that I'm out of practice in dealing with that side of things.' He wasn't about to tell Helena all about the personal difficulties he'd been having. He knew it wasn't worth trying to defend himself. It was much better to get her on side by being contrite.

'I was under the impression that you were the person contracted specifically to deal with those things.'

Seb bit his tongue. She was absolutely right, but at the same time she was grinding his gears and it took everything he had to say, 'You're right, I'd dropped the ball but please, rest assured that it's all under control now.'

Her face softened slightly. She flipped open the folder on her desk, which he saw contained a printout of their EMP with various notes scrawled over it. The writing was loopy and not easy to read upside down.

'I'm happy to share my initial thoughts with you. I usually have a pretty good idea of how it'll go with the SAG meeting at this point. I'm hardly ever wrong.'

Seb didn't doubt it for a minute and also felt lucky that he'd grovelled just enough to make her rethink her first impressions of him.

'Thank you, Helena. I'd value your thoughts. We're very happy to take on board any suggestions you might have.'

She rolled her eyes at him and said, 'You can give the sucking-up a rest now, okay? It's a great document and I can tell that despite earlier indications, you do know what you're doing.'

He didn't know what to say, and was slightly put out that his sucking-up had been seen through.

Helena began going through page by page, muttering under her breath about the notes she'd written. 'Ah yes, this one. You have the campsite on the fields at the back of the park and the access is across some council land. Correct?'

'Yes, that's right.'

'Leaving aside the permissions which I assume you have or are pending, there's going to need to be some work to make that a suitable access point. Basically, you'll need to breach the natural boundary of the park by making what is essentially a hole in the hedge. Correct?'

He nodded, although he hadn't quite thought about it in that much detail yet.

'It might need planning permission.'

'What? Really? It's council land.'

'It is, but that doesn't mean they'll agree to designate the land for a use of that nature.'

'But if we can't access the campsite that way, the only other way is down the street.'

'And we wouldn't allow that. You'd end up with people wandering in the middle of the road, not to mention that the residents might have something to say about their street becoming part of the festival.'

'Okay. I'll find out about the land. That's not something that would come up at the SAG, is it?'

'No, it's a separate issue. The only thing that I've flagged as an SAG issue is the proposed demographic of the public attending.'

'It's been difficult to pin that down,' said Seb honestly. 'If we use the library book club as a guide, it could be literally anyone, but we anticipate it to be families, groups of women and single people, mainly.'

'That's just about everyone,' Helena said, laughing.

'I suppose it is,' Seb grinned, not having realised before. 'What's the impact of not narrowing it down to a particular group?'

'Having a niche makes it easy for them. Say you're having a rock festival, you know it'll likely be loud, but a pretty well-behaved crowd with a few wrong-uns in the mix that the police might need to look out for. If you're having a dance music festival, it's a younger crowd. The police will worry about drugs and residents will worry about that too. With a folk festival, there's nothing for anyone to worry about.'

'It's a book festival. I'd take a stab in the dark that it most closely fits with the folk festival type of thing. These are book people,' he said, hoping to emphasise the point.

'I take your point,' said Helena, 'but it's a new thing for this area. You could do with submitting some comparable information from a similar event, like Hay Festival, that's the most obvious one. See what you can find out about their demographics, maybe even see if you can get hold of someone from their SAG who might talk to someone on ours. In fact, I could give my counterpart in Powys a call. That might be the most straightforward thing to do. I'll see if I can get hold of an EMP for it, off the record.'

'That'd be amazing, thank you,' said Seb, chuffed that Helena seemed to be warming to their event so much that she was going above and beyond.

'Look, I want this to be a success. Don't think for a minute that I won't be pulling you up on every tiny thing when you get underway, but I want you to have the best chance of success, even if you are bloody idiots to think that a few months is long enough to organise something like this.'

'Honestly, Helena, I can't thank you enough.'

'Alright. I haven't done anything yet,' she said, blushing. 'And there are plenty of other things I need to flag up, so let's get on with it.'

By the time he left the council offices, Seb was armed with information and a whole new set of priorities, his top one being calling in to the drop-in session at the planning department the following day to get their take on whether the access from the campsite and car park to the main festival site was going to be a problem. They didn't actually know how to apply for permission, but Seb had been hoping that, as a local architect, Matt might be able to use his contacts to put them in touch with the right person. Now, knowing that the success of the whole event depended on getting this tiny thing sorted out, he decided to take it in hand himself. He needed to take responsibility for the event, not call in favours to get things done. At least not yet.

As it was almost lunchtime and he knew Jess was on her own at the haberdashery all day, he popped into Oliver's and picked up toasties and coffee for them both. He'd done a couple of trips between the unit and Archie's barn the day before and had sold some old metal signs to a scrap dealer. It made a nice change to have money in his pocket and, as well as buying lunch for Jess, he left some money in an envelope for Oliver as a first payment towards the rent.

The haberdashery was buzzing. There were a couple of people sat at the table looking through knitting books, by the looks of it. Jess was busy pulling out fabric to show three women who were enthusing about almost everything, and another couple of people were walking around with armfuls of wool while they continued to browse.

Not sure where to go, Seb went behind the counter. As soon as he put the coffees down, a woman came over and put a book down on the counter in front of him. She smiled expectantly and hovered her phone near the card reader.

'Oh, sorry,' he said, realising that she thought he was going to serve her. 'Unfortunately, I've got no idea what I'm doing.'

The woman laughed. 'You do look like a rabbit in the headlights. That's okay, I can wait for your girlfriend.'

Seb opened his mouth to object and then just smiled. Jess *was* his girlfriend, and even if he hadn't really thought about it until now, he was very happy for it to be the case, and equally happy for everyone to know.

Realising that this was going to continue to happen, he snuck into the kitchen instead and leant against the worktop while he munched his toastie.

'The coast is clear!' Jess called a few minutes later.

She'd served the woman, along with the yarn-carrying customers. Only the fabric perusers were left and they were quite happy looking by themselves for now.

'Perhaps I should teach you how to use the till?'

'I think knowing that could be the least of your problems if I set foot in here. Imagine if someone wanted anything except to pay? Nightmare.'

Jess finished a mouthful of toastie and rolled her eyes in delight. 'This is delicious, thank you. Probably a good ninety-nine percent of customers come to the counter for a non-paying reason to be fair.'

'See? Neither of us has time to devote to getting me up to that kind of speed.'

Jess put her food down to serve the women who had finally decided.

'Sorry to drag you from your lunch,' one of them said, obviously not sorry enough to keep browsing for five minutes while Jess finished eating.

'Oh, it's fine,' Jess said. She was smiling as if she really didn't mind. It was interesting to see her in action. The last time he'd been to the shop, she'd been the only one there.

He found himself pasting a fake smile on his own face a few minutes later when the customers left the shop, admittedly having spent enough money to make the interruption to their lunch worth it. 'I don't know how you manage to be polite to people day in, day out.'

Jess laughed and looped her arms around his neck. 'I know you seem to have trouble being nice for its own sake sometimes. So tell me, did you summon up some charm for Helena?'

'I tried, but she saw straight through me.'

'Ha, that probably serves you right after the last time.'

'Probably,' he admitted, pulling her closer and giving her a long, lingering kiss.

'Hey, I'm at work,' she said, chastising him, although the smile on her face and the kiss that followed told him she didn't mind at all.

'I'd better leave you to it. I've got some more stuff to move over to Archie's this afternoon before the meeting later.'

'But you haven't told me what Helena said.'

'You can wait until later to find out like all the other

traders,' he teased.

'Do you want to stay at mine tonight?'

'That'd be great.' Jess's place was cosier than the flat above the coffee house. Seb loved the stove that warmed the whole cottage, and the position on the side of the hill was stunning. It was exactly the kind of place he would have pictured Jess living if he'd had to guess. He loved that her things were everywhere. It was tidy but lived in. There had been a weaving loom, of all things, on the coffee table in the lounge along with a bowl full of fabric hexagons that she was in the middle of stitching together. There was a basket of knitting wool, the needles sticking out of it, in the corner of the lounge. He didn't think he'd ever seen anyone with so much of themselves gathered into their living space. Most of the things he bought were tools, which obviously didn't end up in the house anyway, although he'd definitely be keeping his favourites in the corner of the lounge at his flat rather than subject them to the leaky roof of Archie's stables.

He had time to take a couple of truckloads of kit over to the stables before the meeting. While he was at the unit, he took some pictures of some stuff he didn't think he'd need again. It was always tempting to keep things that were going begging at the end of a job, just in case they came in handy one day. They usually didn't and a lot of what he needed to find a home for was exactly that kind of thing. Once he'd locked up, he headed back to Croftwood for the traders' meeting. They had achieved a lot in the past few weeks and hopefully such a positive report from Helena would encourage more involvement and volunteering closer to the event, as well as giving the traders confidence that putting their time into getting involved would pay off. Knowing that Helena was backing them, he finally felt like he was getting somewhere.

30

Jess had been seriously impressed by Seb at the traders' meeting. He'd clearly laid out exactly what was going to happen and where. He'd answered everyone's questions satisfactorily and then handed over to the other committee members for their updates.

At the end of the night, the two of them, exhausted but happy, piled into Madge and headed to Jess's house.

'Perhaps we should have taken the truck,' said Seb, attempting to push the passenger seat back before realising that it already was as far back as it would go.

'I can't leave Madge in the car park overnight,' said Jess, immediately regretting referring to the car by name. She could feel Seb's mirth even without looking at him.

'Your car's called Madge?'

'Yes.' She tried to sound very matter of fact about it.

'Why?'

'I like the name Madge, it suits her.'

'I think I was asking why a car would have a name rather than querying the choice of name.'

'You'll see when you get to know her a bit more.' Jess pulled up in the space next to the cottage, switched off the engine, and climbed out.

'I'm not sure that's going to happen now you've outed yourself as a nutter,' Seb said, stretching his arms over his head as if he'd been in the car for hours, rather than ten minutes.

Jess grinned at him over the roof of the car and gave it a pat. 'Careful, you're not quite ahead of Madge in my affections yet.'

'I'm not sure Madge will be able to compete with me after tonight.' He came around to Jess and looked at her, making her knees weak with longing at the thought of what he might mean. Then he took her bags from her and backed away, teasing her with a sexy half-smile.

'You'd better show me what you mean,' she said, happy to kiss goodbye to any thoughts she might have had of getting any sleep.

Later that evening, they sat on the sofa together, wrapped in a couple of Jess's homemade quilts, drinking hot chocolate in front of the fire, which Seb had stoked back into life when they'd finally ventured out of the bedroom.

'You know we've sold out of the early bird tickets already?' Jess told him. 'Patsy's sent me a WhatsApp. That means you can put first your invoice in. With the ticket money and the grants that Toby's got, there's more than enough, even after we've paid the deposits.'

Seb put his arm around her shoulders and drew her closer to him. 'I will. At least I feel like I'm getting somewhere now, and can justify it.'

'What are you up to for the rest of the week?'

'I need to get the access sorted out from the park to the campsite. I had a quick look at it after I met Helena, and it looks as if the allotments are at the other end of the site. It's literally almost scrubland, the part we're proposing to use. I was wondering about suggesting some kind of deal where because we're clearing the land anyway, we offer to clear it thoroughly so that the allotments can expand. They all looked well-tended, so I bet there's a demand for them. Then the council get to make a bit of extra cash out of the festival too, in a roundabout way.'

'I love that idea. I bet it'll make all the difference if you go to them with that idea rather than just asking to knock a hedge down and create a temporary track through there.'

Jess had been absolutely right. The planning officer that Seb spoke to was as enthusiastic as you were likely to find a planning officer getting about anything and agreed to support the plan to remove the hedging, creating a path from the park to the campsite at the next meeting of the planning committee. He seemed to think that cultivating the land and marking it out for allotments would be all that would be required in return since apparently it was on the council's wish list to increase their allotment offering; it was one of those things that would never be a priority. He also suggested that they might want to look into funding a gate between the park and the allotments as an alternative to replanting the hedging, just in case the festival became an annual event. That would need planning permission, but since running the festival wasn't contingent on that, Seb felt quite comfortable agreeing to take the request to the festival committee.

After the meeting, he called into the haberdashery with lunch for him and Jess. It was quite busy, and someone he'd not seen before was running a knitting workshop around the big table. Jess was chatting to the ladies while they ate their sandwiches, although a couple of them seemed more interested in looking at wool than eating their lunch.

'You don't look like a knitter,' said the woman in charge.

'Correct,' he said, feeling slightly overwhelmed since they were all looking at him now. He felt as if he ought to announce himself. 'I'm Sebastian, Jess's partner.'

Jess beamed across the table at him, which was reassuring since it still felt strange referring to her like that.

'Fi. Knitting tutor, nice to meet you.' She held her hand out for him to shake, which he did.

'Ah, Fi of the cruise,' he said.

She laughed. 'Amongst other things, yes. I'm not sure I remember Jess talking about you,' she said, shooting Jess a look.

'I didn't have time!' Jess said, coming round and taking his hand, leading him towards the kitchen. 'We were too busy workshopping.'

Fi and all the other ladies smiled and stared at them as they backed into the kitchen.

'I'm sorry,' Jess smiled. 'I wasn't expecting you, otherwise I'd have warned you off.'

He kissed her slowly, still thankful every time that he did. 'It's fine. I don't mind parading around for your knitting ladies.'

'I think they enjoyed it. It's a nice surprise to see you,' she said, looping her arms around his neck and leaning in for another kiss. 'And you look pleased with yourself.'

'I think I've got the permission sorted for the path. They loved the allotment idea.'

'Brilliant! And I've emailed Fliss, and she's thrilled to be taking part. I've offered her somewhere to stay. I know we haven't planned this stuff yet, but perhaps we ought to look into a glamping option?'

'I'll put it on the list.' He rolled his eyes. 'You knock one thing off and another one slides into its place.'

'I can see us glamping, can't you? I'm much keener to camp on that basis.'

'If we can have mates' rates, yes,' he laughed. He could think of nothing nicer in the world than spending a night under the stars with Jess.

'Anyway, I'd better get back. I'll chaperone you to the door.'

'I bought you a sandwich, but if you've already eaten…?'

'At the risk of sounding ungrateful, you take it,' she said. 'I've eaten about nine packets of biscuits this morning. I love the sentiment, but you're doing me a favour by eating it for me.'

They walked to the door under the watchful eye of Fi and the knitting ladies, their conversation turning hushed, leading Seb to assume that they were probably whispering about him and Jess. So, uncomfortable with an audience, rather than kiss her goodbye, he squeezed her hands and said, 'See you later? Come round to mine after work if you can.'

She nodded, her eyes sparkling, and he wondered if he'd be able to wait until then to see her. She was like a drug that he couldn't get enough of. The high never diminishing, however much he had.

'Oh my god,' Fi said later on, when the knitting ladies had all left for the day. 'Where did Sebastian spring from?'

'He runs the events company that is organising the Croftwood Festival. We only got together recently,' Jess explained. 'We didn't start seeing each other until after the Bruges cruise.'

'You're a fast worker,' Fi said, laughing as she collected the mugs together to take into the kitchen.

'It's not like me at all. I mean, I couldn't stand him when we first met.'

'Ah, he's a grower. I can see that in him.'

Jess laughed. 'I suppose he is.' He was certainly growing on her more quickly than she'd thought possible.

'What's this festival? Is it worth coming to?'

'Yes, I'm organising it and there will be knitting, I hope, but definitely craft of some sort, as well as a book club and some good music. It's the third weekend in August.'

Rob was keeping the music line-up very close to his chest, insisting that any credible festival made a thing out of announcing the acts bit by bit. Only Patsy had challenged him, insisting that she needed some names to go on the website and the posters, but so far, nothing had been forthcoming.

'A book club, what is it like Hay or something?'

'Not really. It's based on a book club they run at Croftwood Library.' Jess explained the concept. 'We've asked William Templeton and FL Thorne to come along and do talks since their books will be two of the choices.'

'No way! Paddy's just finished reading an FL Thorne book and left it on my bedside table insisting that I read it next. I bet he'll be keen to come if I tell him she's coming. Books for him, knitting for me. What do you think you're going to do on the craft front?'

'I don't know yet,' confessed Jess. 'The book club needs properly advertising whereas the craft is a kind of extra thing that doesn't need as much thought.'

'You need something along the lines of how they run The Handmade Fair, you know that craft festival-type event that Kirsty Allsop used to run? They had a massive tent where loads of people can do a craft workshop at the same time. I printed a tea towel when I went once.'

'I love that idea. It'd be great to do something like simple stitching or learn to knit and crochet,' Jess said, her imagination beginning to fire up.

'You could sell kits then, in case anyone got hooked and wanted to carry on over the weekend or when they go home. I'll help you organise it.' Fi's eyes were bright with enthusiasm.

'Really? Because I love that idea, but with the book club stuff, I've got a lot to organise already. I don't want it to be an afterthought.'

'Definitely. You did me a massive favour filling in on the cruise at the last minute, and it's no hardship to come to a festival and craft all weekend.'

'You and Paddy can have free tickets,' she said, making a mental note to add that to her list of things to discuss at the next committee meeting.

'Brilliant! Paddy loves camping, brings out his Boy Scout side,' Fi said with a wink, making Jess laugh again.

Once they'd finished tidying up, Jess locked up and said goodbye to Fi, promising to be in touch with more information about the festival. She headed to Seb's. For once, it would be nice to spend the evening together with no pressing festival business to discuss.

'Fliss emailed me,' Seb said, all excited and bouncing over to the door as soon as Jess went into the flat.

She was puzzled. 'But she's already emailed me to say yes and we've sorted out a few details.'

'No, this was about something else. Well, it's festival related, but she wanted to see what I thought about an idea she's had.'

It was getting more cryptic by the minute. 'And?' Jess's eyes were wide, trying to coax him to tell her whatever it was that he was bursting with.

'She knows Ned Nokes. He's a friend of her partner's and he's willing to play for us.'

The moment that she should have been enthusiastic about Seb's news was overtaken straight away by practicality. 'We can't have Ned Nokes at the festival. Can you imagine? We'd sell out the minute the tickets went up for sale and no-one would be interested in books.'

Seb looked so sad that Jess wasn't on board, that she wrapped her arms around him and kissed him, hoping to take the sting out of what she'd said.

He pulled away. 'What if we didn't tell anyone? Fliss said he and Brun, that's her boyfriend, play together all the time. Why don't we promote Brun on the line-up and then just have Ned play as well, like a surprise.'

'You don't think Ned Nokes fans would see through that?' she said doubtfully. 'Does this guy Brun even play his own gigs? Isn't he normally with Ned? They had a number one a while ago.'

'I don't know. I think it's an incredible offer, though. Shall we see what the rest of them think?'

It was only fair to go to the committee to get a consensus, but Jess already knew that Rob wouldn't take kindly to being forced into taking a musical act he hadn't handpicked.

'It is a great offer and you're right, we ought to see what everyone else thinks. I'm just being protective of the book club. It's not because I don't think it's an incredible opportunity.'

'To be honest, I'm quite pleased that you're not as excited as I was. I might have been a bit paranoid if you couldn't wait to meet him.'

Jess looped her fingers into his belt loops and pulled his hips towards hers. 'Nope, weirdly you're sexier than Ned Nokes,' she said.

Seb laughed softly. 'I'm wondering what kind of pheromones I'm giving off if you think that's true.'

Jess couldn't believe her brain could come up with something so cheesy, but she said it anyway; it fitted in the moment. 'Maybe you should leave me with a very strong reminder just in case I do bump into Ned Nokes sometime soon.'

'Happy to oblige,' he said, putting his hands under her

bottom and lifting her. She gripped her thighs around his waist and her arms around his neck while he carried her into the bedroom.

31

The next couple of weeks whipped by in a blur of activity. Every ticket release sold out within a matter of days, all on the back of the book club, which had now confirmed Alexis Diamond as well as Bill and Fliss. Jess was secretly pleased because it had never been the intention that the music would be the focus. It was there to give added value, and fill the evenings with something for the festival-goers to do. Everything was moving in the right direction.

Seb was on standby, waiting to hear from Helena about how the Safety Advisory Group meeting had gone. It was due to finish at five o'clock, but by the time Jess came to meet him after she closed the shop, he still hadn't heard and was jittery, to say the least. She'd been expecting him to come to the shop as soon as he heard, so when that hadn't happened she texted him, finding out that he was waiting in Oliver's with Matt, Toby and Oliver. They were all sitting around Toby's regular table, catastrophising about all the things the SAG meeting could be finding fault with and by the time Jess joined them, they'd as good as convinced themselves that the festival would have to be cancelled.

'Oh, come on,' Jess said, 'Didn't Helena say there was nothing that could trip it up?'

'Way to jinx it, Jess,' Seb said, as if she'd as good as sabotaged it herself.

'I'm just saying, I'm sure it'll be okay. We've spent weeks listening to Helena's recommendations and aside from her being able to visit the festival itself and give it her seal of approval, I'd say we're as good as there.'

Seb glowered at her, and she had to stifle a laugh. They'd all been sitting here too long to have any sense of perspective left.

'If we get the sign off from this meeting, don't you think we ought to go out and celebrate?' she suggested.

'I've got the kids,' said Matt, 'so no celebrating for me, unless you guys want to come round to mine? We could have a few beers around the fire pit in the garden.'

Seb's phone rang. He answered it before the second ring.

'Helena?'

They all waited with bated breath, staring at Seb to see whether his expression would give them an indication of what had happened.

'Oh, that's great,' he said, his face breaking into a huge grin. 'Thanks so much. For everything. Okay, yes. Bye.' He put his phone down on the table, exhaled and said, 'Looks like we're celebrating then!'

'Yes!' said Oliver, holding out a fist to Seb, who bumped it before pulling him into a brief hug. 'We've bloody got it over the line. Nice one, Seb!'

Seb shook his head. 'It's been all of you. You guys and the rest of the committee are the ones who have done just as much of the hard work as me.'

Jess smiled at him. That might have been true a few weeks ago, but now Seb was the driving force behind the festival. If Jess had to guess, she'd say that before he came to Croftwood, he'd lost more than his home and his business. He'd lost his mojo. She wasn't sure when the change came and wouldn't credit herself with it. But gradually, every bit of progress he'd had, every little win, had all contributed to drive him on. In the past couple of weeks, Jess and the rest of the committee had breathed a sigh of relief because Seb had taken on all the things that they'd put in motion; the traders' stalls, the food vendors and even some of the logistical arrangements for the music, although Rob had insisted he needed to be the main contact for the artists, which was fine by Sebastian. He still involved Jess in the book club since that was easy, as they were together most of the time anyway, and he said he didn't know enough about how it was supposed to work. She suspected he knew how much she was loving being involved with the authors, speaking to their publishers and liaising with the library, and she loved him for seeing that.

She'd also been having fun working with Fi to devise the plans for the craft workshops. Patsy had offered to be their crochet person, and between the three of them, they had brainstormed some great ideas.

'I'm going to go. We'll have the kids fed and in bed by seven if you guys want to come around then,' Matt said, standing up.

'Can I bring Hilary?' Toby asked.

They all looked at him, all with the same question on their minds.

'We've been seeing a bit of each other,' he said, blushing slightly.

'Of course you can bring her,' said Matt. 'Is Lois coming too?'

'I'm supposed to be picking her up after work, so yes. We'll head home via yours,' said Oliver.

'We can order in some pizzas later,' said Matt, before he left.

Toby packed up his laptop and headed off too, while Oliver chatted to Jack, and Seb and Jess headed up to the flat.

'What a relief,' Seb said, slumping into the corner of the sofa, the big grin still on his face.

'You'd thought of everything,' Jess said. 'You must have been quietly confident.'

'I would have been back in the day, but things are different now. I don't want to take anything for granted. Things have felt hard-won lately, so this feels good.'

'It's a huge win,' Jess said, coming to sit next to him. She leaned into his side and laid her head on his chest. 'I'm proud of you.'

She felt him gulp, and he laid his hand on her head. 'Thanks,' he said, his voice thick with emotion.

She shifted so that she could look at him. He had tears in his eyes, which he quickly wiped away with his thumb and fingers.

He gave her a tight smile. 'Sorry, I don't know why it's made me emotional.'

Jess reached up and stroked his cheek, using her own thumb to wipe away a stray tear. 'It's because it feels to you as if everything is riding on this festival. It's more than a job. It's how you're going to rebuild your life.'

He nodded, gently pulling her head back into his chest so that she couldn't look at him anymore. 'It always felt like the last chance to save the business, to turn things around. But now it doesn't feel like that's what I'm doing. That's all gone now and whatever happens next is going to be different.'

'Because of us?' It took a lot for her to say that. It felt as if she was exposing herself and how she felt when maybe it was too soon.

'Yes,' he said, exhaling, his chest falling beneath her as if he'd released a ton of tension from his body. 'That's a big part of it. I wasn't looking for this and it's changed what's important for me. I don't want to be the person who spends his life blagging contracts, not knowing whether I can deliver them. When you finished off that EMP for me, I realised that I'd become paralysed by the fear of failing. That's why I'd procrastinated about it, because somehow, not finishing it meant that I hadn't failed yet.'

'I know what you mean. It's not the same at all, but that's why I haven't been on holiday for years. It felt like if I did, it would finally mean that Jon was gone. It wasn't until I went to Dorset in April that I realised that wasn't true.'

Sebastian scrambled to sit up. 'Who's Jon?'

Jess knew she hadn't told Seb about Jon. For a long time it hadn't mattered. Then when they started spending most of their time in bed, the right time had never come. But now, with Seb pouring his heart out, it felt like the right time. But also, Jess was painfully aware that she should have already told him.

'Jon was my first boyfriend. And my last. Until you. He died almost ten years ago.' She watched Seb's face for signs that he was cross with her for not sharing this information before, but he didn't look cross. 'It wasn't until I went back to Dorset when you were poorly that I felt I'd got any closure. I'd been frightened to go back there, scared that it would bring everything back and it would seem like I'd lost him yesterday, all over again.'

'Oh, Jess. I had no idea.'

'I know. It's okay. Nobody knows except Patsy. I came here and started again. Being in a different place made it easier to forget, and it wasn't until I started to have feelings for you that I knew I needed to go back. To kind of make sure I was ready to move on.'

Seb took her in his arms and they sat for a few minutes, saying nothing.

'It must have been hard to go back and face that after such a long time,' he said, making Jess wish she'd told him before. She'd worried that it would seem strange to talk to him, of all people, about someone else she loved. It was unusual to embark on a relationship with someone when you still loved someone else, would always love someone else, but she knew now that Seb wasn't the type of man to be jealous of a ghost.

'Deciding to go was almost the hardest part, but working on that mini-cruise with Fi gave me the excuse I needed. That had felt like a massive step too.' She told Seb about that last summer. 'It seemed too close to the idea of a holiday and I was worried it would be hard to not think of Jon all the time, but we were so busy, it definitely felt nothing like a holiday.' She smiled, taking Seb's hands in hers. 'I'm sorry I didn't tell you all of this before.'

'Do you mind if I ask what happened to Jon?' He sounded uncertain, worried perhaps that it might upset her to talk about it.

'He had a brain tumour.' She explained about those last months of Jon's life and how seeing Zac had helped her come to terms with how she'd been unable to be part of them.

'God, Jess. I don't know how you get over something like that. I thought I'd had it bad, but it's insignificant in comparison.'

'It took me years to get over it. I didn't think I had, but when I went to Dorset, it all felt so far away from now.'

Seb took a deep breath and began to speak. 'I didn't just lose the business and the house. I had a partner until a few months before the pandemic. She's with one of my friends now.'

Jess knew by now that Seb was slow to share. Not because he was hiding these things from her on purpose, it just took a long time for him to trust anyone. And now that he trusted her, little by little she would discover more about him.

'That's awful, Seb.'

He shrugged. 'Nobody died. I can't imagine what that was like for you.'

'What happened to you, Seb, it's not insignificant. It's just a different kind of loss, something you still need to come to terms with, grieve about, even.'

They sat looking at each other, both taking in what they'd learned.

'Come on then,' Jess said, standing up and stretching. 'Tonight's supposed to be a celebration and we're missing the party.'

Seb groaned. 'Are you sure you don't want to celebrate here instead?'

Jess laughed. 'Later. A beer and pizza in the sunshine is calling my name.' She pulled on his hand forcing him to stand up. He took her in his arms again.

'I love you,' he whispered into her hair.

She pulled back, searching his face and seeing complete sincerity said, 'I love you, Sebastian.' A wave of euphoria washed over her and she grinned. 'I actually do.'

He laughed, 'Thanks for the confirmation. You sound surprised.'

'I am a bit. It feels too soon, but it feels amazing to say it, like it's letting something out of me that was trapped inside.'

'Come on, you,' he said. 'Let's go. You're lightheaded from lack of beer and food.'

They strolled across town in the sunshine to Matt and Patsy's. Jess had forgotten that Seb hadn't been there before and they had to pause on the driveway so he could take in the huge, beautiful house, getting all the shock out of the way before they knocked on the door.

'Come in!' Patsy said. 'We're outside. Ollie's just about to order the pizza. Do you both want beer?'

Patsy paused at the fridge to grab some beers as they walked through the kitchen to where the huge bi-fold doors were open and had been pushed aside, turning the house and the garden into one space. Matt was lighting the fire pit while his son, Sammy, stood watching with a serious expression on his face, listening as Matt patiently explained that they could stay up for pizza but that there would be no marshmallows on a school night. His twin sister, Flo, was busy begging Oliver to help her climb up the rope ladder to the tree house.

'I'm really good at climbing up, but it's wobbly,' she said.

'Flo, don't be bossy. Let Oliver enjoy his beer in peace,' said Patsy. 'One of us will help you in a few minutes.'

'How many is a few?' Flo asked.

'Come on,' Matt said. 'If it means a minute's peace!' he said, making both of the children squeal as he growled, then chased them over to the corner of the garden where an impressive tree house nestled in the branches of an enormous oak tree.

'Are grown-ups allowed in there?' Seb asked.

'Sometimes,' Patsy said, laughing. 'I don't know why Matt built it with the rope ladder, it freaks me out as much as Flo, so I've only been up there once or twice.'

Seb swigged his beer, then grinned at Jess before heading down the garden.

'How's things?' Patsy asked once he was out of earshot. She sat down next to Jess in the chair Seb had just vacated.

'Things are great,' Jess said. 'Really great. Now that the festival's coming together, he's throwing himself into it. It's like he thrives on organising the chaos.'

'A bit like Ollie in that sense,' Patsy said. 'What's he got lined up for after this?'

Jess paused, then looked at Patsy. 'I don't know, actually. We haven't talked about what happens after the festival.'

'But you must wonder what his plans are? Do you think he'll look for work around Croftwood?'

'I'm not sure it works like that in his industry. I guess he'd base himself somewhere. He used to have a place in Cheltenham.'

'Oh, god,' said Patsy, getting up. 'I've forgotten to put the rest of the beer in the fridge. Won't be a sec.'

She left Jess wondering how it was possible that she had fallen in love with Seb without having even discussed what might happen next? Maybe it was because neither of them had been expecting to fall for each other when they'd both avoided anything like this happening for a long time, for fear of getting hurt again. But maybe they were existing in a bubble of the Croftwood Festival and once that was over, would that mean their relationship would be too? That wasn't what Jess wanted at all. She wanted to picture a future for herself with Seb in it, but she wasn't naive enough to think that their lives would meld together without anything changing. Seb had had such a period of upheaval, she could hardly expect him to continue living in limbo in Oliver's flat waiting for some elusive contract that might keep him in Croftwood. No, it was too much to expect from him.

'That treehouse is next level,' Seb said, helping himself to another beer from the ice-filled bucket that Patsy had brought outside.

'What will you do after the festival, Seb?'

He looked at her in surprise. 'I'm not sure yet. Why?'

She bit her lip. 'I suppose I'm wondering whether falling in love with you means we're together now. Or whether it means we're together… for now.'

He took a deep breath. 'After everything that's happened, it's hard for me to think that far ahead, Jess.'

She cut him off before he could say anything else. Her heart was on high alert for a bump in the road, and she could see this one coming. 'I get that,' she said, trying to sound as if she was completely on board with him not being able to commit to her in the way she'd hoped. It was ridiculous to have expected that. 'I know you're not going to find enough work to stay in Croftwood, I just wondered if you'd got anything definite yet.'

He took her hand. 'Nothing definite yet, no.'

Jess managed a smile. 'I'm just going to give Patsy a hand with the pizza,' she said, getting up.

'Jess…'

'It's fine, I was just asking.'

She went inside and ran upstairs, finding the family bathroom where she locked herself in and let herself cry for a minute or two. What had she expected? A happy ever after where Seb miraculously found the everlasting contract of his dreams in Croftwood? She'd let herself fall for him without thinking that she might lose him. Dying wasn't the only way to lose someone, after all, and Seb knew that already. His heart was better equipped to deal with that happening again, especially since this time he was going to be the one choosing to leave. While Jess stayed in Croftwood with all the memories they'd made together, with nowhere to escape to this time.

32

Why did they decide to spend the night at Matt and Patsy's? It had seemed like the best idea in the world the night before, but now, Seb wished more than anything that he was in his own bed nursing his hangover rather than here.

Jess had left earlier, although he'd only been vaguely aware of her getting up. She had the shop to open and he could only assume that she'd had the sense to drink a lot less than him, otherwise he was sure she'd still be next to him, regardless of the opening hours of the Croftwood Haberdashery. As he lay there, he remembered the conversation she'd started out of the blue about his plans after the festival. He'd been too tipsy to grasp exactly what she was getting at but something must have prompted it. They hadn't discussed what might happen after the festival, mainly because he didn't know.

He glanced at his phone, which only had ten percent of its charge left. It was eight o'clock. The twins' chattering carried through the house. He didn't relish the thought of dealing with two enthusiastic seven-year-olds while he was feeling like this, although he'd had fun with them last night until Matt had wrangled them up to bed. But he couldn't stay here either. He needed coffee. Lots of coffee and probably some toast.

His phone pinged with a message while he was gingerly getting dressed. He smiled, expecting it to be a message from Jess, but it was from someone else.

All thoughts of his hangover forgotten, he went downstairs in search of Oliver, Matt, or anyone else who he could share his panic with.

'Hey guys,' he said, smiling at the children who were sitting at the breakfast bar eating cereal.

'Hi Seb!' they chorused. 'Do you want some of my Cheerios?' Sammy added shyly.

'Thanks, buddy. I think I'll have a coffee for now.'

Patsy put a cup of coffee under his nose almost instantly. 'Can't make them fast enough this morning,' she said, smiling. 'Feeling fragile?'

He nodded, with a bashful smile. 'Has Oliver left?'

'Yes, he was opening up this morning. I think he regretted not asking Jack to do it, but it was too late by the time he realised he'd... had too much fun.'

'Why are all the grown ups tired, Patsy?' Flo asked, thoughtfully. 'Did you all go to bed too late?'

'That's it exactly Flo. We were having too much fun, and we didn't realise what the time was. You know how that can happen.'

Flo sighed. 'It always happens,' she said. 'I wish we could have played in the tree house for longer last night.'

'And had marshmallows,' Sammy added.

'We didn't have marshmallows without you,' said Seb.

'Marshmallows at the weekend, you two,' Matt said, smiling at his children as he came into the kitchen. He kissed Patsy and relieved her of the latest coffee she'd made.

'Hey, Matt. I've just had a text about the big marquee. It's come off a lorry and is too badly damaged to repair. They've cancelled our booking.'

'Any other options?' Matt asked.

Seb shook his head. He'd fought hard to get the marquee at a price they could afford in the first place. 'By now, any alternatives will be booked up.'

'What's a marquee, Daddy?' Flo asked.

'Come on, you two, time to get dressed or we'll be late,' Patsy said.

'It's a big tent that we need for the festival,' Matt explained.

'Like the circus?'

'Yes, it is a bit like that,' Matt said.

Matt and Seb looked at each other. 'It's got to be worth looking into at this point?' Matt said.

'Thank you, Flo, you've given us a very good idea,' said Seb.

Flo skipped upstairs with a grin on her face, not caring what the idea was, just happy that Seb was pleased.

Seb headed back to the flat, wishing he'd got some sunglasses with him. It was a beautiful day to walk through the leafy streets of Croftwood, but not if you had a hangover. Still, by the time he was home, the fresh air had cleared his head, and he was ready to take on the challenge of finding a replacement for the marquee. He called a few conventional places, just in case they'd had a cancellation on one of their hires, but as he'd suspected, it was nearing the height of the season and no-one had anything.

He chuckled as he typed "circus tents to hire" into his search engine, fully expecting to be presented with a list of actual circuses. But he was pleasantly surprised to find a list of companies with exactly that sort of tent to hire. After a couple of hours, it became clear to him that it wasn't quite the innovative idea they'd first thought. There was no availability because it was the height of the festival season, he kept being told. As a last resort, he called the company at the bottom of his list. They provided big tops for hire and a circus to go with it, if you wanted.

Half an hour later, he'd secured a replacement tent, but at a cost, not all of it financial. Even though he'd been clear that the circus element wasn't required, the only tent available was a big top that was being used by a travelling circus. Happily, they'd told Seb, the circus was having a couple of weeks off either side of the festival weekend. The circus was willing to transport the tent to Croftwood and help put it up at a very reasonable cost, but they would need somewhere to stay. With the festival campsite full, Seb's only option if he wanted the tent was to find some other land where the circus could camp for a week or so. Thankfully, he'd been assured that there were no animals in this circus, but there were a lot of people and a lot of vehicles.

He sighed. He'd had about twelve hours of feeling like he was winning, that was all. Now, he was back to troubleshooting a problem that might put an end to the festival, at least as it was currently planned. Archie Harrington was his only hope.

'Ah, quite a predicament,' Archie said, rubbing his chin thoughtfully after Seb had explained what the problem was.

'I don't suppose there's any chance at all that you have some more spare land anywhere? Our campsite fields are full and I know there's an issue with the estate land because of the trust.'

'And if you can't have this tent?'

'I don't think we can run the festival without it. We can't rely on the weather being good. With the cinema and the tent, we can shelter everyone if it rains, otherwise I think we'll have to think about refunding ticket holders and reducing our numbers to however many we can fit in the cinema.'

'Goodness, that would be a shame, especially now that you have William Templeton confirmed.'

Seb tried not to smirk. He loved that that was Archie's primary concern.

'Unfortunately, I don't have any other land I can offer.'

Seb's heart sank.

'But I do have a tent.'

Seb frowned. 'Of that kind of size?'

'I was a small boy the last time I saw it, admittedly,' Archie said, 'But yes, I remember it being capacious. Used to be used for holding the annual get together for the estate workers.'

'Wow, that sounds like just the thing,' said Seb.

Archie held a hand up. 'Now, before you get excited, it has been in a barn for god knows how long. It could be riddled with mice-nibbled holes for all I know.'

'Can we have a look?'

Since the barn was on the other side of the estate, Seb offered to drive. Archie directed him further along the road, towards the big house that Seb hadn't seen before.

'Quicker this way than going around the outside,' said Archie.

'The house is incredible,' said Seb, slowing down as they came closer. It had too many pretty twisted brick chimneys to count, numerous gabled roofs adorned with decoratively edged tiles and ornate ridge tiles. There were lots of mullioned windows and the whole house was surrounded by a moat which was full to bursting with waterlilies.

'It's a money pit,' said Archie, laughing. 'But a beautiful one. Take the road to the right at the end here.'

They drove along until the road ended and Archie instructed Seb to continue around the edge of a field, where the grass was short thanks to a flock of sheep who ran as far away from the truck as they could get.

'Here we are.'

They pulled up to a brick barn, with gaps between some bricks that made a decorative pattern. In comparison with the stables in the courtyard at the estate office, it was in good repair. It gave Seb hope for the state of the tent. Archie led the way inside to the back corner, where something huge was covered by an old tarpaulin.

'Here she is,' he said, patting it.

Between them, they pulled part of the tarp back to reveal the tent underneath. There were a few holes, but they looked to be on the outer layer only and were all quite small.

'How do you get it out of here?' Seb asked.

'I think it was manhandled onto the back of a tractor, from what I recall,' said Archie. 'I'm not sure you'd get away with that these days.'

'If I can arrange to have it moved, would you be willing to let us use it?'

'Of course. It's wonderful to help,' said Archie.

Seb spent the rest of the day getting quotes from various companies to have the tent transported from the barn to the park. It wasn't a straightforward thing to organise at all. The other problem was that they'd have to find people to help put the tent up. A tent that no-one, not even Archie, as it turned out, had any idea how to erect.

He was keen to tell Jess about his day and although they'd made no firm plans, he'd expected her to call around to the flat once she'd closed the shop. But by six o'clock, there was still no sign of her.

'Hey, are you still at the shop?' he asked when she answered her phone.

'I'm at home.'

She didn't sound like his Jess. There was no warmth in her voice.

'I'd love to see you tonight. Can I come round?'

There was a pause before she said, 'Okay. I'll cook something.'

'No, don't worry, I'll bring some fish and chips.' He

wanted to ask if everything was okay, but she'd say yes, even though he was sure something was up.

He picked up the fish and chips on the way to Old Hollow and they sat on a picnic rug in Jess's tiny front garden, eating in silence, watching the sun dipping lower in the sky, though still giving enough warmth to enjoy. Jess had lent him a spare pair of sunglasses since he had no idea where his were. Most likely in a box in the corner of his lounge, but which one he couldn't begin to guess.

She cleared the fish and chip papers and went inside to make a pot of tea since neither of them especially wanted anything stronger after the night before.

Jess came back outside with the teapot and mugs on a small tray. Seb told her about his day rather than launch straight into an inquisition about why she was being distant with him.

'Archie is like the fairy godfather of the festival,' Jess said, after Seb told her about the tent.

'He is,' Sebastian agreed, 'and he doesn't want anything for it.'

'You said his mum is keen on meeting Bill. We ought to do something special for her.'

'I also got some quotes today for glamping options. There are a few companies who will do the whole shebang, so we're kind of outsourcing it but it's expensive. Otherwise we'd have to set it up ourselves.'

'It's one less thing to think about. Do you think what we could charge would cover the costs?'

Sebastian nodded. 'Definitely. And given how many tickets we're selling, we don't need to have that many glamping tents, anyway.'

'Presumably you've got a tent?' Jess asked. 'For us?'

'I have. It's in Archie's stable block at the moment, hopefully not being devoured by anything else that's in there.

It's quite small, though.'

Jess turned and grinned at him. 'I think that'd be okay.' She looked beautiful with the sun glinting off her hair, and her Audrey Hepburn sunglasses. Her sundress was pooled across her thighs because she was lying with her knees bent. 'What do you think you'll do after the festival?'

Ah, suddenly he remembered her asking him something similar at Matt's last night. They'd barely discussed life, how it might look for them in the future, whether they saw themselves in that future together.

'I know you asked me last night and I think I said I don't know,' he said gently. 'We haven't talked about what happens next, have we?'

'No, and that hasn't mattered. But with the festival coming up, it's been on my mind. I'm starting to feel as if we're somehow linked to that and that when the festival's over, we're over.'

Seb turned onto his side, desperate to reassure her, but at the same time unsure of what he could say with any certainty. 'I have a couple of things in the pipeline. Nothing's certain yet.'

'It won't be long until you get your final payment from the festival. I suppose I just wondered whether you're planning to get somewhere else to live? Whether it might be in Croftwood?'

He could hear in her voice how hard it was for her to ask him whether he'd considered staying. They both knew she was asking if he would stay for her.

'I haven't thought that far ahead.' It was lame. Not what she wanted to hear, he knew that, but it was the truth. 'Oliver's been good enough to let me stay in the flat indefinitely, and I can start paying him proper rent now. Any other decisions can wait until I know what direction the work is going to go in.' It was impossible to tell what she was thinking with her eyes hidden behind her sunglasses. 'I'd love to be all in, Jess. I'd love to know what's going to happen next so that I can tell you I'm staying, but I can't do that.'

'It's okay,' she said, keeping her gaze firmly fixed on the sky above. It would have been more reassuring if she'd turned and smiled at him. But he wasn't giving her anything to be reassured about .

'I can't offer you anything until I've got my life back into some kind of order.'

'I don't need anything, Seb. All I want is to not lose you.'

He knew what she meant by that, and his heart broke for her. He didn't want to put her through any kind of heartache after what she'd been through. No-one deserved that, especially not Jess.

'I want to promise you won't lose me, Jess, but I can't do that. You mean everything to me, but I didn't plan this. I've had no control over my life for a long time and you're the only part that has turned out to be good in all that time. I don't want to lose you, but I need to get my life back before I can promise you a future with me.'

She sat up, leaning her elbows on her bent knees. 'I can't pretend it's not shit, because it is. I don't want you to leave.' She sniffed and wiped her nose on the back of her hand. 'There. That's where I am. I don't need you to be the man who can make my dreams come true by offering me a stable future. An amazing job and salary isn't what I care about. I have my own money, and a house and business already. Don't leave thinking that you have to achieve anything before I'll want you, Seb.'

He sat up and reached for her hand. 'Jess, I know that stuff doesn't matter to you. That's one of the things I love about you. The fact that you fell in love with me when I have nothing.'

She turned and smiled. He'd never been so glad to see her

smile, but then she pulled her sunglasses off and he saw tears in her eyes.

'Oh, Jess. I'm sorry.' It broke his heart that he'd made her cry. But it would break both of them if he made promises he couldn't keep. If he gave her hope for a future he couldn't be confident of. That had happened to her before, with Jon.

She turned and cupped a hand around his jaw. 'I understand why you can't promise me anything. But I want you to stay,' she said simply.

'I'll do my best to factor that in,' he said softly, leaning up to kiss her.

'But until you have any plans, you'll be here?'

'Yes.' It was the only promise he could make; to be here until the end of the festival.

33

It hardly seemed possible that the festival was due to start in just a few days. Croftwood Park had been closed early on Monday morning and deliveries of fencing, toilets and tents had begun to arrive. The aim was to have the infrastructure in place by late Wednesday so that they could give access to traders on Thursday for setting up.

Seb was overseeing the delivery of the tent from Croftwood Court. The low-loader lorry that was transporting it had reversed along the main path in the park as close to the spot where the tent would be sited as it could get before it was craned off onto the grass.

'Can I get some help to unpack this?' he called to the group of people he'd hired to help with the fit-out. They were busy erecting the perimeter fence, but he was keen to see if there was any major damage to the tent that would need addressing before it was too late. Archie had been confident it had been packed away in pristine condition and that aside from the mouse holes, it would be perfectly serviceable, but it had been keeping Seb awake at night, worrying that after all this, it wouldn't be up to the job.

Six of them heaved the canvas, unrolling and unfolding it until it was spread across the grass in the middle of the park.

It was as large as Archie had promised, but riddled with more than a few mouse-nibbled holes in some places.

Seb thanked the team and sent them back to what they were doing. He texted Jess to see if she could come over to have a look. She had Fi and Penny in the shop today preparing for the craft workshops, so hopefully she'd be able to slip away. They'd hardly seen each other for the past couple of weeks, since he'd been so busy now that the festival was almost here and it was nice to have an excuse to see her.

'Mmm,' she said, squatting down and picking up the edge of the canvas, holding it so that the sun shone through the holes. 'It's like a sieve. I'm not sure there's much we can do about that.' She took her sandals off and walked onto the canvas in her bare feet, squatting down again in the middle to assess what looked like the roof. 'This part isn't as bad, but there are some tears along the seams and a few bigger holes.'

'Is it salvageable?' Seb asked.

'If it was going to rain solidly all weekend, I'd say no, but I think we can patch it up and it'll be okay. It doesn't matter if the sides have holes in and I think between me, Fi and Penny, we can make it good enough that we won't need buckets underneath the roof to catch any showers.'

He reached out to take her hand, steadying her as she pulled her sandals back on.

'Thanks,' he said. 'I've missed you.' Because he had. Distancing himself from Jess now wouldn't make it any less heartbreaking to leave her, if that's what he had to do. They were already in too deep, but at least they both knew where they stood.

'Me too.' She leant up to kiss him. 'Will you have time for a lunch break? We're having a delivery from Oliver's if you want to join us.'

'Better not,' he said, kissing her back. 'I've got to be at the campsite to meet the glamping company once I've got everything sorted out here, and Helena's meeting me over there at four so that we can get that signed off.'

'Already? That's good.'

'That's the easy part,' he said. 'There's only the electrics for the lights over there. Everything else is straightforward. I don't think she'll have any issues with any of it.' They'd had a head start on the campsite over the weekend, with volunteers helping to set things up in exchange for heavily discounted tickets and food provided by the Croftwood WI. 'I'm more worried about getting this tent up just in case we find out the poles have got woodworm.'

Jess laughed. 'I'm sure they won't have. Look, why don't we come back after the shop closes and we'll repair the canvas. It's a lovely evening to sit in the park and sew.'

'That'd be amazing, thank you.'

They'd barely seen each other over the past few days. He'd missed her but was all too aware that he needed to get used to seeing less of her. Surely that would make it less painful if he had to leave.

When he left.

'Are you guys up for an old-fashioned repair job tonight?' Jess asked Penny and Fi over their sandwich lunch. It was just as well that the shop was so quiet during the summer months because they had all but taken it over with their preparations for the festival. There were small balls of wool, and pieces of fabric in piles over any and all available surfaces. It was hard to believe, but there was a system amongst the chaos and they were all enjoying themselves.

'I'm up for anything, and since I'm staying at yours, where you go, I go,' said Fi.

'What are we mending?' Penny asked.

'The big tent that we've borrowed from Lord Harrington.

It's got a few holes in and some of the seams need whipstitching back together where the fabric's rotted over the years.'

'The seams will be a doddle with one of those curved needles and some button thread,' said Penny. 'But how are we going to mend the holes? If we patch them by stitching, it'll leak through the needle holes.'

'I wondered about using spray adhesive,' said Jess. 'It doesn't need to last longer than a few days, and the rubberiness of the glue will help with the waterproofing.'

'It's not going to rain,' said Fi.

'Hopefully not,' Jess said. 'But we need to be on the safe side.'

They spent the rest of the day packing kits, and then gathered the supplies for the mending job before they left the shop for the day.

'I think a bag of sweets might make this go more smoothly,' said Penny. 'I'll pop to the shop and see you in the park.'

'And I think we'll deserve a glass of wine when we get home,' Fi said, 'so I'll come with you.'

Jess grinned. 'You'd better be quick. I'm not doing all that mending by myself!'

She carried on to the park, having to walk around the perimeter to the temporary entrance for the festival. There was a man sat in a garden chair under a parasol which Jess imagined was probably a makeshift site office.

'Hi, is it okay to go in?' She asked out of politeness because she had every intention of going in anyway.

'Name?'

'Jess Taylor.'

He consulted a clipboard. 'Ah yes, you're here to mend the tent.'

'Yes, I am,' she said, surprised that they'd managed this

level of organisation on the first day.

'I'm Roger. Site manager until the festival opens and then I'm off the hook.'

'Nice to meet you, Roger. I've got a couple of friends coming to help, too.' She wrote their names on the clipboard where he indicated, then carried on through the park, which was looking distinctly dishevelled.

The tent was exactly as it had been earlier in the day. Jess stood with her hands on her hips and exhaled. It might take longer than an evening after all.

'I've brought back-up.'

She turned to see Seb walking towards her with Patsy, Lois and Oliver behind him.

'What are we doing, then?' Patsy asked.

Jess explained what she thought, and they decided on a plan so they could be sure they were systematically checking the canvas. It was too big to be laid out on the grass while there was so much other activity going on around the site, so it had remained only partially unfolded.

'The main thing is the roof, so if we start at this end where we can see, and work our way along, unfolding the other end and folding this one as we go,' Jess suggested, just as Penny and Fi arrived.

Jess made the introductions, since Seb was the only one of the group to have met Fi before. Then they all manhandled the canvas to expose the first portion of the roof. There were several parts that needed stitching to join the roof back to the side and a couple of large tears, but otherwise, it wasn't too bad. Jess explained how she thought best to mend it and they all got started.

'Call me when you're ready to move it again,' Seb said. 'I want to show Oliver what we've done over at the campsite.' They headed off while the women sat down, ready to start.

'It's all coming together so quickly,' Lois said as she cut a piece of fabric with some pinking shears.

'They've done a lot even since this morning,' said Jess. 'Seb says the campsite is as good as ready, apart from the glamping section.'

'We're glamping,' said Lois. 'I don't know if Oliver told you, but the British Library had a sponsor who will pay for all the speakers to glamp for the weekend so I booked it for all of them and Oliver thought it'd be nice if we were around to host them.'

'Eunice and Bill are going to glamp?' Patsy asked, incredulous.

'Apparently so! I suppose they're not too far from home if they change their minds. And the glamping bit has its own posh loos, which is the main reason we're doing it.'

'We're doing the normal camping,' Jess said. 'But I've told Seb the loos had better be up to scratch.'

'We're camping too,' Patsy said. 'We've got the twins. They've never been camping or to a festival, so they're beyond excited.'

'We ought to make sure we're all pitched together,' said Fi, who was camping with her boyfriend Paddy who was arriving on Friday morning with their camping supplies. 'Can we have priority pitching? Is that allowed?'

'What do you think, Jess? Will Sebastian let us?' Patsy asked. 'It'd be so much more fun if we all camp together.'

'I feel like we're going to miss out now,' Lois said.

'I'm sure camping in the lap of luxury will take the edge off your FOMO,' Patsy laughed. 'Anyway, you can always sneak over and visit us if you get bored hanging out with Bill and Eunice.'

'Right, has everyone finished their bit?' Jess asked. 'Do you think we can shift this by ourselves, or shall we call Seb and Oliver over?'

'Let's give it a go,' said Lois.

The five of them pulled the heavy canvas along the grass, folding it at one end, and unfolding the other to expose the next section of mending.

'This part doesn't look as bad,' said Fi.

They all settled down again to work. Lois sat with Jess, pulling two pieces of canvas together while Jess stitched.

'I've been meaning to say thank you for what you've done to include the book club in the festival,' Lois said. 'When we first talked about it, I didn't think it could work, but you've really brought it to life and made the concept work.'

'Don't jinx it,' said Jess. 'We won't know whether it works until Friday.'

'It will, I know it. And the British Library said they'd like to sponsor it if we do it again next year. They'd like to be involved at the planning stage. From what I've experienced, they don't throw their weight around at all. It's very collaborative.'

'Wow, that sounds amazing,' said Jess. 'If it goes well, we ought to do that. It'd be brilliant publicity. We'll have a longer lead time for next year, if we do it again, so it'll be easier to involve them. Plus, we know what we're up against now.'

'Do you think we'll be patching a tent up at the eleventh hour next year?'

Jess laughed. 'I hope Seb's ready to book the tent for next year the minute this weekend is over!'

Dusk was falling by the time they'd finished. Jess was looking forward to seeing it once it was up. She had a feeling it would look fantastic with the bright fabric they'd used to patch the roof.

'I'm ready for a glass of wine,' said Fi, stretching as she stood up. They were the only ones left, waiting for Seb and Oliver to reappear from the campsite.

Jess texted Seb to let him know they were leaving. Goodness knows what he and Oliver had been doing all this time.

When they got back to Jess's, Fi settled herself in the spare room, then they both changed into cosier, more comfortable clothes and took the bottle of wine out into the garden to watch the sky turn from orange and pink sweeps of colour, into a clear, starry night.

'This is beautiful,' said Fi, who lived in Bristol. 'I've never seen so many stars. Thanks for letting me stay. Cheers.' They clinked glasses.

'Cheers. You're welcome. Thanks for coming to help.'

'So you and Sebastian are still going strong?'

'For now, although we've not seen much of each other over the last couple of weeks. He's been too busy.'

'Why "for now"?'

'He's had a tough few years. He almost lost everything after the pandemic. This is the first contract he's had on his way to building his business up again. I'd love it if he stayed around here, but honestly, he needs to go where the work is.'

'Oh, Jess. You two seem so great together. Do you think you can do long-distance?'

Jess shrugged. 'It's the first proper relationship I've had for almost ten years. I wasn't looking for anything like this, and before, I would have said it'd be easy to do long-distance. Before Seb.' She sipped her wine, feeling relaxed and finding it cathartic to discuss this stuff with Fi. 'But now, I think it'll be devastating to let him go, even if I know he's coming back because I don't know when that will be.'

'And you deserve more than waiting at home for your man.'

Jess wasn't sure what she deserved. It was still hard to believe that she was in this situation. After being single for so long, to now being all in with Seb.

'I get why he needs to do it, for his own self-worth. I just wish he could find something that meant he could stay in

Croftwood. I'm nearly thirty-two and having had a glimpse of what life could be like, you know, love, marriage, kids, all of that, after spending years thinking I'd lost any chance of that, I don't want to sit back and watch it slip through my fingers.'

'And you see all of that with Seb?'

Jess nodded. 'It's Seb or no-one. Although I thought that before and it's turned out not to be true. But this time, it's different. It's Seb.'

'So, will you wait for him? Will he wait for you, do you think?'

'I don't know if either of us should expect that from each other.'

'You need to discuss it at least,' Fi said.

Fi was right. Having had the conversation that established what Seb wanted, what he felt he needed to do next, Jess was aware that she hadn't had the opportunity to tell him what she wanted. Perhaps he assumed that since her business was in Croftwood, long-established and still growing, that she would have no ambition to do anything differently.

But things were different now. Jess had spread her wings over the past few months, and because Seb had been there through all of that, right from the start, he had some idea of how much she'd moved on. But he had no real idea of where her starting point had been. That was what she needed to explain to him. She wasn't the woman who barely ever set foot outside of Worcestershire any more. She wanted to explore new opportunities and that meant that while a few months ago she might have been happy to wait in Croftwood for Seb's return, now she realised that this was the opportunity for her to forge her own future. Her reasons were different to Seb's, but nevertheless similar in that she needed to feel as if she'd achieved something other than running away to Croftwood.

The only regret in her life was that she and Jon hadn't had longer together, but that wasn't anything she could change. But she hadn't influenced what came after Jon enough. That's what she knew now. So maybe on some level, Seb was doing her a favour by not allowing their relationship to define his future. Jess had allowed a relationship to define the last ten years, and she didn't want to do that again.

34

Having been signed off by Helena the day before, the festival campsite opened on Thursday at noon for those people who wanted to camp the night before the festival officially opened on Friday morning. The weather forecast looked favourable, if not promising endless sunshine for the entire weekend, and everyone was relieved about that.

Seb and Matt had pitched their tents that morning as close to the glamping area as they could, and had saved enough space for Fi and Paddy's small tent to join them the following day. Toby and Hilary were glamping, while Jen and Rob had decided to opt out of camping altogether and both lived close enough to the park to be able to walk.

The big tent had been hauled up the day before and everyone had stopped work to watch, cheering when it was finally up. It looked amazing, with its patched roof nestled under the branches of the nearby trees. It was the perfect workshop space and in the evenings, they planned to clear the tables away to provide extra space for people to while away the evenings with a drink or two from the bar while the children played.

Rob had set up all the sound equipment for his music acts on the stage in the cinema. Because of the licence, all the music had to finish before ten o'clock every night, but since it wasn't a music festival, that was okay with everyone. Rob had booked a mix of local bands, along with two well-known acts from the nineties indie scene who would perform as headliners on the Friday and Saturday nights.

Steph was due to arrive with the mobile library, which had been emptied of library books by a small army of volunteers the night before, and the shelves restocked with Bill's, Fliss's and Alexis's books and plenty of copies of Alexis and Fliss's backlist books which Jess had negotiated on a sale or return basis from their publishers.

If there was anything that they hadn't thought of, it was almost too late now, and everyone on the committee was looking forward to it being underway.

Seb was outwardly calm, troubleshooting all the last-minute problems as if they were a tiny hitch in his day, even when that wasn't always the case. Helena had yet to make her final site visit which was planned for late on Thursday afternoon, by which time everything should have been set up. He was waiting at the gate with Roger for one last delivery. The retro gaming arcade. He was sure that Jess had forgotten about it since their conversation months ago. But he hadn't. Ever since then, he'd been waiting to take her up on the challenge of playing each other at the dancing game, and he couldn't wait to surprise her.

'Here we go,' Roger said, readying himself to approach the driver's window with his clipboard.

'Brilliant,' said Seb. 'You know where to send them?'

Roger rolled his eyes. 'Course,' he said, then went to interrogate the driver.

Seb made his way over to the only spare piece of park left. He'd planned it carefully since the arcade people weren't able to get to them any earlier after packing up their last festival, which had been on the Isle of Wight. It had worked out well since Jess had already left the park for the day.

Roger had sent the driver into the park and the lorry was crawling along behind Seb, who was waving them into the right spot so that they could unload right where they were going to set up. After a quick chat to the two guys who were in charge, he felt satisfied enough to leave them to it and headed back to the campsite.

Matt had decided that two nights in a tent with his children would be more than enough, so had gladly allowed Seb and Jess to use his tent for the night so that Fi could use theirs since Paddy wasn't arriving until the following day. Seb was looking forward to spending his first night with Jess in more than a week. It wasn't only that Fi had been staying with Jess for the past few days, but after their heart-to-heart, he felt there had been an unspoken agreement to cool things between them. Neither of them wanted it to end, but anything more intense than what they already had would make everything more difficult.

Their little area of the campsite had been decorated to within an inch of its life. There was bunting strung between all the tents, fairy lights twirled around guy ropes and even a flag fluttering in the breeze at the end of a fairy-lit flagpole. It already looked fantastic, and it wasn't even dark yet. Various camping chairs were arranged haphazardly in the middle, with a couple of blankets ready for when the temperature dropped later on.

Jess was sat alone, reading. A bottle of beer was hanging lazily from her fingers, and Seb smiled when he saw her looking so relaxed. She hardly ever stopped, except when she sat down to sew.

'Hey, help yourself to a beer,' she said, smiling when his shadow fell over her book and she realised he was standing there.

'Better not. I've still got the sign-off meeting with Helena later on.' He wanted nothing more than to sit and be with Jess, but it wasn't likely to happen until the other end of the weekend. He was also struggling to find the right time to tell her that he'd accepted a contract to run a corporate event for a British beer brand at Oktoberfest in Munich. It was a relatively small contract and only for a few weeks, but it started right after Croftwood Festival and he would be away until the end of October. Though Germany wasn't far away, the contract involved an intensive build schedule that Seb knew would leave no time for any visits back to Croftwood. Ten weeks away from Jess. It was doable, but what he didn't know was what was going to come after that. This one-job-to-the-next situation could go on for a while until he established his reputation again, and he didn't want to leave Jess with such uncertainty.

So at the risk of spoiling the weekend they'd both been looking forward to and working towards for so long, he decided that with no-one else there, the time had come.

'I've accepted a contract, Jess.' Having a swig of beer to take the edge off was tempting. He watched her face for any sign of what she might think. She'd known it would happen, but none of the detail.

'Where?'

'Germany.'

'When?'

'I start the week after next until the end of October.' He waited for her to say something but the urge to fill the silence won out. 'I didn't expect it to be so soon. I'm sorry.'

She gave him a tight smile that didn't reach her eyes. 'It's okay. That's what the plan was all along.'

'What does it mean for us?' he asked, desperate to have some idea of where he stood.

'I don't know, Seb. What do you want to do?'

It wasn't as if Jess had the blueprints for their life in front of her. Neither of them knew what it meant. But they needed to decide what they were willing to accept from each other.

'It's different for me. I'm the one leaving you behind. I can't ask you to wait.'

'I don't know what to say.'

But she hadn't said she'd wait.

Later that night, Seb crawled into the tent, grateful for the fairy lights that had made it easy to find his way to their camp. Helena had signed everything off with the only glitch being one of the food vendors who had a food hygiene certificate that was out of date. It had taken a long time for Helena to make her checks, and there had been small things to address as they went around, so although Seb was exhausted, he was massively relieved.

He shuffled himself into his sleeping bag and cuddled up to Jess. He wasn't sure she was friends with him after his bombshell earlier, but since she was asleep, he took advantage of that.

'Did she say yes?' Jess mumbled, shifting herself so that she was facing him, although her eyes were closed.

'Yes,' he whispered.

'Good. Love you,' she said sleepily.

'Love you too.' He smiled, glad that things between them were still okay for the moment. The weekend was too important to them both to spoil with thoughts of what was going to happen afterwards, even if they knew now what that was. And he was too tired to think straight.

The festival opened at noon the next day, with Roger opening the gate and announcing the festival open in the manner of a town crier. It was fantastic, and the people waiting in the queue all cheered as they streamed into the park. The local brass band were playing in the old Victorian bandstand giving a carnival atmosphere from the beginning.

Aside from a couple of long-distance glimpses of Seb across the festival site, Jess hadn't seen him that morning. It was going to be impossible to spend any time together. That made her grateful that he'd told her about Germany yesterday. She would have hated finding out afterwards that he'd known all weekend and not mentioned it. It was bad enough that he was leaving without bringing any more angst into it or springing it on her at the last minute. And after the festival, it would almost be the last minute.

Jess went straight to the cinema, where the first book club meeting was starting in a couple of hours. She'd arranged to meet Fliss Thorne in the foyer. Seb had wanted to be there, but not knowing what he might be doing from one moment to the next, Jess had offered. Fliss wanted to watch Bill's talk as she said she was nervous about what to expect. Jess found it amazing that a best-selling author would have any qualms about anything like that; she knew Fliss had done lots of things like that before, but she also didn't mind hanging out with FL Thorne for a while.

'It's lovely to meet you, Jess, after all those emails!' Fliss gave her a hug.

'Lovely to meet you, too.'

'This place is fantastic,' said Fliss, taking in the art déco features of the cinema foyer from the golden bannisters to the ticket kiosk.

'Is it too early for a drink?' Jess asked, fully expecting Fliss to politely decline.

'I'd love one.'

They took two glasses of Prosecco from the bar and then made their way into the stalls.

'Oh my goodness, there's William Templeton,' said Fliss.

'And Seb!'

They were on the stage chatting to someone else, who Jess knew was Bill's publisher and was doing the interview with him. The interviews with Alexis Diamond and Fliss were going to be done by Lois but she was stuck at the library today.

Seb put a hand to the floor at the front of the stage and jumped down once he saw Jess and Fliss walking towards him. He had a huge grin on his face and pulled Fliss into a hug.

'It's great to see you,' he said.

'You too, Seb.'

'Have you been over to the campsite yet? Your name should be down and they'll show you where to go.'

'Don't worry,' Fliss said, 'We're all sorted. I've left Brun over there unpacking the car. He's my partner, and a couple of our friends have tagged along too.' The look on her face when she talked about Brun wasn't lost on Jess.

'I'll look forward to meeting them later.'

'It won't be weird, will it?' Fliss said, looking worried. 'Duncan's your family.'

Seb shook his head. 'You don't deserve how Duncan treated you. Family's got nothing to do with it. Are you staying to watch Bill?'

'If that's okay?' Fliss said, looking at Jess for confirmation.

'Of course,' said Jess. 'Where would you like to sit?' she asked Fliss, looking around. They had their pick of places at the moment since the doors didn't open for another hour.

'I've got a surprise for you guys,' Seb said with a bashful smile. 'Follow me.'

He led the way back to the foyer and then upstairs to the circle.

'Welcome to the VIP area!' he said, holding his arm out.

The circle was always a luxurious place to watch a film

from, but now, in between each pair of chairs was a small table with a champagne bucket, glasses and bowls of snacks. Another table near the door was loaded with some of Bill's books and some signed photos of him.

'The champagne will be here a bit closer to the start time,' Seb promised.

'This is amazing,' said Jess, wishing she could take Seb in her arms and thank him properly.

'Lord Harrington and his mother will be joining you, and so will Eunice and a couple of people Lois has invited from the British Library.'

'Fantastic,' said Fliss.

'Look, I must go. I'll see you later.' He planted a quick kiss on Jess's cheek before he left.

'Oh, you and Seb!' said Fliss, settling herself into one of the most comfortable chairs you were ever likely to find in a cinema, and sipping her Prosecco.

'Yes,' Jess said, sitting down next to her. 'We've been seeing each other for a few months.'

'Is he staying in Croftwood now?'

Jess didn't know how much Seb had told Fliss about his plans or his situation in general, and it wasn't her place to say all of that. 'I don't know. His next job is in Germany until the end of October.'

'Oh no. So you're thinking of doing some commuting? Brun and I did that for a while. We still live between here and Iceland, but we're together a lot more now that I can work from anywhere. I still had a day job when we met,' she explained.

'I run a shop here, so it's not easy to be flexible about where I live.'

'And I suppose there aren't many events around here to keep Seb busy.'

'I don't know where we go from here,' Jess said, feeling

able to be honest with Fliss.

'Don't lose hope. Sometimes a solution presents itself when you least expect it.'

Jess highly doubted that she hadn't already thought of every conceivable route through the maze that was her and Seb's future, but she smiled and nodded at Fliss because she liked her and was looking forward to spending the best part of the day together.

By the time Bill came onto the stage, the cinema was packed to the rafters with eager book-clubbers. In Lois's absence, Oliver had volunteered to compère and he gave a brief rundown of how the book club element of the afternoon would work before he introduced Bill and his publisher to overwhelming applause.

'William Templeton. Still a dashing man,' the Dowager Countess whispered to Jess.

'He certainly is,' she said, smiling and topping up their glasses with the chilled champagne that had been delivered.

'Go steady there, Mother,' Archie said. 'If you want to camp tonight.'

'Are they?' Fliss mouthed to Jess.

Jess shrugged and giggled before their focus was drawn to the stage where Bill's publisher began asking him about his early film career.

After the talk, Bill was whisked away to the mobile library van to do his book signing. Jess and Fliss followed Archie and his mother downstairs and out of the back of the cinema into the heart of the festival.

'I'm desperate to explore,' said Fliss, 'But I promised Brun I'd go back to the campsite to meet him. Do you know how I get there?'

'I'll come with you,' said Jess, in no rush to be anywhere else for a while. Fi was running the craft workshop that had been going on at the same time as Bill's talk, so she'd have finished by now, too.

'It's so nice to see Seb happy,' Fliss said, as they strolled through the park towards the campsite.

'He's been brilliant. We'd never have got this off the ground without him.'

'I mean, he seems happy with you. That's rare for him. For someone who came from a relatively privileged background, he's had a hard life.'

Jess was acutely aware that she knew almost nothing about Seb's background, but she didn't want to admit that to Fliss. It hurt that that was the case.

'He doesn't talk about his past much.'

'That's not surprising. He's always worked hard to distance himself from his father. Wouldn't accept any help from him back in the day, and I doubt that's changed.'

Jess was shocked that Seb would rather have ended up homeless than ask his family for help. Her parents would be the first ones she'd turn to in the same situation. She couldn't imagine not feeling able to.

'Did you meet his last girlfriend?' It was a calculated risk. She should ask Seb this stuff but it was easier to ask Fliss.

A brief look of disdain flicked across Fliss's face as she turned to look at Jess. 'That woman wasn't in love with him. She was out for herself. We saw them at a wedding of another cousin and she was flirting with Duncan. He's my ex, and probably invited it, knowing what he's like, but still. Poor Seb. So I knew it wasn't going to last.'

They emerged from the park onto the path that crossed the allotments, heading to the campsite.

'I know I shouldn't ask you this, but you know him better than me. Do you think he's someone who can be all-in?'

Fliss stopped walking. 'He's always guarded himself against anything that might make him happy. He's been hurt a lot in the past, not just by Maria, so he protects himself against getting close to anyone. Actually, he can come across as a bit of an idiot when you first meet him. But I can honestly say he looks happier than I've ever seen him. He was thrilled about surprising you with the VIP area this afternoon. He's in as much as he knows how to be, I would imagine.'

'Thanks,' Jess said. 'It must seem odd that there are things I don't know about him yet.' But one thing she could understand was that Seb had found it hard to let her in. That much they had in common.

'Not at all. Brun and I are constantly finding things out about each other. But if Seb hasn't told you about his family, it's because he doesn't think it's important, not because he's holding back for some other reason.'

'I don't know much about this kind of thing, anyway. My last relationship ended ten years ago.'

Fliss couldn't hide her surprise. 'Sorry. I'm sure there's an explanation and that you're entirely normal.'

Jess laughed. 'You'd have to ask Seb. But yes, there was a good reason why. Some other time?'

Fliss nodded and linked her arm into Jess's. 'I'm ready for another glass of champagne. Do you think that's included in our glamping package?'

The campsite was a hive of activity. Tents were being erected at an astonishing rate, and flags, bunting and fairy lights were everywhere.

'There's Brun!' said Fliss, happily.

'Oh my god, is that Ned Nokes?' Jess asked.

Fliss put a hand on Jess's arm. 'Is that okay? I know you were worried he'd attract the crowds, but he's going to keep a low profile. Coincidentally, his partner Anna is doing the PR for the band that's headlining tonight, so they fancied tagging along.'

'It's fine. I wasn't expecting to come across a celebrity in the campsite, that's all.'

'What do you mean? Me and Bill are camping with you,' Fliss teased.

'But Ned Nokes, Fliss.'

Fliss laughed. 'I know. It's a common reaction. When you get to know him you'll feel differently.'

'Really?'

'No, not really. Everyone loves him. What you see is what you get.'

'Hey, Fliss! We've bagged the tent next to you,' Ned said, coming over to them and kissing Fliss on both cheeks.

'This is Jess. She's part of the festival team and Seb's partner.'

'Great event you've put on here, Jess,' Ned said, shaking her hand. 'This is Anna.'

'I feel like we're gatecrashing,' Anna said, smiling. 'But it's not often we get to see Fliss in her natural habitat whereas she has to put up with going to Ned and Brun's gigs all the time.'

'You're definitely not gatecrashing,' Jess said, warming immediately to Anna. 'The more the merrier.'

'We were just about to head into the festival,' Anna said. 'I've arranged to meet the band before their soundcheck.'

'The book club should be out of the cinema by now,' Jess said.

'Shall we come with you?' Fliss suggested, looking at Jess to see if she was going to tag along.

'Yes, let's leave the boys here to sort the camp out.' Anna said. 'The sunshine is making me crave a cold beer.'

'There's a bar in the cinema, that's where your band will be too, I expect,' said Jess. 'I'll come and see how Bill's book signing's going.'

They strolled back to the festival site while Fliss and Anna caught up on what they'd been up to since they last saw each other. They explained bits and pieces to Jess so that she could follow their conversation, and Jess thought how lovely it was to have only just met these women and immediately feel as if they were friends.

The three of them queued for drinks in the backstage bar, then with Prosecco in hand, Anna went inside to meet the band, who were fine-tuning their equipment under Rob's strict supervision, while Fliss and Jess went to investigate the mobile library van. The queue had dwindled enough for Fliss and Jess to get inside.

'Oh my goodness!' Fliss exclaimed when she was confronted with shelf after shelf of her books. 'This is surreal. There's no way we'll shift all of these. It's a good job you have them on sale or return.'

'You might be surprised. Those shelves were full of Bill's books earlier on.'

Bill looked shattered but happy as he signed the last few books for his fans. Eunice was sitting in the driver's seat reading an Alexis Diamond book, and Rosemary was sitting next to Bill, handing him the books one at a time, opened to the right page.

'Hello, Jess,' said Rosemary. 'If you want a book, please take one from the shelf, write your name on a Post-It note, then hand it to me. You pay on the way out.'

'Thank you, Rosemary. We just popped in to see how it was going. This is Fliss Thorne.'

Everyone in the van turned to look at Fliss, who turned bright red. 'Lovely to meet you all,' she said.

Bill smiled and nodded, then went back to his signing with Rosemary acting as photographer for his fans. Eunice came over and warmly introduced herself. 'We're camping with you,' she said.

'Gosh, that's brave,' said Fliss with admiration. 'I must

admit I was planning to stay in a hotel, but Brun persuaded me it would be fun.'

'I confess we're not quite glamping,' said Eunice. 'Bill has hired a camper van for us. Our friends Dottie and Alex are driving it here for us and then are going to take our glamping tent for the weekend.'

'That's a very smart idea,' Fliss said. 'Still, we should all be alright. It's supposed to be lovely weather all weekend.'

Jess had a text from Seb while Fliss was chatting to Bill once he'd signed his last book. Seb had gone to the campsite and was heading back over with everyone, including Brun and Ned, so that they could listen to the music.

Everyone arrived at the cinema and once the introductions were out of the way, they all made their way through the queues waiting to be served at the backstage bar and bagged a space halfway down the room. Matt had Sammy on his shoulders, and Oliver had Flo on his. The twins had noise-reducing headphones on and were beyond excited.

'How's day one been?' Oliver asked Seb.

'Is it still only Friday?' Seb laughed. 'It feels like the longest festival in history, but yes, it's going well.'

'It's brilliant,' said Fliss. 'I can't believe I haven't been going to festivals. Lazing around in the sunshine surrounded by books and music is my idea of heaven.'

'We've been very lucky with the weather,' Seb admitted. 'It'd be a different story if it was raining. I'm not sure we'd be well set up for that.'

'You're wrong, mate,' said Matt. 'As if Helena would have signed it off if your wet weather contingency plan was lacking.'

'It's true!' said Jess. 'It's probably the best organised festival in the world with Helena checking it all.'

'Is she coming?' Patsy asked.

'She's coming tomorrow on a day ticket,' said Seb.

'You made her pay?' Patsy asked incredulously.

'She insisted! She likes to do everything properly,' said Seb.

Brun and Ned appeared with a couple of jugs of beer and a stack of plastic glasses, and it wasn't long before the music started. Anna's band was on first and everyone agreed they were brilliant and that Anna would have a hit on her hands.

'She does have a knack for picking the gems,' Ned said proudly.

The nineties indie band were fantastic too, with everyone marvelling at how many of their songs they'd remembered, having thought they might only know one or two. By the end of the night, everyone was dancing and singing along. It was the best night.

Once the music stopped, and after the cheers had subsided, Rob wished everyone goodnight and asked everyone to make their way to the exits.

'I'll catch you up,' Seb said, kissing Jess.

By the time they all got to the campsite, the twins were over-excited at the prospect of a night under canvas, and Matt quietly suggested that if everyone pretended to go into their tents, that might speed the bedtime process up. Once the twins were in the tent and they could all hear Matt's hushed tones reading them a story, everyone gathered quietly in the circle in the middle of their camp and waited, enjoying the ambience of the campsite beginning to settle down for the night.

'The coast's clear,' said Matt, crawling out of the tent. 'They're sound asleep.'

Ned produced a bottle of whisky from his tent and a stack of small coloured shot glasses. 'Anyone for a nightcap?'

The bottle was passed around. Even Eunice and Bill's friends came to join in since their little boy was fast asleep in their nearby tent.

'I can't believe you're camping,' Anna said to Dottie, who

was heavily pregnant.

'I'm at that stage where I'm not sleeping well, so I don't think it'll make much difference. And it's something nice to do with Bert before the baby comes.'

'He seemed to enjoy running around with Sammy and Flo,' Matt said. 'You guys ought to come round to ours sometime. The kids have a treehouse that I bet Bert would love.'

'Thanks, that'd be great,' said Dottie. 'We don't know that many people around here. We moved form London a couple of years ago and Alex is still down there a lot.'

'You weren't tempted to play a set, Ned?' Dottie's husband, Alex, asked.

'Don't encourage him!' Anna said, making Ned laugh. 'Honestly, he'll take any opportunity. An event like this without having to be a groupie is a rarity.'

Once they'd polished off the bottle between them all, everyone said goodnight, and Jess crawled into bed and lay with her eyes closed, listening to the sounds of zips being zipped and unzipped. By the time her tent was unzipped and Seb appeared, she was dozing off.

'You waited up for me,' he said with a tired smile.

'I don't feel as if I've seen you much today.'

'I forgot what it's like. The whole time you're planning it, you concentrate on the start date as if it's the finish line, when really, it isn't.'

'That's true.' Jess snuggled into Seb's arms while he arranged himself so that they were curled together in their sleeping bags.

'How was your day? Have you enjoyed it?'

'Yes, it's been fun hanging out with Fliss and Anna.'

'Did Fliss tell you all my secrets?'

Jess looked at Seb and even in the half-light she could see the worry in his eyes.

'She told you about Maria?'

It was a relief to realise that Seb had thought this through. That he was aware he'd told her hardly anything about his life before they'd met. 'Yes.'

'I should have told you, but I didn't know what to say. It's meaningless compared to what you went through with Jon.'

'It hurt you. That's not meaningless.'

He nodded and pulled her closer. 'I will tell you all this stuff, Jess. It's just not that important to me anymore.'

It was important to Jess because she wanted honesty in their relationship, but she knew the fact Seb hadn't shared everything with her wasn't because he was deliberately hiding anything. 'It's okay. I don't need to know everything about everything. That's the fun part of getting to know each other.'

Germany hung in the air between them. As much as she'd love to have a proper conversation about what they were going to do, she was no further forward in her own mind about what she wanted. And besides, it wasn't the right time. She wrapped Seb's arm around her waist and pressed her back against his front.

'Night, Seb. Love you.'

'Love you, Jess.'

35

Apart from spending the night together in their tent, which was more a case of Seb falling into an exhausted, coma-like state as soon as he sat down, he and Jess hadn't seen each other at all on Saturday. They'd made a plan to meet at Fliss's talk in the cinema on Sunday afternoon in an attempt to try to enjoy at least some of the festival together.

Jess had a new appreciation for the behind-the-scenes work that went on at an event like this. It meant that the public could enjoy themselves without noticing the mechanics of it all. She was so proud of Seb and was desperate to tell him, and sorry that they would only have a few days to relax together before he went to Munich.

She spent the morning in the big tent with Patsy and Fi where they were running a drop-in and sew, knit or crochet session. It was a lovely, calm atmosphere with people chatting to whoever they ended up sitting next to. Everyone was helping each other and looking forward to Fliss's talk in the afternoon.

Penny, Linda and Mary from the knit and natter club were sitting near the end of one of the long tables and when she had a moment to sit down, Jess sat and stitched some fabric hexagons together until someone needed a hand with their own sewing.

'Have you got a moment to have a word, Jess?' Penny asked.

'Of course, shall we go outside?'

They headed out to the park and, against all the odds, found an empty bench in the sunshine.

'I've got a proposition for you,' Penny began.

Jess was intrigued. 'Okay.'

'Would you be interested in taking me on as a business partner? You know I love working in the shop and I know you don't like asking me to do more than a couple of days a week. I also know that the shop is a tie. And I think until now, you've not minded that. But now that you're with Seb… You're young, Jess and you deserve to have fun without the shop holding you back.'

'I love the shop.'

'Of course you do. So do I. A lot of people love your shop and that's because of you. I hope what I'm trying to suggest is that you can have the best of both worlds. Yes, you could pay me to do extra hours but I'd love to be more involved. If that's something you'd like, too.'

Jess grinned and threw her arms around Penny. 'Thank you. It's a wonderful idea, but are you sure you want to take it on?'

'I've spoken to Mary, and she's keen to do some hours. That'll spread the load a little bit.'

Jess had never thought to actually ask Penny what she wanted. She'd assumed a few hours a week were as much as she'd be prepared to do, and here she was solving Jess's biggest problem.

'Let's sit down together next week and make a plan. I'd love to work something out. But I'm not planning to run off into the sunset with Seb.'

'You could if you wanted to,' Penny said. 'You should be

able to take some time off without worrying about the shop, and I assumed you'd want to spend some time with Seb after the festival's over.'

Since things had become more serious with Seb, Jess had been wracking her brains about how she could contribute to their lives being flexible enough to make their relationship work. If Penny had suggested this before he'd told Jess he was leaving, she'd have been over the moon because it would have seemed like the perfect solution. But just because he'd made that decision without factoring her in, it was no reason to stop thinking about a more flexible life for herself. One that would allow her to grab opportunities when she wanted to, and do some exploring again.

'Seb's leaving. His next job is in Munich and he starts the week after next. Anyway, I've waited ten years for the time to come where I'd feel as if I wanted something more than what I have in Croftwood and now that time's come, I don't want to stay here and wait for Seb and I can't go with him either. But your offer means I can think about doing something different, whatever happens with me and Seb.'

'I'm thrilled!' Penny said. 'Come on, let's buy a jug of Pimms to share with the others before we head off to hear Fliss's talk.

By the time they'd packed everything away from the craft workshops, Jess, Fi and Patsy were among the last to arrive at the cinema. Seb had texted her to say he'd saved their seats in the circle. There were too many people for it to be a VIP area this time. There were even people sitting in the backstage bar with no hope of seeing the stage, but happier to listen in than miss it altogether.

'Hey,' said Seb, kissing her as she sat down next to him in the seat he'd saved her. He squeezed her hand. 'I've missed you.'

His eyes sparkled and Jess wondered how she was going

to feel when he left. It was one thing planning what she might do now that Penny was going to help more with the shop, but now that she was here, next to him, she realised that's all she wanted.

'I missed you too. You promised me that camping with you would be romantic and all you've done in that tent is sleep.'

He grinned. 'I know, and no-one is sorrier about that than me. But tonight's the night. Roger is supervising the vendors who want to pack up and leave tonight and everything else can wait until tomorrow.'

'Hi, do you mind if we grab those seats?'

Jess looked up to see Brun, Ned and Anna, who was pointing to the seats along the row.'

'Not at all,' Seb said.

'I'm am looking forward to this,' said Brun to Jess. 'I watched Fliss do talks like this in Iceland. That is how we met.' He looked so proud, it made Jess's heart swell.

Lois came onto the stage, and everyone clapped. 'This is our final date-with-a-book club meeting of the inaugural Croftwood Festival, and we're going out with a bang by welcoming FL Thorne to the club.'

The place erupted with cheers as Fliss walked onto the stage. Despite having told Jess she was nervous, she didn't look it now. She looked self-assured, as if it were something she did every day.

Jess could have watched Fliss and Lois chat all day. It was fascinating to hear about how she got started as a writer, the thrill of finding out her books had been a hit in Iceland when she'd sold next to none in the UK and had thought her career was over before it had even begun. Once they'd finished talking, Lois announced that the date-with-a-book club would begin and last for an hour, after which time Fliss would be in the mobile library van for the book signing.

'Come on,' Seb said, taking Jess's hand. 'We'll see you back at the campsite,' said Seb to the others.

'Where are we going?' she asked.

Seb had led her out of the front door of the cinema, which was quiet thanks to most of the festival-goers being in the cinema and presumably spilling out into the big tent for the book club part.

'It's a surprise.' He led her along the path to the opposite end of the park where she'd not had chance to venture yet.

'Oh my god, it's the arcade!' she said, seeing the sign above the entrance to the tent. 'We hadn't even talked about this since that night in your flat, right at the beginning.'

'I was hoping you'd forgotten.'

'I had! Do they have the dancing game?'

'That's literally the only reason I booked it, although it's been a massive hit all weekend. I had to wait until I knew everyone would be busy doing something else.'

When they went in, it wasn't quite empty. There were a few teenagers on the machines, including two girls on the dance game.

Seb went to stand nearby, then said loudly to Jess, 'I wonder how Ned Nokes knew about this festival?'

The girls stopped dancing and whipped around to look at Seb. 'Ned Nokes is here?' one of them asked.

'Oh yes, just see him in the cinema.'

The girls looked at each other and abandoned the game, along with the couple of other girls who had been in earshot.

'You're so naughty,' Jess said, laughing and climbing onto the dance platform.

'What?' Seb said, feigning innocence.

'Okay, what are we dancing to?'

'Something easy to warm up.' He started jigging on the spot.

Jess giggled. 'Oh, you're taking this seriously.'

'I hope you are too,'

'I've had a glass of Pimms so you've probably got a head start.'

The music started and Jess did her best to concentrate on what the screen was telling her to do, but it was years since she'd done anything like this and by the time the song ended she was no better than she'd been at the start.

'Best of three?' she said. Seb had a slightly better score than her, but they were pretty evenly matched. At least that meant he was struggling just as much.

'Okay. Shall we stick to the easy level?'

'Definitely. I've got no hope if it's harder than this.'

After Seb won the next two rounds as well, Jess was happy to call it a day. 'You were a worthy winner,' she said.

'My misspent youth finally pays off,' Seb said with a smile.

'You weren't that good!' Jess laughed, knowing from what Fliss said, that his misspent youth had probably been pretty limited.

They went back out into the sunshine and found a quiet spot under a tree. They lay, their faces shaded by the tree canopy.

'I wish I wasn't leaving,' he said.

'No you don't.' She turned her head but he was looking straight up to the sky.

'But this is what I want. Everything that's here in Croftwood, especially you.'

Hearing that somehow made the prospect of him leaving seem easier. Because he didn't want to go and would rather be here, with her. That made it easier to bear than if he'd been leaving without a backward look.

'I'm not going to be here waiting for you, Seb.'

He turned now, his eyes full of hurt. Then he sighed. 'And I can't ask you to do that, Jess. I know it's me who's blowing up the best thing thing that's happened to me for a long time.'

'Don't regret the decision you've made,' she said, leaning up on one elbow and resting her other hand on his chest. 'It's been the best thing to happen to me for years. The reason I won't be here waiting is because I'm going off on my own adventure. I've emailed about working on one of the craft cruises. It's only for three weeks but it'll be the longest I've been away from Croftwood and the shop since I came here.'

'And Penny will cover you for all of that time?'

'Yes,' Jess said happily. 'We're going to arrange things differently so that she'll be more like my business partner. But the thing is, I thought the shop was the only thing stopping us from being together when actually, when she offered and that wasn't in my way, I didn't immediately think about following you. I wouldn't do that anyway, I know you're away for work, but it made me realise that I'm free to do other things as well.'

'So, you're not waiting for me in Croftwood, but we could say we're open to meeting each other when our paths cross?' Seb still had a worried look.

'More than that , I want to be together whenever we can. Be open to what each other is doing, make allowances for the fact that we won't always be in the same place but that doesn't mean we're not in a relationship. Let's be like Fliss and Brun.'

Seb laughed, 'Right. I suppose at least we're not living between continents.'

'And you could live at my house when you're not away.'

'Are you asking me to move in with you? Because that's a big deal and you've slipped it into the conversation as if you're asking me to dinner.'

Jess dipped her head and kissed him. God, she was going to miss him. 'Move in with me, Seb.' She wasn't even worried that he'd say no. He wouldn't, so it didn't feel like a risk to ask. They'd been living between each other's places for weeks.

'I'd love to,' he said, pulling her head back down towards him and kissing her deeply. 'I wonder if we've got time to head back to the campsite before anyone else gets there?'

After more kissing under the tree, they strolled back to the campsite. People were beginning to spill out of the cinema and there was still a long queue outside the mobile library, but no-one else seemed to be heading back to the campsite just yet. It was the last day of what had been a fantastic festival and everyone wanted to drink in the last of it before it was over. Jess and Seb were more interested in drinking in as much time as they could in their last week together, so all thoughts of doing anything apart from heading back to their tent went clean out of their heads.

They giggled like teenagers when they heard the others arrive back at the campsite a couple of hours later. Reluctantly they pulled on their clothes and unzipped the door to join everyone else.

'Have you been having a nap?' asked Flo, who had glow stick bracelets stacked up on her wrists while her brother had a single blue one on his.

'Yes,' said Jess. 'Seb had to get up very early this morning.'

Patsy smirked at her. 'Did he?'

'We've brought a load of food to share,' said Lois, depositing a couple of trays of loaded fries on the picnic blanket in the middle.

'And I picked up some cold beers out of the cinema fridge,' said Oliver, putting a cold box down.

'Brun, will you play a song?' Flo asked.

Brun had his guitar with him and had played a couple of Icelandic songs for them the night before, telling the children Icelandic folk tales as well, which Matt was grateful for since it did a good job of calming them down after the excitement of the day.

'Let's have tea first, Flo,' said Patsy. 'And then you can ask again nicely with the magic word.'

Once they'd finished eating, Brun disappeared to fetch his guitar, and returned with two.

'I brought yours too, Ned. Thought we could have a sing-song,' Brun said, grinning, knowing he'd backed Ned into a corner.

'Yes, please!' said Flo, who presumably had no idea that a few years ago Ned had been one of the most famous popstars in the world. Jess was pleased Flo had insisted, for the benefit of the adults who would have been too shy to suggest it.

Brun and Ned began to play and sing the song, which had been all over the radio the year before. As they played, other campers began to gather around to listen until there was quite a crowd of people, all stood in silence listening to the beautiful music.

Jess sat in front of Seb, leaning back onto him, her head on his chest. His arms were wrapped around her, and he rested his bottle of beer on her hip. It couldn't have been more perfect. The music, their friends around them, the starlit sky and the happy kind of tired that came from the deep sense of satisfaction at pulling off the festival successfully.

'This is what you meant,' she whispered, looking up at Seb, seeing his eyes full of the same emotions as hers. 'Why it's not a festival without the camping.'

He nodded. 'I love you so much,' he said, dropping a kiss onto the top of her head.

She smiled, thinking that this was the best memory of the past few months. The perfect way to remember what she and Seb had when they were apart. 'Love you too.'

36

Epilogue

Three Months Later

The day had finally arrived. Seb was back from Germany and was on a train back to Croftwood. Jess was so excited to see him, she was a bag of nerves. She'd suggested picking him up at the airport, her mind full of romantic notions about running into his arms at the arrivals gate, but Seb had insisted there was no need, and that it'd be better to be together the moment he was back rather than have to drive an hour before that could happen.

She closed the shop at five o'clock as normal, incredulous that the time had finally come after so many weeks of waiting, then she pulled her coat, hat, scarf and gloves on and headed for Madge.

It was strange to think that in the weeks since Seb had left, the weather had turned from the last days of summer to being almost winter. It was freezing, and she had piled the stove high that morning with some long-lasting night briquettes, so she wouldn't be taking Seb home to a cold house.

They'd moved his things up to Jess's house — their house — in the few days between the festival ending and Seb leaving for Germany. So they'd only lived there for a couple of days together. They'd decided not to attempt any rushed weekend reunions while he was working away. With the uncertainty of train strikes and airline cancellations, they'd agreed it wasn't worth it for what would amount to just a few hours together.

But she'd missed him so much. It had been the longest ten weeks of her life. She'd distracted herself by throwing herself into making the new arrangements with Penny work. Jess was determined not to take advantage, and they'd worked out a fair way of sharing the burden so that even when Jess was away for almost a month working on the cruise with Fi, Penny had plenty of time off when Jess got back. The workshop programme was in full swing now that there was no gardening to distract their customers and Fi had started working in the shop on a regular basis as their knitting guru.

Jess parked in the station car park and headed for platform two where all the trains from Birmingham stopped. The station had recently been renovated back to its Victorian splendour. It was in the heart of the oldest part of Croftwood, near where Toby and Hilary lived, where the houses were beautiful. They were mostly built from granite quarried from the Malvern Hills like Jess's house but they were huge, elegant and sat on tree-lined avenues. The station was also built from the same stone, but its crowning glory were the ornate ironwork canopies that sheltered the platforms. Newly painted, their colours were vibrant, and Jess took a few photos of the intricate metal flowers that decorated the tops of the pillars while she waited.

The train pulled in and Jess scanned the people who were alighting, looking for Seb. When she saw him, her heart ballooned in her chest and the ten weeks of desperately missing him were suddenly worth this moment when he was hers again. She waved and headed along the platform towards him. He'd put his bags down and was waiting with open arms and a huge grin on his face. Jess pressed herself against him and felt his arms around her, holding her tightly. He was warm and solid and smelt just as she remembered. He dropped a kiss on the top of her head and she pulled away, watching his eyes sparkle as he took her in.

'God, Jess. I've missed you.'

She could hardly speak. 'Me too.'

He heaved his bags up onto his shoulder and pulled her into his other side. 'Let's go home.'

She grinned up at him. 'Your hair's different.'

'It was getting unruly.' He ran his hand through it self-consciously.

'It looks good.'

'You look good.'

They got back to the cottage and Jess managed to stoke the fire back to life and chuck a couple of logs on it before she was in Seb's arms again. They spent the next hour or so showing each other exactly how much they'd missed each other, before they realised how hungry they were.

'I bought some fresh bread. Do you fancy cheese on toast?'

'Perfect,' said Seb, filling the kettle.

They took their tea and toast into the lounge to eat in front of the fire. It was so cosy, more so when Seb was there as well. Jess snuggled into his side and pulled a blanket over them.

'I don't even mind that it's winter if we get to do this,' she sighed happily.

'I've been dreaming of being here with you.'

Jess looked up at him. The way he was looking back at her made her heart melt. Maybe she could cope with him being away for weeks at a time if it was like this when he came home. 'And we've got nothing else to do for at least a couple of days.'

'Actually, I've signed my next contract, and that starts this week.'

Jess sprang away from him. 'You did that without talking to me about it?' It was one thing to know that Seb was going to have to go where the work was, but if this was how they were going to live, there had to be a discussion at least.

'Only because it was too good an opportunity to pass up.'

'Seb…' She wasn't going to cry. Not on his first night home.

He reached for her hand and squeezed it until she met his eye. 'Jess, it's here. In Croftwood.'

'So you're not leaving?'

'No. I don't think I can. It's too hard being away from you. And now, I don't have to be.'

'But how long is it for?'

He shrugged. 'I'm not sure. It's kind of an open-ended arrangement.'

Jess frowned. 'That doesn't sound very contracty.'

'It's for Archie Harrington. He wants to have a Christmas market at Croftwood Court and he knows what I can pull off in a tight time-frame.'

'Really? That sounds amazing.'

Seb nodded. 'We've already made some arrangements, I wrote the EMP in the evenings while I was away and Helena's already signed off the plan.'

'Oh my god, Seb. We'll have our first Christmas together.'

'I hope the first of many.' He turned away to reach for something on the coffee table. He held out his hand and there was a ring in the middle of his palm.

Jess looked at him, then reached for the ring.

He clasped his hand closed. 'Hold on, I have to ask you before you get the ring.'

'Ask me what?' This was incredible, and she was willing to play the game so that it wasn't over too quickly.

'Jessica Taylor. Will you marry me? I want to have all of my Christmases with you. All of my everythings with you.'

He held his hand open again, and this time let her take the ring. It was a beautiful vintage diamond eternity ring.

'Oh, Seb.'

'No, let me do that,' he said, taking it from her and holding it ready to place on her finger. 'You haven't said yes, yet.'

'Yes,' she said, putting her hands on his cheeks and pulling him towards her. 'I want everything with you too. The ring is the most beautiful thing. I love it. And I love you,' she said, smiling.

'It was my mother's. Is that okay?'

'It's perfect. It means even more to me.' And when he slipped it onto her finger, it fitted perfectly and looked like it was made for her.

'I love you so much, Jess.'

The following day, Jess and Seb headed to Oliver's for breakfast. They'd decided to have a lazy day to celebrate Seb's return and their engagement, but they had no food in the house.

'Morning, nice to see you back, Seb,' Oliver said. 'What can I get you?'

They ordered and sat at a table near the window. They were the only ones there apart from a couple of people with headphones on who were working on their laptops.

Oliver brought their coffees over. 'Jack's sorting the breakfast toasties. Mind if I join you?'

'Not at all. In fact, you can be the first to hear our news.' Jess looked at Seb, who gave her a small nod and smile of encouragement. 'We're engaged!'

'Oh, wow! That's great news, congratulations!' They all

stood up to exchange hugs.

'Hey, what's going on?' Matt and Toby had come in.

'They're engaged!' said Oliver.

The hugs and congratulations started all over again, then the food arrived and they all sat down.

'If you're staying in Croftwood, we ought to talk about next year's festival,' said Matt. 'We've finalised the accounts and we can afford to pay a salary to a festival director.'

'Subject to approval from the committee,' Toby added.

'I'm very happy to throw my hat in the ring for consideration,' said Seb, munching his breakfast.

'We'll set up a meeting. Good to see you back, mate,' said Matt.

Jack brought a fresh round of drinks over for everyone, and then Patsy and Lois burst through the door together, both out of breath.

'Oliver texted us,' Lois said. 'Congratulations!'

'Let's see it,' Patsy said, keen to see Jess's ring. 'Wow, that's a beauty. You chose that?' she asked Seb who just laughed. 'Well done.'

'Thanks. It's a family heirloom.'

'When's the party, then?' Patsy asked.

Jess raised an eyebrow at Seb who shrugged and smiled.

'I'll organise it,' Patsy declared. 'We'll have it in the backstage bar. I'll let you have some dates to choose from.'

'That sounds amazing, thank you.'

It had been lovely to share the news with their friends but after not having seen each other for weeks, Jess and Seb couldn't wait to be alone again, so made their excuses and left.

'A party?' Seb said.

'I don't think we have any choice. And it might be fun. Perhaps we should invite our families?'

'Oh, no, no, no,' Seb said, 'At least not mine. That's not

something we want to rush into. But I can't wait to meet your family. Why don't you take me to Dorset? It'd be nice to have met them before the party.'

'Really? I'd love to take you,' said Jess.

'I'd love to see where you grew up. Where you and Jon used to hang out.'

Jess thought her heart might explode with love for Seb in that moment. He genuinely didn't mind Jon being part of her life. She leant over and kissed him. 'Thank you,' she said softly. 'We can sleep on the beach and eat mushy pea fritters.'

'We're not sleeping on the beach until at least June, but you can tempt me with a fritter. Come on, let's get home.'

Seb put his arm around her shoulders, and Jess snuggled against him.

This was everything.

The End

Sign up to my exclusive mailing list to find out about new releases, special offers and exclusive content. Go to www.victoriaauthor.co.uk

Also by Victoria Walker

Croftwood Series
Summer at Croftwood Cinema
Twilight at Croftwood Library

Icelandic Romance Series
Snug in Iceland
Hideaway in Iceland
Stranded in Iceland

The Island in Bramble Bay

Author's Note

Thank you for choosing to join me at Croftwood Festival! If you enjoyed it and you have a few minutes to leave a review, I'd be so grateful. Reviews are the best way to help other readers find out about books they might enjoy.

I'm a latecomer to the festival scene and definitely not brave enough to go to Glastonbury or anywhere else where the loos might not be up to scratch, but I have dealt with my fair share of festival mud, rain and heatstroke. I wanted Croftwood Festival to be like the Hay or Cheltenham festivals but one where you might have a fighting chance of having heard of the authors. As an avid reader of mainstream fiction, it's rare that I see any authors that I love listed to appear at those events. Although Marian Keyes is going to Hay this year, but I think she's the exception that proves the rule.

* * *

If you've read my Iceland books, I hope you enjoyed Fliss popping in for a cameo as much as I enjoyed writing it! I was tempted to let Ned be a headliner, but he does have a tendency to turn most things into the Ned Nokes show.

In August 2023, at the Underneath the Stars festival, I found out by chance that the friend of a friend we were with was the licensing officer for a city council. I could not believe my luck when she agreed to answer my festival-related questions, and once I had the answers I couldn't believe that she would ever want to go to a festival! I'm sure she must walk around noticing everything they could have done better. Helen, thank you for your thorough answers to my questions. I couldn't have written the book without you. Any mistakes are mine. In the interests of the story, I have ignored Helen's main advice: you can't decide in March to have a festival in August the same year. In real life, she would do her best to talk anyone out of doing that, and with good reason.

Thank you to Berni Stevens for another fab cover and to Catrin for editing and proofreading. You're both stars and I love working with you. Thanks to James and Claudia for proofreading and story advice. Along with Jake, they are my original festival buddies.

If you're going to a festival, have a fab time! Let me know which ones are your favourites. You can find me in these places:

Facebook - Victoria Walker Author
Instagram - @victoriawalker_author
www.victoriaauthor.co.uk

Printed in Dunstable, United Kingdom